May 2015

THE LYNCHPIN

Also by Jeffrey B. Burton:

THE CHESSMAN

THE LYNCH PIN

JEFFREY B. BURTON

MP PUBLISHING

THE LYNCHPIN

Published in 2015 by
MP Publishing
12 Strathallan Crescent, Douglas, Isle of Man IM2 4NR British Isles
mppublishingusa.com

Library of Congress Cataloging-in-Publication Data

Burton, Jeffrey B.
    The Lynchpin / Jeffrey B. Burton.
    p. cm.
    ISBN 978-1-84982-308-1

1. Serial murder investigation—Fiction. 2. United States. Federal Bureau of Investigation—Fiction. 3. Suspense fiction. 4. Murder—Minnesota—Fiction. I. Title.

PS3602.U76977 L96 2014
813.6—dc23

Cover design by Alison Graihagh Crellin

ISBN 978-1-84982-308-1
10 9 8 7 6 5 4 3 2
Also available in eBook.

For my wife, Cindy.

"A murderer is less to fear. The traitor is the plague."

Marcus Tullius Cicero (106–43 B.C.)

PROLOGUE

Though the dark-haired man wore a special pair of latex gloves, he tapped the disarming code into the in-home security system with the cap of his BIC pen. He'd worked his magic on the cellular unit during the dry run that morning.

But that morning the house had been empty. He'd watched from the tree line as the target left for work in his Escape Hybrid. Then he sat without moving for another thirty minutes, watching the home and monitoring a GPS transmitter he'd attached above one of the Escape's back wheel wells to verify there'd be no unexpected U-turn to pick up misplaced work papers or a forgotten lunch. At last he skirted the long driveway that fortuitously hid the front of the house from the street. The nearest neighbor lived a quarter mile down the road. The target's desire for privacy made this particular job a cakewalk.

Now it was 3:00 a.m., and the target, who lived alone, was asleep in the master bedroom. The dark-haired man slid out of his Timberland boots, leaned against the wall in the split-level's sizeable foyer, and shut his eyes. He listened for several minutes, accustoming himself to the sounds of the house settling. After another moment he nodded and opened his eyes. He slipped his SIG Sauer P228 into his belt holster and retrieved the inhaler from the inside pocket of his black windbreaker.

It was to be an in-and-out, five minutes tops, but the dark-haired man figured he'd make it six or maybe seven for personal reasons. He knew it was a character flaw—it wasn't as though he'd done this too often—but a quick spray into one of the target's nostrils or into his snoring mouth would rapidly induce cardiac arrest.

He liked to watch.

The target would begin to flutter about, twisting in the bed sheets. Inevitably, the eyes would snap open. The dark-haired man liked that his targets saw him in their final moments. Perhaps a few more wild shakes or a jerk for the phone on the bedside table, and then it would be over. The chemical would dissipate, untraceable in the autopsy. Natural causes, the coroner's office would conclude; cardiac arrest brought on by a sudden heart attack.

The dark-haired man slipped down the carpeted hallway, pressed against the wall to keep any errant floorboards from creaking. The door to the master bedroom lay open and he could make out a crumpled quilt and dark hills of pillows…and then it was almost *his* heart that came to an abrupt stop.

The target's bed was empty.

A toilet flushed and the dark-haired man spun sideways. A figure stood in the doorway of the master bath, staring back at him. The dark-haired man dropped the inhaler and reached for the SIG, but the target was already in motion, charging him like a defensive end, and the two men slammed hard into the bedroom wall and tumbled to the floor.

The dark-haired man snapped his left elbow upward into the target's jaw and scrambled for his gun, but the target grabbed his wrist with one hand and locked his other about the dark-haired man's neck, cutting off his air. The intruder bucked, rocked, kicked up with a knee, trying to shake the bastard off him, but the target squeezed his throat harder still. The dark-haired man panicked, brought both hands up to pry the bastard's hand off his throat, but that freed up the target's other hand, which quickly joined the first around his throat, securing the deadly grip.

The dark-haired man twisted his head sideways toward the empty hallway. His eyes bulged and he kicked limply at the hardwood floor. His bladder unclenched in a rush of urine.

And then he died.

PART ONE

The Lookalikes

CHAPTER ONE

"So she was embalmed and tossed into Lake Superior?" Special Agent Drew Cady of the Federal Bureau of Investigation looked at the county medical examiner, a beanpole with a black mustache named Wallace Foeller. He hoped the ME could not only answer this query, but also the myriad questions that lay beneath it.

The cadaver, a brunette in her early twenties, lay atop the stainless-steel examination table, only her neck and face exposed above the body sheet. She was—final identification had been made the previous day by a devastated father chauffeured up from Newton, Iowa, by a family friend—twenty-three-year-old Katrina Mortensen, also of Newton, Iowa, who had last been seen by a bartender downing strawberry margaritas at a nightclub called Daffodils in Des Moines. Mortensen had been attending a three-day conference on implementing best practices in dental hygiene, the headline event at the Des Moines downtown Marriott the previous week. She had disappeared the second night of the conference. Mortensen's movie-star looks lent her disappearance the media legs that it otherwise might not have received, and Cady had followed the story in both the *Star Tribune* and the occasional non-update update from some talking head on a news channel out of the Twin Cities.

Cady hadn't needed the father's verification. He knew it was Mortensen.

"These marks near the collarbone," Foeller said, indicating the right side of Mortensen's neck, "that's the incision made to get at the artery. Looks like an aneurysm hook was used to split apart the tissue above the artery. Your perpetrator used suture strings as a ligature to tie off the blood vessel once the arterial cannula—that is, an arterial tube—was inserted into the artery. The ligature remains. This is the artery that was used to inject the embalming and arterial fluids. This is where they pumped her full of formaldehyde."

Cady shifted his feet, slightly off balance in the Duluth branch of the St. Louis County Medical Examiner's Office. ME Investigator Foeller's office and examination room were hidden in a little-traveled hallway in the bowels of the University of Minnesota Medical School, Duluth campus, and Cady counted himself lucky that Police Chief Skip Weflen and Lieutenant Deb Rohr of the city's Violent Crimes Unit had hung around during the examination, despite having already been through the autopsy findings with Foeller earlier that day. On his own, Cady would have needed a trail of breadcrumbs to find his way back to his car.

"How are those chemicals pumped in?"

"Embalming machines allow you to regulate pressure and flow. A hose from the machine is attached to the arterial tube."

"How did they pump out her blood?"

"Drainage is much like injection, just at the other end. Once the jugular drain tube is inserted and a hose is attached, a ligature ties off the blood vessel. Dyes in the arterial fluids, which eventually flow out the drain tube, let the embalmer know when it's done."

"Draining the blood and injecting the formaldehyde is done at the same time?"

"Yes." Foeller waved his hand over Katrina Mortensen's throat and glanced at Cady. "This was done neatly. Professionally. The person who did this has had some practice."

"So our killer may work at a funeral home? Or be an expert in human body preparation?"

"I'd say he or she has great knowledge when it comes to arterial embalming. But as for the rest, nothing was done with the cavity, no setting the face. None of that."

"This is all very interesting," Police Chief Weflen said, "but it begs the question: what the hell did they do with her blood?" Weflen had the dour face of a replacement card dealer, the kind sent in by a desperate pit boss to stop the bleeding.

"That part's on you," the ME answered.

After the initial identification made it clear that Katrina Mortensen had been kidnapped in Des Moines, taken across state lines to some point along Minnesota's Northern Shore—likely between Duluth and Two Harbors—murdered, embalmed, and dumped into Lake Superior, where she almost immediately washed ashore, much to the mortification of a Cub Scout troop earning their Webelos badges by picking up garbage along the shoreline, Chief Weflen had made a phone call. He'd contacted the SAC—Special Agent in Charge—of the Minneapolis Division of the FBI and requested Special Agent Drew Cady be sent to Duluth to review the most bizarre autopsy results he'd ever seen. Cady did most of his work with the Minneapolis field office, even spending a week each month with forensic accountants in the Twin Cities. Technically, though, since he lived in Itasca County, he reported out of Duluth's satellite office, more commonly known as the Duluth Resident Agency, located in the Federal Building off First Street.

After a quick bureaucracy-cutting phone call from Minneapolis, Cady made arrangements with Chief Weflen to meet at the North Arlington Avenue Office—the Duluth Police headquarters. He had hightailed it the eighty-odd miles to the city that squatted on a hill above Lake Superior—Minnesota's answer to San Francisco, only with snow tires. Fortunately, it was still the first half of September, and he might have another ten minutes before he needed those.

Cady had met Chief Weflen, briefly, at the Duluth Resident Agency earlier that summer. The somber-looking man was waiting for him in the parking lot at headquarters; after a brusque handshake through the rolled-down window, he introduced Cady to Lieutenant Deb Rohr. *It's the damnedest thing*, Weflen told him as he and Rohr slid into a squad car. *I'm going to let the ME tell you because it's the damnedest thing.*

While Foeller walked him through the autopsy, Lieutenant Rohr scribbled notes on a legal pad, though this was the second time she'd heard it. If meticulousness kicked off a scent, Cady figured, there'd be no place Rohr could hide. She looked to be in her mid-forties, of average build, with a face that looked lived in and a nose that'd been broken somewhere along the line.

"Tell him about the bruising," the police chief instructed the ME.

"Chafing and contusions about her wrists and mouth are indicative of duct tape, likely used to subdue her in the abduction."

"Bound and gagged," Chief Weflen said, stepping away from the table.

"Nothing remarkable in the rape kit. No semen in the vagina or anus. No indications of sexual molestation. As absurd as this sounds, apart from the poor girl washing ashore naked, no evidence of a sex crime in the traditional sense."

"You get a TOD?" Cady asked.

"An accurate time of death in this case is all but impossible," the ME explained. "Lake Superior trumps body temp, embalming trumps blood pooling, et cetera, et cetera. And no blood sample, obviously, so I took urine from the bladder for the tox screen. Prelims indicate no blood alcohol content, so they kept her alive long enough for those margaritas to wear off. Didn't feed her, though—at least nothing partially digested in the stomach contents." Foeller shook his head. "It takes about eighteen hours to digest a meal, so I'd guess she lived at least a day after the abduction. Perhaps we'll get more from the samples taken from the liver and spleen, but I doubt it."

"How did she die?" Cady asked.

"I'm sorry if I was unclear earlier." The ME stared at Cady. "She died from loss of blood while being injected with toxic chemicals. Take your pick—both will kill you."

"The embalming process, what you described…they did that while she was still alive?"

"Far as I can tell."

Cady digested that piece of information in silence.

"I'm going to kill whoever did this to that pretty young girl." The ashen-faced chief of police broke the hush. Weflen had two daughters about Mortensen's age. "And if either of you bring what I said up at the inquiry, I'll plant evidence to make it look like you were involved."

Cady hadn't known the police chief long enough to tell whether the man was joking.

CHAPTER TWO

"It's kind of sexy." Terri Ingram was taking assorted leftovers out of the fridge, which she placed on the counter for Cady to microwave.

"My carrying a gun?"

"Yeah, in a James Bond sort of way."

"I'm afraid to ask how you feel when you see policemen."

"Street cops lack subtlety," Terri replied. "Between pepper spray, Tasers, cuffs, and whatever else, their utility belts rival Batman's."

"Batman's not sexy?"

"I was never a comic-book geek, unlike a certain someone who shall remain nameless." Terri rapped her knuckles on the countertop. "So that's why you ordered me the Catwoman costume."

"I bumped into it online and thought it might complement your eyes."

"I don't even want to know where you *bumped* into it online. It looks like Catwoman costumed by Hugh Hefner. I live in fear of checking your browser history." Terri thought for a second. "Hey, doesn't the FBI have filters on their PCs for pervs like you?"

"I can get around them."

"I swear, G-Man, if we weren't engaged, I'd have you committed."

Cady had popped the question on a pontoon boat in the middle of Bass Lake on the Fourth of July. It would have made for an uncomfortable ride back to the lake house had Terri said no. Fortunately, Cady was spared finding out how uncomfortable.

Cady would never go into specifics and Terri didn't pry, but he'd let her know that Duluth caught a bad one and the city's chief of police had requested he be brought in to consult. Terri excelled at reading between the lines.

"Are the creepies drawn to you like moths to flame? Or do you gravitate toward them?"

"I'm from Ohio, Terri. These are your Minnesota kin I'm dealing with—your friends and neighbors."

"Don't make me Google. I'll have a list of Buckeye State whack jobs so fast it'll make your head spin."

"Buckeye State whack jobs?"

"Yes, and you're at the top of the list. Now stop changing the subject—the point is, you're still in PT and they've got you hunting a monster."

Special Agent Drew Cady had first crossed paths with Terri Ingram the previous year, during an investigation into the Chessman copycat killings—a nasty piece of work that ended with Cady once again suffering through a series of surgeries on his already gimpy right hand. Over a long career, he'd been dumb enough to dive headfirst into a veritable briar patch of serial killers and lucky enough to come out the other side. The only silver lining in his latest case was that, once through the brambles, Cady found himself going through physical therapy at the Grand Itasca Medical Center in Grand Rapids while staying with Terri at her lake house, all of fifteen minutes away in the northern Minnesota town of Cohasset.

Two months into rehab, Cady tried to help Terri with the daily chores at Sundown Point Resort, the string of cabins she managed along Bass Lake; hoisting and securing boat motors with one hand proved all but impossible. He'd eventually settled on snapping pictures of triumphant fishermen returning to shore with their prizes or taking group photos of relatives renting cabins from Terri for family reunions. And he killed more time with the hobby he'd grown into during his first attempt at retirement: American numismatics— collecting rare US coins. But even though he'd gotten excited over a few acquisitions, including an uncirculated 1819 half dollar with virtually no wear, the hobby hadn't managed to fill his days. After a third month of inventing busywork, Cady was bored stiff.

Terri, sensing his restlessness, had voiced her concern.

"I don't want to see you placed in harm's way ever again—tracking Mexican drug lords or hunting Al Qaeda cells—but you following me around all day like a newborn puppy is driving me ape. Aren't there some white-collar pussies you can chase down?"

"White-collar pussies?"

"You know, the ones who'll pee their pants when you come to arrest them instead of hacking at you with a tire iron. The ones who serve time at those country-club prisons where they let them play badminton. I mean, Jund owes you that much."

Cady feigned ignorance of any collusion when Roland Jund, an FBI assistant director in the Criminal Investigative Division and Cady's old boss, *coincidentally* had called him that same evening to "check in" on how Cady's physical therapy was coming along.

After five minutes of chitchat, Assistant Director Jund cut to the chase. "So what do you think about all of these white-collar pussies?"

Cady realized then where Terri had gotten the expression.

"I think I need to put them in jail, sir."

And with that, Drew Cady was back in the game.

He worked on the Medicare Fraud Strike Force out of Minneapolis, which, like similar groups peppered about the country, kept the FBI's dance card full attempting to recover billions scammed by felons committing healthcare fraud. It was an eye-opener for Cady, and he found himself thrust into the world of doctors penning needless prescriptions for kickbacks, patients leasing out their Medicare numbers, fraudulent wheelchair sales, fake physical-therapy claims, phony DME charges for nonexistent durable medical equipment, bogus invoices for unused drugs—a seemingly endless buffet of fraudulent billing schemes set up by Medicare cheats to bilk the already overmatched federal program. Cady's new colleagues in Minneapolis were a team of forensic accountants. They spent most of their time looking into patterns of irregular billing. And when the time came to have a face-to-face with a person of interest in a current investigation, Cady never felt threatened; the hair on the back of his neck had yet to rise, and he'd never been attacked with a tire iron—not even once.

Then came the call from Duluth Police Chief Skip Weflen about the bloodless cadaver Lake Superior had coughed ashore.

He'd spent most of the drive back from Duluth lost in thought. They'd kept Katrina Mortensen's embalming from the media, but who knew how long that would last. And once that disquieting factoid came out—and it would come out—the investigation would become Ringling Brothers. The finesse, as Cady had explained to Chief Weflen and Lieutenant Rohr, was to get the perpetrator into custody so they could own the factoid and not have the factoid own them.

Due to formaldehyde's acute toxicity, as well as it being a known carcinogen, the Occupational Safety and Health Administration regulated formaldehyde's use in funeral homes. That was a starting point, Cady thought. OSHA might surprise him, could be a quick turn. Rohr would be working the Mortensen timeline while her people checked the funeral homes, in person, within fifty square miles of Duluth.

Cady welcomed Terri's banter upon his return home from Duluth. He couldn't tell her any more than she'd already heard on the news— it wouldn't be appropriate—certainly not how the Mortensen girl was drained of blood. This time of night, he should be hungry. Starved, even. But, unsurprisingly, he wasn't.

Cady's cell buzzed. A flick of the screen showed it was Special Agent Elizabeth Preston—Assistant Director Roland Jund's right hand at the Bureau in Washington, D.C. Agent Preston's calls were never for small talk or mirth, and Cady sensed immediately that something was up. Though their relationship had been strained over the years, stiff, even take-your-sister-to-the-dance awkward, the events of the past year had proven that Agent Preston had his back, and Cady had hers.

"Hey, Liz, where's the fire at this time of—"

The special agent from D.C. cut him off mid-salutation. Cady shut up to listen.

"You're kidding," Cady said, although he knew that Preston never joked. "He did what?"

Terri turned from the microwave to stare at him. Cady crooked the phone against his shoulder so he could ransack the kitchen drawers for a pad of paper and a pen, then stopped abruptly with a spatula in his hand, straightening slowly to his full height.

"Jund said he needs to see me in person?"

CHAPTER THREE

"You strangled him?" Cady asked.

"I didn't have a baseball bat handy."

Assistant Director Roland Jund—rumpled and weary, looking as though he had not slept since the Second Boer War—sat across from Cady in a half-deserted Starbucks off East Market Street in Leesburg, Virginia. Jund was on paid leave and this was not Bureau business. Not officially, anyway.

"Strangling is so up close and personal," Cady said. "An intimate death."

"It's not like I had a lot of options. You get up to take a leak in the middle of the night and find a man hovering over your bed with something in his hand. Clearly my night visitor wasn't there to read me a fairy tale."

Cady thumbed through the photocopy of the police report Jund had given him.

"But the police didn't find this thing he'd been holding?"

"It looked like an inhaler, for asthma or something, but he dropped it when he went for his gun. If I hadn't moved, you'd be thinking up pleasantries for the wake."

Cady shrugged. "You get into a fight with an unknown intruder in your house at 3:00 a.m. There are a few *oddities* for the police to look into, but it's classic self-defense. Justified. Won't ever see a courtroom."

"I'm lucky I take after my father. Man had the strongest hands in the world. I watched him pull up tree roots as a kid."

"Did they dust your home security system?"

"Yes. A collage of partials. Mostly mine. JoAnne's. A blur of my sons'."

"There you have it."

"Have what?"

"I want your security code, so when you're downstairs playing pool I dust the unit with fluorescent powder, flash it with a UV—a black light—and jot down the numbers with fingerprints on them. Take me less than a minute."

"But you wouldn't know the sequence."

"Come on. There are a limited number of combinations." Cady thought for a second. "You ever punch it in with guests standing around?"

"I don't know. Over the years—maybe."

"Perhaps when we come in, I stand at an angle and see the first number. That narrows it down."

"Pretty thin."

"What's your code?"

"1-9-8-4."

"Jesus," Cady said, tossing a hand in the air. "The first one he tried, no doubt."

Jund averted his eyes, nodded.

"Passwords, codes, PINs are easy to crack in the age of Facebook. Birthdates, anniversaries, pet names. Even your mother's maiden name is no longer sacrosanct. And that's all aside from the fingerprint trick."

"What if it was an inside job?" Jund asked.

"You didn't know the guy, did you?"

"Never seen him before in my life."

"You have any dinner parties lately?"

"Liz tell you JoAnne and I are separated?"

Cady nodded. "I was sorry to hear that."

"It's been three months and some coming. Haven't entertained for work or relaxation since before my youngest left for Syracuse last fall."

"Have you been seeing anyone?"

Cady and his ex-boss stared at each other.

"I'll take that in the affirmative."

"JoAnne and I have been seeing a counselor, trying to make it work. Neither of us want a divorce, the separation's proved that. Evidently, when I come home at night, all I want to do is drink scotch and fall asleep on the recliner. There's not much for us to talk about since the boys are away at college. She's got a righteous beef, I guess, but the job kicks my ass. I imagine you know of what I speak," Jund said, alluding to the failure of Cady's previous marriage.

Cady nodded.

"With all that said, there is someone I've seen, briefly, a handful of times over the past month or so. JoAnne doesn't know and I'd like to keep it that way."

"You've had this person to your house?"

Jund shrugged. "Twice. Late nights when there wasn't a risk of JoAnne swinging by." Jund shook his head. "Don't judge, Agent Cady. It was JoAnne who left me in the first place. That's my rationale, anyway."

"I'll need the woman's name."

Jund nodded.

"Tell me about the man—your intruder."

"Thin. Maybe forty. Black hair. Like I said, I've never seen the son of a bitch before. I only got a look at him after the attack, when they body-bagged him away."

"They got a name yet?" Cady asked.

"A Detective Keene at Leesburg PD will call if the fingerprints get a hit. But due to the *unique* nature of his demise, they're performing an autopsy."

Jund had a spacious six-bedroom shrouded by woodland in Loudon County, Virginia, outside of Leesburg—the county seat—and a mere thirty-mile drive from Washington, D.C. Not a bad commute, considering Jund's daily grind in the nation's capital rarely aligned with rush hour.

"They didn't find a gun." Cady began rattling off facts from the police report, more for his own benefit. "He wasn't wearing gloves. He had no wallet, no ID, no keys, nothing in his pockets. No dropped inhaler about his body or found under the bed."

Jund twisted in his chair. "I don't know what to say about that."

Cady said nothing, thinking.

"I had single malt the night before, probably why I had to take a leak, but I wasn't intoxicated, Drew. Everything in my statement is the gospel."

"That means someone else was in the house. The man had a partner."

Jund nodded. "It's not a random home invasion like the cops seem to think, not some meth head trying to steal my plasma TV."

"I'll crawl out on a limb and say we can rule out a sex crime."

"I didn't get the impression he held any amorous intentions. I also doubt he was there to pre-op something that involves an ice-filled bathtub and missing kidneys. I'd be a goddamned imbecile not to see how this situation points back to my role at the Bureau."

Cady didn't quibble.

"Anyway, I appreciate you coming here. I need someone from outside the bubble, someone I can trust. Someone who knows how to take names and kick ass." Jund's eyes darted over the scattered java addicts sharing the coffee shop with them, then settled back on Cady. "That's why you're here."

"My ass-kicking days," Cady said, holding up his gimp right hand, "vastly overrated as they were, are long gone. But maybe we can piece together a name or two. Let's go back to that night. You run downstairs, you grab the kitchen phone on your way outside and 911 it from the driveway. Then you stay outside to wait for the police."

"My heart was beating like a bongo drum. I was scared to death."

"It took the police about five minutes to arrive?"

Jund nodded again. "I told them what had happened before they went in."

Cady looked out the Starbucks' window. "The silent partner is involved in another task; he hears the struggle, but for whatever reason does not get involved, which, believe it or not, may be the luckiest thing that happened to you that night. Then the silent partner has about five minutes to doctor the scene and slip out the side or back door."

"Had to be the back. The side is too near where I was pacing in the driveway. I'd have seen him."

"So he slips out the back, off to wherever they hid their car, and escapes into the night."

Jund's phone buzzed and he held up a palm.

"This is Jund," the AD spoke into his cell. "Hello, Detective—what's the word?"

Cady slid his chair back and rubbed his eyes. Jund was right—
something bigger was at play. Something coordinated, and with
purpose. Something, Cady felt as he half-listened to his old boss
talk to the Leesburg detective, that could bite a big chunk out of AD
Jund's ass.

"No, Detective. Never heard of him." A pause. "You're shitting
me." A longer pause. "Yes, I find that peculiar as hell." Longer still.
"Absolutely not. That's not my division." One last brief silence. "I'm
sure you will." Jund clicked end call and stared at Cady. "Christ."

"What?"

"The noose is starting to tighten."

"What?" Cady repeated.

"Turns out my night visitor was a fellow FBI agent."

Cady's jaw dropped.

"His name was Steve Parrish."

Drawing a blank, Cady shook his head.

"I'm going to need a lawyer, Drew. That woman I told you about,"
Jund said, "the one I'd been seeing…her name is Dayna Parrish.
And I think she's his wife."

CHAPTER FOUR

Cady stood alone in Jund's master bedroom, staring at the spot near the king-size where the FBI assistant director had strangled his nighttime intruder, who turned out to be a fellow FBI agent. And *strangled* was not an entirely accurate word. Agent Parrish's larynx had been crushed.

Agent Liz Preston had gotten Cady a copy of the ME's report as well as a handful of photographs, copies most likely, of Steve Parrish's cadaver that had been taken by the forensic photographer for the Leesburg PD in this very spot. Preston hadn't told Cady how she'd gotten copies of either and, given that it was a case in which she had no jurisdiction and one helluva conflict of interest, Cady hadn't asked.

Everything looked as Jund had said. Jund comes out of the bathroom to see an intruder at the side of his bed. With a shot of adrenaline, Jund brings the fight to the intruder and ends up killing the man. It is Jund's home. It is the middle of the night. Jund calls the police as soon as he feels safe and goes outside to wait for them in the driveway. A no-brainer case of self-defense if there ever were one.

Or was it?

The intruder turns out to also be an agent in the Federal Bureau of Investigation. And to make matters even murkier, the dead agent is the husband of the woman with whom Jund has recently been having sex. Jund claimed he'd observed Parrish with something in his hand, something which the Leesburg police did not find during a thorough search of the crime scene. So either Jund was lying, which Cady did not believe for a second, or the intruder had a partner that night who tidied up while Jund waited for the police in the front yard.

Cady sat on the corner of the king-size and placed the three pictures of Steve Parrish on the bed in front of him. The first was a medium shot of the dead man, on his back, arms sprawled at his side, head sideways. The other two pictures were almost identical, close-up shots of Parrish's right profile as his eyes—wide and bulging—stared sightlessly into Jund's hallway. Cady thought about the trajectory of the agent's head. Parrish spent his last few seconds on Earth twisting his head as though…

His thoughts turned to the silent partner.

You're here with Agent Parrish, but in a different part of the house, doing God knows what. You hear a loud commotion, two men crashing to the floor. Why not come to your accomplice's aid? If Parrish were there for the kill—the wet work—what were you there for?

Cady thought about Jund's suspicions, about how this was not an arbitrary burglary gone awry or, as the facts were seeming to imply, a love triangle turned deadly, but something that snaked its way back to Jund's position in the Bureau.

Jund's home computer was in the study on the main level of the house. The silent partner likely had a different skill set than Parrish, a different job to perform. The partner could have been there to break into Jund's PC. During the scuffle, Parrish's silent partner no doubt panicked and went into hiding. Then, with Jund out of the house, the silent partner put in a minute's work of scrubbing the scene and then escaped through the sliding-glass door from the entertainment area in the lower level, across the backyard, and off into the woods.

Cady stood on Jund's lower floor, absentmindedly spinning the cue ball on the assistant director's Glenwood pool table—or, as Jund would demand it be called, his billiard table. The sliding-glass door, Leesburg PD notes indicated, had been found shut but unlocked. Jund maintained that, though he rarely ventured downstairs these days, he was sure the door had been locked. And it didn't help matters that the home security system had been shut off.

So what had Parrish's silent partner taken from the scene?

Jund assumed Parrish had carried a handgun, which was why the assistant director went after Parrish like a pit bull smelling blood. But if it were a crime of passion and Parrish was there intending to shoot Jund over the affair with his wife, how hard would it be to pull the trigger and put Jund down in midstride? FBI agents were well trained in firing handguns. But if he hadn't had the gun in hand at that moment, if it were something else he was fingering, something that required administration upon a sleeping and defenseless Roland Jund…it had been three in the morning, after all. Why go to all the trouble of breaking in and disabling the alarm system when you could simply ring the doorbell and shoot Jund when he opened the door?

It wasn't his area of expertise, but Cady had read of inhalants or serums that could induce an abrupt heart attack in a healthy person. Undetectable poison. Undetectable murder. Jund had a pressure cooker of a job, a collapsing marriage, was well into middle age and was already on meds for high blood pressure and cholesterol. *He was a ticking time bomb*, colleagues and family members would mumble at the funeral. *It was just a matter of time.*

Cady slid open the glass door and stepped outside. The backyard turf was rich green, weed-free, and screamed of a professional yard service. He followed the shale patio as he stepped out from under the shadow of a deck the size of an aircraft carrier and into Jund's lower backyard. To the left, tiered boulders and cobblestone steps wound up a flowered walkway toward the upper deck, where the swimming pool lay and where the catered events and politicking took place. Down here, the lawn angled toward the tree line and the six-foot privacy fence of brown metal that defined Jund's property line.

Parrish's silent partner had to have known he could not go out the front door, had to know that exiting via the side garage door would be iffy with Jund standing guard in the driveway. So he would have fled this way, spurred on by the motion detector light that would have come on once he hit the patio. Getting into the woods quickly would be imperative, even if Parrish's silent partner had to circle back to the getaway car.

Cady stared into the shade of the woods—a gauntlet of ignored brush, undergrowth, uprooted trees, rock outcroppings, packed dirt and muck that angled down into what Jund had described as a ravine containing a thin trickle of water. Jund said no one in his family had ventured beyond the fence line since the boys were out of middle school, and he'd seen nothing back there in eons except for the occasional white-tailed deer or coyote—the nearby homes were too far away for children at play, and Jund claimed he'd never once had to chase away unruly teenagers who'd snuck out there to smoke weed or play doctor. Cady stared off across the lawn. It hadn't rained since the night of the incident; if the silent partner had left any trace behind during his escape, at least there was still some chance of finding it.

Cady looked down at his black Florsheims. He'd been in too much of a hurry to catch the last flight out of Minneapolis to think of packing his hiking shoes or an old pair of sneakers.

In Jund's kitchen, Cady rummaged around until he found a drawer containing serrated steak knives with wooden handles. He tossed a half dozen in a plastic bag from the walk-in pantry. Cady left through Jund's side garage door, worked his way to the lower west side where the privacy fence began, slipped around the outer side, and began hiking the property line, head down, looking for any disturbances in the brush or packed dirt.

About sixty yards in he found what he was looking for: the spot where Parrish's silent partner had leapt over the chain link. Two almost-parallel indentations in the dirt where the intruder had to have landed after scaling the six-foot barricade, ostensibly meant to keep neighbor kids and other feral animals from trespassing into Jund's rear yard. Cady squatted and surveyed the area. A couple of feet in front of the indentation that Cady took for a right shoe was a round divot, most likely the landing place of the intruder's right kneecap. Two feet farther in he found two smaller depressions that he figured were made by the intruder's palms. Cady looked up at the fence. It appeared as if the UNSUB—unknown subject—had come down hard, hard enough to leave these marks in the packed dirt. Not surprising, since he would have been panicked about getting caught, moving fast in the dark night and making a hasty retreat over unfamiliar terrain. Actually lucky, Cady thought, not to have made the leap a few feet farther down the fence line, where the intruder would have landed atop a jagged bed of rocks that might have put a damper on his escape.

Cady tied a flex cuff to the fence rail. He'd call Agent Preston and have her send a forensic team to dust this section of fencing for prints. If anything came of it, Liz could feed the results to Leesburg PD. Cady stuck one of the steak knives into the ground beside the intruder's right footprint as a marker. The lab boys might be able to pull the UNSUB's shoe size or weight, or whatever other magic they worked tucked away in Forensics. Cady lifted his foot and let his size 11 hover over one of the indentations. The print seemed a couple sizes smaller—food for thought.

Carrying the bag of knives, Cady headed down into the ravine.

After twenty minutes Cady surfaced from the ravine, God knew where, and nearly tripped over a gravel road. He hiked north, figuring that, unless his sense of direction was completely turned around, he'd eventually intersect with the county road that led back to Jund's estate. The gravel road turned to dirt, and over a crest Cady came upon a housing development, what appeared to be a string of single-family homes, an upper-income neighborhood in its infancy.

At this stage the houses were little more than cement foundations and lumber frames on what appeared to be two-acre parcels of land, plenty of space to spit up trees, bushes, and fences so future owners wouldn't have to see one another outside of the occasional nod or neighborly wave from their cars. Workers' pickup trucks were littered about the makeshift road, and Cady could see construction activity at each of the eight homes. The first house was farther along than the others. Cady followed a barrel-chested man pushing a wheelbarrow full of red bricks and smoking a cigarette.

"It's the model home," the mason, Denny, explained after Cady flashed his badge and introduced himself. "The real estate agents will use it to sell the others. These units are already sold, but this row's just the beginning." Denny waved an arm in the direction from which Cady had come.

They say people look like their pets. Denny looked like his brick-laden wheelbarrow: short, stocky, capable of getting the job done. He had a crushing handshake, not unlike Jund, that made Cady think anyone breaking into Denny's residence in the dark of night would be in for a similarly nasty surprise.

As if reading his mind, Denny asked, "You here about the dead burglar?"

Cady weighed that in his mind. What he really thought was that this would be the perfect spot for Parrish to park before approaching Jund's home. "Just checking to see if anyone saw anything suspicious or out of the ordinary."

"That's all we talked about at lunch. No one brought anything up, but if you talk to the guy who killed the fucker, tell him a bunch of us would like to buy him a beer."

Cady nodded. "Any cars come by that shouldn't have?"

"Hell if I know. Got architects and general contractors stopping by, those realtor agents I was telling you about, and subcontractors like myself, here for the brickwork."

"Hear of any cars abandoned or towed away?"

Denny shook his head.

"Is there a set place for parking?"

"You park wherever you need to get the job done. And don't block others or you'll get barked at."

"Any security cameras set up?" Cady asked, taking a wild stab.

"Nah—this is the only house with any electricity so far," Denny replied. "The only thing we're worried about is assholes stealing our gear."

"What do you do about that?"

"Fenced in at night." Denny pointed at a metal structure halfway up the makeshift road that looked like Stalag 17 for construction material.

Cady thanked Denny for his help, got five seconds' worth of directions confirming he was on the right path, and headed back toward Jund's house, which amounted to walking another city block north and cutting through the line of trees. He'd have Liz Preston send the FBI technicians through this section of woodland, too, just in case. Cady was out of steak knives, as he'd hit pay dirt down by the ravine, near where the water flowed.

The UNSUB's left shoe appeared to have gotten suctioned off in the muck. The intruder must have panicked, numerous marks indicating where he'd scratched around the sludge in a desperate attempt to find the errant shoe, not wanting to leave any evidence behind, or, perhaps worse yet, complete the night's nature walk with one stockinged foot. The UNSUB had eventually found the lost shoe and yanked it from the mud, but the shoeprint, as well as a wayward footprint from the UNSUB's flustered search, were both telling.

He'd thought of Terri as he hovered his foot over the depressions left in the mud. He thought of how he was always stepping over Terri's shoes in the entryway of their lake house, about the certain shape of her shoes when she left prints in the mud leading up to the cabins. Parrish's silent partner was not a man.

Cady was tracking a woman.

CHAPTER FIVE

"In the absence of legal counsel, I've been instructed by my attorney to tell all inquisitors to go piss up a rope."

Although Dayna Parrish's face might not launch a thousand ships, her body could bust up more than a few friendships. But she had a tongue on her that would make the ancient Greeks scamper aboard ship, pull anchor, and head back to Sparta.

"Mrs. Parrish," Cady said, attempting a disarming smile, "I think we've gotten off on the wrong foot."

"I'm not on any wrong fucking foot and I know exactly who you are, Special Agent *Drew fucking Cady*. You're chummy with the bastard that murdered my husband. And if you're not off my property in five fucking seconds I'm going to start screaming rape at the top of my lungs."

So much for his disarming smile.

Cady stepped off the front stoop, took another backward step, then crossed his arms and stared up at Mrs. Parrish in the doorframe of her Kings Park, Virginia, suburban rambler. The next-door neighbor in the denim shorts and dress socks mowing his lawn and the teenagers tossing a Frisbee across the street would have a case of cognitive dissonance when they heard a blood-curdling scream but witnessed a man in a dress suit and tie standing passively on the sidewalk.

"Then I guess it all comes out sooner rather than later," Cady said, hoping he'd called her bluff—that Mrs. Parrish wasn't truly and loudly neurotic, that she'd be the one who'd have to live in the neighborhood after creating a horrible scene. They stared at each other for several seconds.

"What comes out?"

"Your relationship with the assistant director."

"That's bullshit. Those phone calls were between Jund and my husband, not me, just like I told the—" Mrs. Parrish stopped midsentence. "You're fucking up a police investigation. Your ass just got fired, shithead."

"That's an overstatement. I might get read the riot act about the same time you're brought in to explain your fingerprints on the backyard fence."

The staring match continued. Cady watched her eyes and could tell he'd touched a nerve.

"Did you scratch your face?" Cady pointed to the Band-Aid under her left temple.

"In the absence of legal counsel," Mrs. Parrish enunciated slowly, "go piss up a rope."

"Is that wrist a bit swollen?" Cady pointed at her right hand.

"Go piss up a rope," Mrs. Parrish repeated.

"Roland ever see this side of you?"

"On the advice of my attorney—"

"Yeah, I know," Cady interrupted. "Piss up a rope."

Cady sat in his rental car outside the Parrish home. He recognized the number on the caller ID and thought about letting it flip over to voicemail. Then he remembered Katrina Mortensen—the dead girl on the slab in Duluth.

"Where the hell are you, Cady?" Police Chief Skip Weflen's voice came through Cady's smartphone loud and clear.

"Got called to D.C."

"Well, hell, son—I need you here. Got a city council meeting tomorrow night that you should plan to attend. And Lieutenant Rohr has got this goddamned bee in her bonnet that she insists she needs to discuss with you."

"What's the issue?"

"Pure conjecture, but there's no way I talk about it over the phone," the chief said. "In fact, what the lieutenant says to you stays between the three of us. Deb's a great cop, but this thing came out of left field and she's fixated on it. A case of tunnel vision, and I'm hoping you can reason with her."

Cady slipped his rental car into drive and headed to Reagan National.

CHAPTER SIX

"A squad car will accompany each detective on their mortuary visits. I figure in something as morbid as this, they might need help in case they unearth a Bates."

Cady sat in a metal chair across a desk from Lieutenant Deb Rohr. They were in her office in Duluth PD's Violent Crimes Unit with the door firmly shut.

"A Bates?"

"Norman Bates, like in that movie *Psycho*. Whoever did this is a hell of an odd duck, so if someone's in their face asking hard questions, who knows how they'll react." Rohr pushed a stack of paper across her desk. "That's a list of all the mortuaries in Minnesota where they'd have cause to use embalming machines. Hospitals, too. Like you already know, we've started close and are working outward."

"Anything yet?"

Rohr shook her head. "There's also a list of manufacturers for those pumps at the bottom of the pile. It's impossible to figure out the particular unit."

"OSHA got anything useful?"

"Just more facilities for us to check. However, I did learn something new for show-and-tell. Some fartskulls out there lace their dope with embalming fluid."

"You're joking."

"Lacing it with formaldehyde creates a more powerful hallucinogenic," the lieutenant clarified. "Probably a first-rate rush—once you get past the brain damage and vomiting."

"Amazing that anyone even thought that up."

"The beat goes on," Rohr said. "Day in, day out."

"Coast Guard or Port Authority track anything the night of the storm?"

Rohr shook her head again.

"So tell me, Lieutenant," Cady said, "what did you really want to talk to me about?"

"So you think this woman—Nicole Huckle—who went missing from Cloquet five years ago is tied to the Katrina Mortensen case?" Cady asked.

"Yes."

"I'm not seeing it."

"That's because the picture you're looking at was provided by her parents, which was used in the papers and on TV. I'm sure it was a great likeness of her when she was in high school—it's her senior class picture."

Cady looked at an eight-by-ten of a young woman in a red sweater and red glasses, with medium-length black hair parted in the middle and combed down. Nondescript. Any girl, any high school, USA.

"Don't they snap these pictures the summer before, which would make Nicole Huckle seventeen?"

Rohr nodded.

"And Ms. Huckle disappeared when she was, what—twenty?"

"She had just turned twenty-one."

"Those are formative years."

"Nikki Huckle blossomed. I read the case file, Agent Cady. Her dad was a strict disciplinarian—no sign of any abuse—but life in the Huckle household was constricted. So when Nikki Huckle graduated and went off to UW in Superior, she took to nightlife like a duck to water. Managed to get herself kicked out of the dorm in six months after her roommate found Nikki's stash of ecstasy pills and speed. Nikki stayed at an older boy's apartment for a few months, but eventually even he asked her to leave. At that point she had stopped attending class, so back to Cloquet, back home. Nikki's newfound lifestyle didn't agree with her dad and mom, and they soon tough-loved her out of the household."

"Sounds more like she was blossoming into an addict."

"Got dropped at detox on more than one occasion. Got intoxicated at a bar in Sandstone during the Quarry Days celebration and started flashing her tits at the fairgoers. A misdemeanor for indecent exposure. Nikki and her flock of dime-store Paris Hiltons hit every watering hole between here and Hinckley. She hung a lot at Black Bear casino, caught all the concerts, but pretty much considered the North Star State to be Podunkville. She apparently talked a lot about moving to California, modeling or movies…you know the rest of the story."

Cady leaned his elbows on Rohr's desk, chin on his thumbs, wondering about Nikki Huckle's tie-in to Katrina Mortensen, late of Newton, Iowa. From his angle he could see only one of two pictures in a hinged double frame on the lieutenant's desk. Personal photos. The one he could see was a close-up of a young woman who shared the lieutenant's brown eyes and thin lips. Rohr noticed him looking and flipped the attached frames sideways so Cady could see them head on. The second picture was of Rohr and a woman of similar age, both in running shorts and shirts in a crowd of runners.

"My daughter Annie is in a pre-engineering program at St. Thomas down in the cities—biomed and chemical." Rohr pointed at the other picture. "My partner and I ran in the Grandma's Marathon last year. Got okay times, but never again."

Cady said nothing.

"Came out ten years back. Blew a marriage and drove Annie into her father's arms. Annie's had a 4.0 since kindergarten, so I don't figure we screwed up too badly."

Cady nodded, unsure of what to say.

"Anyway—the cops didn't full-court press the Nikki Huckle disappearance, as there was no body and no abandoned car. Just another young 'un who ran off to the big city." Rohr set the dual picture frames back in place on her desk. "One lunkhead officer swore he saw Nikki on a porno site, so that retard and a detective spent an afternoon surfing YouPorn as part of their investigation."

"You're kidding me."

"No shit," Rohr replied. "And I bet they left no stone unturned."

Cady chuckled obligingly. "So what got you looking into Huckle's disappearance?"

The lieutenant kicked a lower desk drawer. "I keep a mystery file in there. Copies of cold cases and other crap that never made any sense." "And what if Nikki really *is* just another young 'un who ran off to the big city?"

"I haven't slept much since this Katrina Mortensen killing. Took my mystery file home and started walking through it when I couldn't sleep. First I noticed Nikki was of a similar age, so I drove to Cloquet and visited a couple of Nikki's old party friends. One of them gave me this photo." Rohr handed Cady a picture. "It was taken a couple weeks before Nikki's disappearance."

"Jesus." Cady's compared the two pictures and looked up at Rohr. Nikki Huckle could have passed for Mortensen's sister.

CHAPTER SEVEN

"That asshole Jahnsen would fill his rag with kiddie porn if it sold papers!" District Two shouted.

"You'll never let that go, will you?" Garry something from District Five baited Dan something from District Two.

"Everyone in this room knows that was complete bullshit. I bought those Bulldog tickets," Dan shot back.

Cady didn't know if it was complete bullshit and didn't care what trivial scandal Dan from District Two had gotten himself into with Alan Jahnsen, the editor of the Duluth *News Herald*. Cady checked his watch again and scanned the faces in the conference room. Nine city council members sat about a mahogany table, mixed in with a walrus moustache from the chamber of commerce, a rotund guy from the board of tourism, a gaunt gent with tremors in a high-end wheelchair, and a string of other city leaders Cady didn't try to make heads or tail of. Duluth Mayor Curt Renquist and Police Chief Weflen sat at the table's head. Cady and Lieutenant Rohr leaned against the rear wall.

Though billed as a city council meeting, there was no media present, no TV or radio reporters, not even the dreaded Alan Jahnsen. And no one appeared to be scribing the meeting minutes. City Council President Sharla Tanner had called the meeting to order and then immediately turned the gavel over to Mayor Renquist, of white hair and wire rims. Mayor Renquist couldn't hot-potato it to Chief Weflen fast enough.

The chief sketched a *Reader's Digest* abridged version of the case, talked a little bit about the victim, Katrina Mortensen, and briefly mentioned that major *oddities* had been noted in the autopsy, but provided nothing to the room on the cause of Mortensen's death. The chief explained the council meeting had been called in order to give city leadership a heads-up on how the freakish nature of the killer's M.O. had the potential to garner headlines that would not paint Duluth in the most positive of lights. Although he couldn't comment on case specifics, his investigators were following up on several leads. Chief Weflen then introduced the room to Special Agent Cady from the Federal Bureau of Investigation.

Cady hadn't anticipated being an active participant in the evening's proceedings. He pushed away from the wall and spoke boilerplate about how the Bureau was prepared to work hand in hand with the local authorities and offer Duluth PD as much assistance as possible in this ongoing investigation. Within thirty seconds Cady was back against the wall. Chief Weflen looked as though he'd bitten into a lemon, but continued onto the next topic.

"I think he wanted more pizzazz," Deb Rohr whispered when the meeting resumed. "But now you know why you're here—to calm the natives, show them the chief is doing everything in his power to get to the bottom of a very ugly case."

"Great," Cady whispered back.

"The mayor's retiring after his term is up," she said. "It's the chief's job for the taking, unless he fucks up a high-profile."

The next topic cut to the chase.

"So if I'm hearing this correctly," the man from the chamber of commerce said, "the *specifics* of this murder are so *horrifically* shocking that there's a good chance it makes the national news, a good chance it's the lead story on the networks and cable, and a good chance that the next time anyone Googles Duluth, they get a thousand hits on this killing?"

"Oh, Christ." District Two again. "It'll live on Drudge forever."

The police chief shrugged.

"That's why we need this wrapped up before the details leak out," said Mayor Renquist.

"What's the media got so far?" asked the council president.

"What we gave them yesterday," the chief answered. "A body washed ashore. It was that girl who'd gone missing in Iowa—heavy emphasis on Iowa. She had been murdered. No further details or comments at this point."

"I've already heard rumors about—" the representative from District One began.

"Who'd you hear the rumors from?" the mayor cut in.

"I'd prefer not to say, but I can't imagine I'm the only person in this room who's heard something."

"There better be no leaking." Renquist scratched at his head. "I'm not facing voters again, and I'll take great personal delight ruining the career of any city employee who goes gabbing to the press about this."

"Realistically, Mayor," Cady said, "you'll be lucky if this doesn't come out by the end of the week."

All eyes turned to the FBI agent.

"And that's assuming every person in this room stays silent." Cady looked at Lieutenant Rohr, thinking about how her detectives were already focusing on funeral homes in a fifty-mile radius. "Too many moving parts in the investigation to keep a lid on for much longer."

The mayor looked at Chief Weflen. "That's why we need an arrest made before the details come out."

"Remember how the flood kicked our asses?" the guy from the tourism board spoke up. "Cars in sink holes, streets like waterfalls, dead zoo animals—we dug our way out in days, but for months we had to deal with empty hotels and cancelled conferences due to those images being blasted across the world."

"The mayor and I will have a heart-to-heart with Jahnsen first thing in the morning," the chief said. "We'll see if we can count on him to do the right thing."

"I'll say *civic duty* a bunch of times in my George C. Scott voice," assured Renquist.

"The mayor does a stellar Patton," Rohr whispered in Cady's ear.

"Twenty bucks says Jahnsen dry humps the First Amendment right in front of you," District Two chimed in.

"Not helpful, Dan." The police chief glared at District Two.

"Mayor Renquist," an attractive brunette seated next to the man in the wheelchair spoke for the first time, "I'd like to thank you, Police Chief Weflen, and the council members for inviting my brother and myself to the meeting this evening."

The mayor smiled. "Of course, Luce. We always count on you and Ev to bring a healthy dose of common sense to a murky situation."

Rohr leaned in toward Cady. "That's Lucinda Quilling and her brother, Evan. Politicians they back tend to get elected."

Cady nodded. Scions of Duluth meant very old money from timber and shipping, even descendants of those who'd dabbled in railroads with financier Jay Cooke and magnate James J. Hill. The Quilling siblings were no exception. Cady had recently read an article in the Grand Rapids paper detailing the Quillings' humanitarian activities, how Lucinda spent most of her time performing philanthropic deeds, giving back to the city that had, since the turn of the nineteenth century, made the Quilling clan exceptionally wealthy. Recent charities rattled off in the article included a grant to restore the opera house to its original condition, donations of new computers to the city library, and an endowment to set up a summer camp for underprivileged children.

The Quilling siblings had also been a guiding force behind transforming Duluth from a dying industrial town to a tourist mecca in the 1980s. Along with lift bridges and big ships, Duluth became known for its retail shopping, antiquing, and banking, as well as premium healthcare for northern Minnesotans. The black-and-white picture in the newspaper article had not done Ms. Quilling any justice. Cady was amazed at how young Lucinda's face appeared for someone who had to be at least fifty, but half a billion in the bank could always be counted on to stem the flow of sand in the hourglass. Brother Evan, who Cady had initially taken for Lucinda's father, had come out on the losing end in his fight with time—evidently a stroke trumped even money.

"I'm not sure I'll be able to live up to your billing, Mayor Renquist," Ms. Quilling said, "but I think we may be overreacting. Quite frankly, I never want to hear how this dear child died and will intentionally ignore the media reporting when it inevitably comes out. It's a tragedy and my heart goes out to her parents. That said, do not forget how our fair city has already established that the site of a double homicide is profitable for tourism."

Everyone in the room knew what Lucinda Quilling was referring to—Glensheen Mansion. Built on the shores of Lake Superior in the early 1900s by Chester Adgate Congdon, mining magnate and one of the wealthiest men in Minnesota history, Glensheen mansion comprised thirty-nine rooms, a boat house, carriage house, and a gardener's cottage, a clay tennis court and grounds irrigated by a nearby creek, even hot running water and electricity—the works. Unfortunately, Chester Congdon's youngest daughter, Elisabeth, and her nurse, Velma Pietila, were found murdered in Glensheen Mansion in 1977. The elderly heiress had been smothered and her nurse brutally beaten to death with a candlestick at the hands of Elisabeth's son-in-law, a man who, after serving time in prison, would eventually open both wrists with a steak knife and bleed to death on his living room floor.

The University of Minnesota in Duluth had inherited the mansion and opened it for public tours in 1979.

"Lizzy was like a grandmother to me. She brought me antique dolls from her trips to Amsterdam. As kids, Ev and I played hide and seek at Glensheen. And the very thought that the site where Lizzy *died* has become a huge tourist trap sickens me to this day. I'd rather it be leveled. Or if I had my druthers, it'd be a home for foster care or teen mothers." Ms. Quilling took a breath and continued, "Now I understand we're all still punch drunk from dealing with the financial repercussions caused by the flood, and the ensuing lack of tourist revenue, but if we take a long, hard look in the mirror, we realize that, now and again, tragedy comes to even idyllic little cities like Duluth. It wasn't too many years back that they were calling Minneapolis *Murderapolis* because the homicide rate there had increased to an all-time high, but I don't recall that blemish bringing economic activity in the Twin Cities to a standstill. I doubt an isolated homicide, which may not have even taken place in Duluth, will show up as a blip on the tourist radar, and it certainly can't compare with the Congdon murders."

"Unfortunately, Lucinda," Chief Weflen said, "the Mortensen case has a certain *unique* aspect that, comparatively, will make the Glensheen murders look like a Sunday stroll."

"Which, again, is why we need this wrapped up ASAP," Mayor Renquist said, looking sideways at Weflen as though the chief should be out prowling the hillside alleyways instead of wasting time at council meetings. "We're throwing everything we have into this investigation. Unlimited overtime. Help from the Bureau." The mayor tossed an arm in Cady's direction. "Hell, I'm five minutes away from ordering the dog catcher and meter maids onboard. But we do not want the media to catch wind of the modus operandi while the killer is still on the loose."

"We're talking only one death here," the city council president asked, "aren't we?"

"The perpetrator screwed up the body dump," Lieutenant Rohr said. "There was a storm the night the victim was dumped into Lake Superior that likely forced a rush job, kept the perp from going out a few more miles and doing it right. So we have a killer attempting to cover his trail, but, that said, we only have the one victim at this time."

"What if there's more?"

The mayor itched his head again. "Then we're fucked."

Cady shook hands with council members and business leaders as they filed out. The meeting had ambled on for another fifteen minutes, mostly council members brainstorming events to pull in visitors to Duluth from the cities and surrounding parts—Shakespeare in the Park, concerts, sailing regattas, that sort of tourist bait.

Lucinda Quilling and her brother were nearly the last to leave.

"Thanks for helping us in our time of need, Agent Cady," the woman said. "Hopefully this unpleasantness will be put to bed in the next day or two and we can toast you at Bellsio's."

"I'd not turn that down."

"Let me introduce you to my brother, Evan. He suffered a stroke last year, but he's climbing back. Ev has trouble with speech, but he's sharp as a tack."

Cady took Evan Quilling's trembling hand in his own busted paw. His time in physical rehab over the past several years had given him a deep respect for the hardships faced by the truly handicapped and made him more direct in his interactions with those less fortunate.

"How's the electric chair working for you, Mr. Quilling?"

Evan Quilling's hand hovered over the wheelchair's joystick, which he used to steer. He looked up at Cady with sad eyes and shrugged.

Lucinda Quilling stepped in. "Evan would prefer to be up on his feet, but the chair's a godsend. So are the stair lifts at home."

"Luce and Ev." The mayor joined the trio, full of broad grins and good cheer, at least for his political backers. "Can I walk you two out?"

After they left, only Cady, Deb Rohr, and Chief Weflen remained.

"You're working out of First Street, right?" the chief asked Cady, referring to the Resident Agency in the Federal Building.

"Yes," Cady said, dead tired from his nonstop travels. "Heading home tonight, back with a toothbrush at first light."

"Good," the chief replied. "I've never heard the mayor swear before."

CHAPTER EIGHT

The widow Dayna Parrish opened the sliding-glass door and the blond man slipped inside. She stared out into the darkness of her backyard—she'd left the outside lights intentionally off—then slid the door shut, flicked the latch, and followed the man into her kitchen. The moon through the closed curtains and a nightlight above the dishwasher provided their only illumination.

"Some of us sleep, you know," Dayna said.

"I used to do that."

The blond man was of middle height, middle size, and, for all Dayna knew, middle-aged. He had his hair cut high and tight, military style, and looked pleasant…at a distance. But up close was a different story. Up close you noticed that a large part of his right eyebrow was missing, which her late husband Steve had informed her occurred in a Chechen detention camp, where mistreating prisoners helped the guards wile away each afternoon's tedium. In this case, the guards had chosen their victim unwisely; a large bribe had been paid for his release, and not long after the guards were each paid a visit in their own home, where accounts were settled in full.

Was any of it true? Steve had shrugged when relaying what little he'd heard to his wife. Who the hell knew?

Face to face you could see his eyes were like sculpted blue granite, and although Dayna had trouble initially putting her finger on it, it finally occurred to her what was awry. His eyes remained devoid of emotion. Even when the blond man smiled or laughed, his eyes most certainly did not. She didn't like to be around him on the best of days, an instinct magnified tenfold in her husband's absence. And Dayna hated herself for feeling intimidated.

"What's the word?" Dayna asked.

"He says to weather it."

Damn, Dayna thought as the blond man sat on a wooden stool at the kitchen island, uninvited, and unzipped his leather jacket. Evidently, the meeting called for longer than a few brief moments of discomfort.

She sat on the stool opposite. "Does he know Jund's pit bull has been poking around?"

The blond man nodded. "Weather it."

"Cady told me they've got my prints on the fence."

The blond man shrugged. "So you dropped Steve off for a meeting at Jund's house on the way to Pilates one night and got the nickel tour. All you really remember from that evening is how nervous you felt around Jund, what with the assistant director staring at your breasts the entire time."

That actually could work. Dayna found herself, remarkably, beginning to relax. Her nerves had been like piano wire since that goddamned night that left her husband dead on a bedroom floor and her stumbling around that fucking briar patch like a goddamned moron. Still, an extremely difficult path lay ahead.

"That fucking Cady scares me. There's shit going on behind his eyes," Dayna said.

"There's not a thing Agent Cady can do to you."

"Weather it, huh?"

"Weather it," the blond man affirmed. "You get anything on Jund's PC?"

"No. I'd just begun when I heard the crash from upstairs. I snuck up the steps, peeked around the corner. Jund had Steve by the throat at that point and…if I'd done anything, Jund would have seen me."

"I understand. You did right to hide and clean up the mess. That was some quick thinking on your part, by the way."

She had a good BS detector—had to in her line of work. Could she really have read the blond man incorrectly? He appeared dead earnest in his attempt to make her feel better about both that night and the unfortunate fallout.

The fact of the matter was, she'd frozen. Steve would still be alive had she thrown herself at Jund, clawing his eyes, pulling him off her husband. Jund's shock at seeing her might have been all that was needed for Steve to recover and complete his task. Days later, Dayna still didn't know what had caused her paralysis. Some innate cowardice? The intimacy she'd shared with Roland Jund in that very same bedroom?

"I could use a beer, and I think you could too," the blond man said. "You have any of those Rolling Rocks Steve liked so much?"

Dayna stared at the blond man. He knew the living hell she'd been through and yet he appeared easy-breezy, bore an all-will-be-A-okay manner, and that the word from on high was to simply *weather it*. And now he wanted a beer. Was there something more in play here? She and Steve had come to the conclusion that the blond man was asexual. Not gay, perhaps loosely hetero, but in a manner that clearly put sexuality itself on the back burner. Dayna somewhat fancied herself fluent in the art of seduction, but when it came to lovemaking and the blond man, there was no there there.

Yet what was she feeling now? A vibe of being hit on? Him wanting to meet at this ungodly hour, settling in at the kitchen island, him comforting her, and now throwing back some drinks? It was out of character and she hoped there wouldn't be any awkward rebuffing in her immediate future, what with her husband's corpse having just been released to the funeral home. Hers and Steve's marriage was one of convenience and she'd done things, done men—Roland Jund for a recent example—that were outside the scope of any traditional wedding vows, but she was still a human being.

"I'll split one with you, and then I need to sleep," Dayna said, walking to the refrigerator. "I meet with the attorney first thing in the morning."

What Dayna didn't notice was how the blond man had slipped on a pair of driving gloves under the island's countertop. She also didn't hear him approach from behind as she leaned into the fridge. Several circles of rope appeared in the blond man's gloved hands, rope that had previously been stuffed under the back of his bomber jacket.

He dropped the noose around Dayna's neck, did an about-face, and yanked the cord over his shoulder, collapsing the noose. The slip knot tightened, cutting off Dayna's air and crushing her screams in her throat. The blond man yanked the rope higher, until Dayna's neck was above his shoulder, her slippers falling off, her toes an inch off the ground. Dayna's hands clawed at the noose, trying to work her fingertips beneath the rope, wasting valuable seconds before sending an elbow into the back of the blond man's rib cage, but by then the strikes were feeble, fruitless.

"'Of all the gods only death does not desire gifts,'" the blond man murmured as the widow Parrish suffered her final throes. "The Greek playwright Aeschylus said that."

By the time he crossed the dining room and opened the side garage door, Dayna Parrish was dead.

The blond man walked to the center of the garage, between her Miata and husband Steve's SUV, Dayna hanging over his back like a sack of dirty laundry. He wondered if in her last few moments Dayna had appreciated how similar her death was to that of her late husband. The blond man looked at the rafters above the Jeep Grand Cherokee.

Perfect.

CHAPTER NINE

Cady was back at Duluth PD by eight a.m. and talking with Lieutenant Rohr by five past.

"Take me through Des Moines again."

"Katrina Mortensen checks into the Marriott at 2:12 p.m. on Sunday afternoon. Although the conference formally kicks off with a keynote Monday morning, most dentists and hygienists arrive during the day on Sunday. There's an informal meet-and-greet with hors d'oeuvres and booze in one of the dinner halls that evening."

"She go to that?"

"Yes. From the interviews, Katrina appeared to be a social butterfly. This was her first conference, and I think she was determined to have some fun."

"In other words, she was young."

"Young and beautiful, eager to let her hair down, but not in a bad way," Rohr insisted. "My take, Agent Cady, is that Katrina was all over that Marriott. She even found time to take a dip in the pool Sunday afternoon. Monday morning keynote, sessions, trade floor, luncheon, dinner, the whole nine yards—she was there."

"High visibility."

"Plenty of time for our perp to spot her."

"But if it wasn't a sex crime, it might not have played out that way."

"It was a sex crime," the lieutenant responded.

"What about what Foeller told us?"

"Wallace Foeller is looking at this with his ME hat on, all vials and blood samples. The rape kit comes back negative, so it wasn't Bubba in the basement with a girl tethered to the furnace. That's the kind of routine crap Foeller deals with every year." Lieutenant Rohr looked at Cady. "A very attractive female turns up naked with the blood pumped out of her but no semen pumped in. Bewildering? Very much so...but it is a sex crime. And with Nikki Huckle from Cloquet looking like Mortensen's twin separated at birth, I'm not getting the sense that this fucker's a one-and-done."

Cady's smartphone was set to vibrate. It danced on the tabletop next to his mouse pad, the name *Agent Preston* on the caller ID. The two had arranged a call at noon his time to discuss the Jund situation, yet it was barely ten o'clock. Cady had a sinking feeling as he brought the phone to his ear.

"Dayna Parrish is dead," Preston said as soon as he answered.

"How?"

"She committed suicide last night. Hung herself."

Cady tried to square suicide with the headstrong woman who had gotten in his face two days earlier. "No way I got that vibe off her."

"She missed an appointment with her attorney this morning and didn't return his calls. He drove to her house, and when no one answered the door, he looked in the garage window. He saw two cars and a pair of dangling legs. He called 911 after he finished being sick."

Cady closed his eyes and tried to recall the stats. "Dayna Parrish is a good decade beyond the high-youth age group. And women generally opt for poison. I'd lay money on Parrish having access to a firearm—hell, I thought she was going to pull one on me the other day. Hanging's just not high on the list."

"Evidently, she'd been under a lot of pressure this past week. Who knows where that leads a person?"

"She just didn't seem like one to crack. No way I got that read, Liz. The woman was more shrew than shrinking violet."

"It gets worse."

"Tell me."

"She left a note," Preston replied. "And it points to Jund."

—

Cady entered Chief Weflen's outer office and was about to speak with his secretary when Duluth's foremost maker-and-shaker Lucinda Quilling stepped out from the chief's inner office.

"A joy to see you again, Agent Cady." Lucinda held out her hand.

"Call me Drew," Cady said, walking her to the elevator. "More of last night's stuff?"

"Something far more treacherous. Politics," she said, smiling. "Nothing that violates any campaign laws too directly; no envelopes were exchanged."

"Next year's election?"

Ms. Quilling nodded.

"The chief seems a good man."

"We share a common vision for Duluth, for its future, but to be honest, I'm playing defense."

"What do you mean?"

"I mean the chief's opponent is an ass."

"Who's he running against?"

"You met him last night."

Cady shrugged, stumped. What he knew about Duluth politics could be stuffed up a bug's nose with plenty of room left over.

"Dan Wetmore—the ham from District Two. Wetmore's not formally tossed his hat in the ring, but everyone knows it's coming. It's only a question of timing."

"Wetmore would be bad for the city?"

"Wetmore would be an unmitigated disaster. I hate to insult asses, because some would say that most politicians are asses. At least asses get things done; often decent things. But Dan Wetmore is a horse's ass. And not much good comes from a horse's ass."

"I need you for the duration," the chief enunciated slowly. "*The duration.*"

"I can search NCIC and ViCAP from the Hoover Building," Cady said. "Hopefully put Lieutenant Rohr's mind at ease that Mortensen's not part of a bigger pattern."

"I've already got my waders on without Deb's bullshit." Chief Weflen was red-faced. "This case is already a goddamned nightmare without her trying to tie another missing girl into it."

"You saw the photos, right? There is a striking resemblance."

"You page through *Playboy* long enough and they all start to look alike."

Cady shrugged. "I'll have the experts at NCAVC construct a profile."

NCAVC stood for the National Center for the Analysis of Violent Crime at Quantico, Virginia.

"I don't need a profiler. For Christ's sake, you saw the autopsy results. We're looking for a fucking maniac. There—that's your profile."

"Like I said, Chief, it's imperative that I go to D.C. I will be working twenty-hour days." Cady knew the strain Weflen was under. "This will be front burner."

"I want daily briefings, Cady. If Deb Rohr or I call, I want it answered on the first ring."

"Understood."

The chief shook his head. "If I get warmed-over stew, I'll go ballistic."

CHAPTER TEN

"I'm radioactive," Jund said, dumping enough sugar into his Starbucks dark roast to turn it into a dessert. "You two need to walk out that door and run as far from me as humanly possible."

The three agents sat in the same Starbucks where Cady and Jund had met five days earlier. The two men sat in the exact same seats, with Liz Preston on Cady's right. Cady noted that Preston's salt-and-pepper was out and a brown tint was now the vogue. The color shaved off a decade. Jund, on the other hand, looked like crops from the Dust Bowl stuffed inside a wrinkled dress suit. Shaving was apparently now optional, the AD's faced lined with gray stubble.

"That's not happening," Cady replied, and Preston nodded her concurrence.

"Look, Drew, Liz, I do appreciate the loyalty, but like I said, I'm literally radioactive. You can see me from Mars. Just ask the ONCIX agents who are no doubt sitting in a sedan out in the parking lot." Jund finished with the sugar container he'd swiped from the cream bar and handed it to Preston. "It's time for attorneys and polygraphs."

ONCIX stood for the Office of the National Counterintelligence Executive. Cady placed the odds at fifty-fifty that the AD's assertion regarding sedans in parking lots wasn't merely paranoia. The case had metastasized from the justifiable use of deadly force during a home invasion—virtually the definition of self-defense—to an issue concerning national security, with a great deal more to it than met the eye.

"Liz filled me in on what she knows in the car on the way here. It took all of thirty seconds." Cady had yet to touch his liquid caffeine.

"What say you fill us in on whatever the hell's going on?"

Jund stared into his cup of sugar as though it were a crystal ball.

Cady sighed. "Dayna Parrish didn't kill herself."

"Of course not." Jund's gaze popped up. "I killed her."

If Agent Preston's jaw had dropped any lower, Starbucks could have used it as a dustpan. "I don't believe that for a second, sir."

"It doesn't matter," Jund said, pointing at the parking lot. "That's what they believe. They think I killed Dayna," Jund paused at the name and then continued, "and made her death look like a suicide, but, apparently, I was too goddamned dumb to toss her PC into the Potomac."

"What's on her PC?"

"I'm being kept in the dark, but—let's see—I assume some recipes," Jund said and began counting his fingers, "a couple of book-club assignments, a treasure trove of classified documents…and, of course, a list of all the times I've threatened to kill her."

Cady suddenly wished he'd ordered decaf.

"Espionage?" The word itself hung on Cady's lip like a bad moustache. "You're not in the National Security Branch."

"Steve Parrish was in Counterintelligence, and I killed him."

Though Cady and Preston were already aware of where Agent Parrish appeared on the org chart, they sat in silence.

"Besides," Jund said, "it's not so much spy versus spy anymore as Intel for Bratva—the Russian Mafia. Those bastards got saturated with ex-KGB operators when the wall came down."

"The Russian mob?" Cady asked, surprised.

Jund looked at Preston, who in turn slid a napkin across the table to Cady. It read: *We'll talk later.*

"Bratva," Jund continued, "would pay through the nose for someone like me inside CID."

CID was the FBI's Criminal Investigative Division.

"So why aren't you in shackles?"

"I get the impression CART is still digesting whatever's on Parrish's computer." CART stood for the FBI's Computer Analysis and Response Teams—computer forensics. "Or perhaps they're hoping I'll lead them to a dead drop, catch me yanking some microfiche out of a pumpkin. Besides, they don't need me in shackles and a jumpsuit, as they've effectively shut me down. My office is closed. My PC, iPad, and smartphone are also being autopsied by CART. And poor Liz here is left to swing in the breeze."

Preston feigned a smile.

"I'm sure my passport's been flagged, and I imagine a SWAT team will descend on me if I try to take more than fifty bucks out of an ATM."

"What did the director have to say?"

"It was a deputy director who ordered me in and sat back while his hired gun explained the *predicament*—that's the word they bandied about, no shit—the *predicament* that I was in. Personally, I prefer tit in a wringer, but that's just quibbling over Beltway semantics."

"Tell Drew about JoAnne's PC," said Preston.

"Ah, yes—the inquiry into my home invasion has evolved. My steadfast colleagues at the Bureau have joined forces with the valiant powers at the Leesburg Police Department, as well as the Loudoun County Sheriff's Office. Good to know I have these newfound friends to aid in any investigation, that is, if I didn't get the distinct impression that they're all looking into me. My wife's computer is one of several items seized from Casa de Jund."

"How is JoAnne taking this?"

"She knows I'm no Russian spy. That part's all clear. But my relationship with Dayna Parrish—even though we were separated, at JoAnne's request for Christ's sake—has gone over about as well as if I'd diddled her sister. Suffice to say the bouquet of roses has gone unanswered."

"What can we do?"

"Must I say it in Swahili? I'm radioactive. I glow in the dark. Unless you want a career enema, the two of you need to walk away." Jund took a sip of his coffee, then returned the cup to the table. "Does the name Brian Kelley mean anything to you?"

"Sounds familiar," Cady answered. "FBI?"

"Nope," the AD replied. "Brian Kelley was a CIA operative, a patriot and a hero. We—meaning the Bureau—accused him of being a KGB mole and screwed his career in the late 1990s. He sat on administrative leave for years waiting to be cleared. It was a travesty and a goddamned shame, especially since the traitor turned out to be one of our guys, one of our colleagues. That asshole Robert Hanssen. You remember him, right?"

Cady and Preston nodded. FBI Agent Robert Hanssen had spent two plus decades spying for Soviet and Russian intelligence, providing invaluable intel and betraying KGB agents who were secretly working for the United States.

"Biggest disaster in Bureau history. Did you know a decade before his arrest, Hanssen's brother-in-law—also an FBI agent—advised the Bureau to investigate Hanssen for espionage because there were wads of cash lying around his house?"

Cady shook his head.

"That heads-up got ignored, along with about a half-dozen other red flags that slipped through the cracks. *The Three Stooges* were better organized. We knew someone was there, hiding in the weeds, and we finally got Hanssen by bribing an ex-KGB agent to get us the mole's identity. In the good old days, we'd have hung the treasonous prick from the Washington Monument."

"So they think you're the new Robert Hanssen?"

Jund sighed. "But in reality I'm Brian Kelley. And it looks like I'll be spending the foreseeable future sitting in my own feces."

CHAPTER ELEVEN

"What's he really want from us?" Cady whispered.

Cady and Preston were jogging a bike trail in the Georgetown Waterfront Park. It was a crisp day and both were decked out in gray sweats, t-shirts, and old running shoes. Cady got the feeling that if they were serious about the jog, Agent Preston would have left him in her wake about two minutes into the run. Preston was working toward her fifth-degree black belt in karate. A few years back, Cady and Jund had attended Agent Preston's exam to receive her fourth-degree black belt, an event at which Liz had to take out several attackers armed with rubber guns and knives. Although the attackers, all of them black belts themselves, wore chest pads and face gear, and weren't, for the purpose of the test, expected to go animal crazy on those testing out, Cady was impressed with how efficiently Liz had put the faux attackers on their respective asses. He'd made a mental note to stay on her good side.

"Not much," Preston responded in a similar hushed tone. "Just prove his innocence, and maybe ferret out the real mole if we have any extra time."

"I love it when you're ironical, Liz."

"I see you're turning into a smartass yourself. That come from Terri?"

Cady gave that a second of thought. "I guess it is. She gives me so much grief, I'm learning to shovel it back."

"Not sure if my two cents means anything, but Terri's the best thing that's ever happened to you. I was delighted to hear you two got engaged."

Cady glanced at Liz Preston, a woman he'd known for years, yet only really knew what she allowed him to see. He took no offense, as it appeared the same with others; she threw up a barrier, an invisible tarp, between herself and, well, humanity. He'd be in serious trouble if someone put a gun to his head and told him, besides karate, to rattle off three of her interests. Preston and Jund were an odd mix that, like gin and tonic, made perfect sense together. Cady knew a large part of Assistant Director Roland Jund's success at the Bureau—up until now—was due to Agent Preston's organizational skills.

"Thanks."

"Try not to screw it up," Preston replied.

"Jund appears to be rubbing off on you as well. By the way, what was all that garbage about the Russian mob?"

"He said that to baffle any prying ears. Something like this, the surveillance goes deep. Roland doesn't believe this has anything to do with Bratva."

"Which is why we're out here?"

Preston nodded. "He's in such an untenable position, and it's breaking his heart. Roland doesn't want to betray the Bureau, but he doesn't want to sit back and take it."

"I was hoping that placing Dayna Parrish at his house that night would force her to come clean with whatever this is about, but now she's dead and we're in a whole new world," Cady said. "Jund is talking espionage and counterintelligence, national security—that's not our forte, Liz."

Preston shrugged. "We catch killers, Drew. There are different motivations at play here than we're used to, which means we'll be forced to learn on the fly. But we're after a killer and we do have our methods."

Cady slowed down but said nothing.

"In fact, we should run a profile on someone who would betray their country, their colleagues, friends, and family—if one doesn't already exist."

"A Benedict Arnold profile," Cady said. "Bryce Drommerhausen has promised an analysis regarding my *situation* in Duluth. I'll talk to him about this. You're a genius, Liz."

The first thing Cady had done after deplaning at Reagan was to contact Bryce Drommerhausen, a supervisory special agent working in the BAU at NCAVC—Behavioral Analysis Unit at the National Center for the Analysis of Violent Crime—and send him a copy of the Mortensen murder file. Cady had long pegged Drommerhausen as the Bureau's best when it came to getting inside an UNSUB's mind in order to ferret out what made the killer tick.

"Hardly, but it's a starting point." Preston slowed her pace to equal Cady's. "Drommerhausen may not want to touch this."

"That shouldn't be a problem. Bryce likes Jund, might even respect him."

"Peas from the same warped pod."

"He asked me about this whole snafu. Said he's heard some ugly rumors and got a big whiff of bullshit."

"What did you tell him?"

"Not a hell of a lot for me to say."

"It's a setup, Drew," Preston said. "Jund's being framed by whatever cell Steve and Dayna Parrish were part of."

"But why Jund, of all people?"

Preston shrugged again. "A patsy to throw others off the scent?"

"That would mean there's a pressure point somewhere along the line, and that pressure point is scaring the hell out of someone. There's a realistic fear of being dragged into the light of day and all the ugliness that would entail. A dead Roland Jund with a home computer full of national security secrets would make all that disappear. However, that arrangement goes south when Jund fights Steve Parrish—there was no time to plant files on his PC—and Dayna Parrish, who could implicate others, is murdered with information left behind to point at Jund." Cady stopped, lost in thought. "But Jund's not in counterintelligence; he doesn't sit in on those meetings, so him being made into a patsy seems misplaced."

Preston jogged in place. "It might not be misplaced."

"What do you mean?"

"Jund's been on a joint FBI and CIA taskforce for most of the past year."

"What taskforce?"

"I don't know." Preston stopped jogging. "Behind all that bluster, Jund takes his job very seriously. No loose lips."

"When the FBI joins hands with the CIA, what does that tell you?"

"National security."

"Who else is on the taskforce?"

"I have no idea."

"At one point in time Robert Hanssen was assigned the task of hunting for a KGB mole burrowed deep within the FBI. In other words, Hanssen was charged with hunting himself."

"Right. Irony of ironies."

"So if a Robert Hanssen exists on this joint FBI-CIA taskforce, that would be the link to Jund. Roland looks around the table at the other members, but one member in particular stares back." Cady looked at his colleague. "We need the names of all the agents on that taskforce."

"Roland won't say boo."

"Misbegotten loyalty aside, Liz, we need those names."

"I'll find a way," Preston whispered in reply. "The only thing I know right now is that when Jund blocks the time off on his calendar for those meetings, he uses a one-word codename."

"Which is?"

"Lynchpin."

The blond man popped the battery out of the cell phone, snapped the back plate back on, and then flicked the phone and battery across the surface of the pond as though skipping rocks. His *client* at the Federal Bureau of Investigation was adamant that *any means necessary* be taken to draw Special Agent Drew Cady away from his pro bono raking about the coals of the Roland Jund affair. The client felt that though he could sufficiently hinder any moves that might be made by Agent Preston, Agent Cady was a wild card. Cady made the blond man's client sweat. And though the blond man's client had been mildly more diplomatic in his assessment of the agent's presence in the nation's capital, he ultimately echoed the concern about Cady best summarized by the late Dayna Parrish—*there's shit going on behind his eyes.*

The blond man headed back to his car. By the time he reached his rental, an idea had already taken hold.

CHAPTER TWELVE

"How did you get this list?" Cady asked, scanning the slip of paper printed with eight names that Preston had handed him as she navigated west on Interstate 66 into Virginia, toward farming acreage north of a town called Marshall in rural Fauquier County. Preston was at the wheel of her Toyota Prius, with Cady riding shotgun.

They were traveling to a three-hundred-acre residence on their way to meet a spook—that is, a retired CIA field operator named Thomas "Eggs" Nolte. When the two agents had gone back to Jund to find out who else sat on the Lynchpin taskforce, their questions had been met only with a tight-lipped shake of the AD's head. When asked what Lynchpin stood for, they got three words and three words only—"Talk to Eggs."

"Eggs Nolte," Preston had informed Cady at the start of the journey, "is a Cold War encyclopedia; a living legend. Nolte goes way back—not all the way to Wild Bill Donovan, but darn close."

William Joseph Donovan—a.k.a. "Wild Bill"—had led the Office of Strategic Services—a.k.a. the OSS—during World War II. Although the OSS was disbanded by President Truman in 1945, its offspring, the Central Intelligence Agency, was founded by the passage of the National Security Act in 1947.

When it became clear that Preston didn't intend to answer Cady's question, he looked over the list of names again and smiled. "It must have fallen off a truck."

—

Thomas Nolte stood waiting for them in the driveway. He looked like a geriatric leprechaun, maybe five two in a pair of unlaced hiking boots, his face a roadmap of wrinkles and his head a mop of graying red. Nolte was compact, looked as though he'd just cut a cord of wood, and had a grip like a snapping turtle when Cady shook his hand.

"I'll be eighty-five next month," Nolte said.

"I hope I look half that good at eighty-five."

"My father cracked a hundred and five. Farmers live forever."

"What do you grow here?" Preston asked.

"Past that county road," Nolte gestured back toward where they'd come, "is mostly soybean and corn, some grain—and that's all mine—but I've got sixty acres socked away for wine grape production. When we get inside, I'll pop a Cab from the winery that takes my harvest."

"You actually work the land?" Preston asked.

"Let's not get carried away. I am retired, after all. Well, practically." Nolte was one of those people who appeared to have a permanent grin. "I rent the land to the real green thumbs. I'm a slum lord."

"It's an honor to finally meet you, Mr. Nolte," Cady said.

"Call me Eggs. Everybody does."

"I bet there's a story behind that nickname, sir."

"Allen Dulles heard I hailed from a tiny farm outside of Meadville, Pennsylvania, and started in with all that nonsense. 'Get Eggs in here,' he'd shout, or, 'Where'd Eggs put that damned report,' and the name stuck. Despite the fact that we weren't an egg farm and didn't have any damned chickens. Anyway, Dulles was the one who brought me onboard, long before either of you newbies were born." Nolte shook his head, and the smile faded momentarily. "I hated that man's guts almost as much as I loved him."

The Dulleses were a family of Presbyterian ministers, Catholic cardinals, international lawyers, and public servants. Allen Dulles had been the fifth Director of Central Intelligence, serving for a chunk of the Eisenhower Presidency and a portion of Kennedy's. Dulles' older brother, John Foster, had been Ike's Secretary of State.

"Welcome to my *Antebellum* room," Nolte said when they reached his large, ranch-style spread and stepped inside. "Otherwise known as the museum." He chuckled. "Every sofa, chair, desk, and table in this room, including the chandelier, is pre–Civil War. Mostly from Southern plantations. Had to embezzle funds to refurbish several of the pieces, but some were purchased in pristine condition, considering their age."

A double pedestal dining table of walnut and mahogany dominated the dining room's center and screamed elegance. Surrounding the table were both splat back arm and side chairs. An oval desk with an attached swivel chair balanced one side, with an upholstered green couch on rounded wood and a decorative end table rounding out the other. The walls were lined with thickly beveled mirrors and pictures of Southern plantations circa 1850. The fireplace mantel contained plaster busts of serious-looking gentlemen Cady did not recognize.

Cady gravitated toward the far wall, where a hefty glass trophy cabinet displayed antique weaponry.

"Didn't take you long to unearth my weapons wall, did it, Agent Cady?"

"I like your double-action revolver," Cady said, and then turned his attention to the long guns. "And that's a sleek-looking musket."

"They changed the face of war, son. Take that smoothbore you're salivating over: that had limited range and precision. As a result, attacking troops would run like bats from hell to get close enough and pray they had enough soldiers on their side to get the job done, even if they had to get up close and personal with their bayonets. But by the Civil War, muskets were rifled—spiral grooves cut inside the gun barrel, you know?—and that made all the difference. That one there," Nolte said, pointing at a different level in his display case, "is rifled, and though still a muzzle-loader, it was incalculably more accurate with a much greater range. A direct frontal assault would be met with a rain of death as far as a half mile out."

Cady nodded, and then waved a hand about the room. "What sparked your interest in all of this?"

"I was the youngest in the litter, so they'd park me with Grandpa when I was small. He was an old coot back then, older than I am now, but sharp as a tack, and he told me stories of the Civil War, where he'd served the Union as little more than a boy. I listened to everything *Ba-pa* told me in flat-out fascination. In school I did all my major

papers on the War Between the States. Fact is, I originally got into
the service as sort of subject matter expert on Civil War–era spycraft:
Rose O'Neal Greenhow, Thomas Jordan, Lafayette Baker and that lot.
But you didn't come here to listen to an old fool ramble on about his
hobby. I'd show you my *Reconstruction* room, but we wouldn't get
around to the business at hand until next week."

Nolte took Cady by the elbow and led him across the room toward
another display case.

"What I really wanted to show off is my limited foray into a
diversion I hear is near and dear to your heart, Agent Cady. Coin
collecting."

"Did Jund tell you that? Usually he gives me no end of mocking
over it."

"There may have been a mild sardonic lilt to Roland's voice at the
time."

Cady leaned toward the display, squinted, and then did his best to
keep his jaw from dropping. "Unbelievable."

"I attended the right auctions at the right time and milked my age
with the other investors for all it was worth to garner some pity wins,"
Nolte said. "You would have been ashamed of me, Elizabeth." Agent
Preston wandered over to look at the coins as well.

The display case contained at least a dozen levels, with each glass
shelf highlighting a particular coin—or series of similar coins—all of
which were enclosed in coin slabs with dark green inserts and labels
above each piece. The coin slabs tilted up and faced forward, and each
came with a detail card and corresponding envelope containing a
letter of authenticity. The top level displayed three 1877 Indian Head
Cent pieces, the two slabs on the outside showing the front side of the
coin and the slab in the middle the backside. The second level was
where it began to get intriguing: a gold 1862 Liberty Head twenty-
dollar Double Eagle, which Cady placed in the ballpark of five grand.
The next level contained a silver 1861 Seated Liberty quarter, worth
perhaps a little less than the Double Eagle, and that was followed by
a gold Indian Head 1859 three-dollar piece. On it went through the
levels in Nolte's display case. Cady looked for five minutes and could
have gotten lost in the detail notes for an hour, but felt Liz begin to
fidget next to him.

"I hope these are insured," Cady said. "For when I sneak back tonight to take them."

Nolte laughed out loud. "Never a good idea to sneak into an old spook's home, son—all sorts of dungeons and dragons at play."

CHAPTER THIRTEEN

"Good thing the Cold War wasn't won based on U.S. spycraft; otherwise, we'd be waiting in lines for toilet paper," Eggs Nolte said before disappearing to make good on his promise of Cabernet Sauvignon.

Cady found a comfortable seat while Agent Preston dutifully took out a yellow pad and pen. Nolte returned with the bottle from his winery and three glasses and, before long, had slipped into talking about Cold War history.

"Top secret Soviet archives were opened in the early 1990s after the Union of Soviet Socialist Republics—the USSR—was dissolved. These archives included the working files of the Central Committee and the Komitet Gosudarstvennoy Bezopasnosti—the KGB—and these archives proved what many of us had suspected all along, but the extent of which was mind-boggling." Nolte shook his head, then took another sip of the Cabernet and continued, "The Venona Project—that is, decrypted messages sent by Soviet Intelligence during World War II—were finally released by the US government in the mid-1990s. The decrypts exposed how hundreds of our fellow citizens had, in fact, spied for the Soviet Union. It was insidious just how deep the penetration went. Julius and Ethel Rosenberg were guilty as sin after all; as was atomic physicist Theodore Alvin Hall. Other intriguing details spilled out as well. But Venona was met with a giant ho-hum. No one cared anymore. The world had moved on." Nolte looked at Agent Preston. "Forgive my salty language, Elizabeth, but the Soviets piss-pounded us."

"I've heard much worse."

"Yep—by the late 1960s, we'd stopped taking Soviet espionage seriously. However, the Soviets remained deadly serious."

"So why aren't we in toilet-paper lines?"

Nolte sipped again and collected his thoughts, looking much like a professor he might have been in another life. "Winston Churchill once said, 'Democracy is the worst form of government except all of the others that have been tried.'" Nolte's natural grin expanded. "You see, the government that allowed the Soviets to be master practitioners in the art of espionage—and it truly is an art form— was corrupt and top heavy. They abolished any religion that hindered their beloved nation-state, expunged free thinking, free enterprise, free press, free anything from their social order. Vanquished individualism and seized private property. No one here remembers the brutality. The gulags, the Berlin Wall built by Communist East Germany, the persecution of Soviet Jews, the daily lies dished out by *Pravda's* propaganda machine. It was truly Orwellian and, as such, it rotted from within. They did it to themselves, and though we didn't see their suicide coming, in retrospect I'm amazed they lasted as long as they did."

"Democracy won out."

Nolte shrugged and then nodded. "By default. Our elections are for the most part fair; the founders gave us divided government in order to toss hurdles in front of potential dictatorships, and, of course, we have freedom of the press, which as far as I can tell in my nearly nine decades, the First Amendment gives the media the freedom to gum up every story they report, including the weather—especially the weather. My point being that open societies like ours are ripe for penetration by our enemies, but closed societies, totalitarian regimes like the USSR, eventually topple of their own weight and brutality. It's a catch-22—they won the spy battles but lost the war."

"I suppose I should feel honored," Nolte went on. "I knew they were Rembrandts of spycraft, while we were only Norman Rockwells. I figured the probability matrix and began to search for their masterpiece. 'Lynchpin' was a word I coined in the late 1960s as the cryptonym for a master spy who had burrowed his way deep into our intelligence services. After a life spent in the National Clandestine Service—and Counterintelligence—my biggest regret was not getting my fingers around the turncoat's throat and cackling with glee as I squeezed the life out of the treasonous bastard." Nolte's grin widened once more. "Sorry again, Elizabeth. I appear to have become highly excitable with age. You know I could have made deputy director back when Poppy Bush held the reins, but being chained to a desk wasn't my cup of tea and, by then, I'd become quite obsessive over the hunt for the Lynchpin. Somewhat like Ahab and the whale."

"So Lynchpin was a high-ranking KGB mole?"

"Much more than that, I'm afraid. Lynchpin was not a solo player, nor did he run merely a cell of double agents. The slippery bastard orchestrated a full-blown network of spies, and right under our noses, no less. He had to be an agent at a high level that not only was passing along highly classified facts and figures, but, and this is based upon the variety of leaked info, he also had what appeared to be unlimited access to our national security data. Our agents in Moscow screamed the loudest, until one by one each met with an accidental death or a questionable suicide or simply fell off the face of the earth, never to be seen or heard from again. We were on high alert by the early '70s. You understand now the codename Lynchpin—the key player who holds it all together. He was high up the CIA's org chart...and he had help."

"What did you do?"

"Much like I suspect Roland Jund's taskforce is doing today, only they have the help of computer programs. We mined the data leaks, and it was as frustrating as untangling the most knotted-up fishing line you could possibly imagine. We traced each leak back to its source area and created lists of all personnel who could possibly have come within an arm's length of the classified data, and then we filtered the list of names, looking for overlap, but by then there were so many names, including numerous individuals in vital positions, that it became valueless. If the threads of evidence point to everyone, you can't find anyone. No doubt Lynchpin foresaw that such a data dump would make us chase our own tail." For once Nolte's grin disappeared. "It was madness. We were the ones chained in Plato's cave and all we saw were shadows. So imagine my surprise when

I reviewed files from the Soviet archives released in the 1990s and found a handful of references to our Lynchpin. The Russian bastards were well aware of our search even back in the day. Like I said, my biggest regret."

Nolte sighed and paused for a moment.

"Periodically, we'd catch a Judas Iscariot, like an Aldrich Ames or a Clyde Lee Conrad or a John Anthony Walker and our paranoia would throttle back awhile until the leaks began again and we'd be back in Plato's cave with our heads where the sun don't shine."

"Did any of these catches, like Ames, cough up anything?" Cady asked.

Nolte shook his head. "It was an era of dead drops and passwords. The hidden one, the person many of our small-fry catches assumed was their KGB control, was more likely our mystery man. He played his own crew so as to leave no fingerprints. And after the wall came down and we sang Kumbaya, however briefly, we went through the KGB files, but there was nothing outside of a handful of fake names that led nowhere. Unfortunately, there were no recordings like in the case of Robert Hanssen, which led to Hanssen's downfall."

"What do you think ever happened to the Lynchpin?" Cady asked.

"Realistically, he's probably been dead a decade or two. Hopefully of pancreatic cancer or something equally long and drawn out. Sorry, Elizabeth."

"This has been educational, Eggs," Preston said, "but why now? Why Jund and this taskforce?"

"Nations have spied on each other since the beginning. You can trace it back to the dawn of man, with cavemen trying to count how many warriors with clubs were in a neighboring cave. And it's not as though the intelligence work stopped once the Berlin Wall came tumbling down. Certainly not for the Russians. Quite frankly, it is part of our nature and it's never going away. Even friends spy on each other. Jonathan Pollard is serving a life sentence for passing along classified data to Israel."

"But for the taskforce to use the codename 'Lynchpin' refers back to your work, to Soviet-era spycraft. Right?"

Nolte shrugged. "Go figure. Vladimir Putin runs Russia. Vladimir Putin was KGB."

—

"It didn't fall off a truck."

It was late afternoon and the two agents were heading back to Washington, D.C. Interstate 66 was heavy with traffic.

"What?" Cady looked over at Agent Preston.

"I got that list of taskforce members from Assistant Director Paul Speedling."

"He up and gave it to you?"

"In a manner," Preston replied. "Those meetings were shrouded in secrecy and held offsite, which was strange, but I recalled Roland heading someplace with Paul once or twice."

"That makes sense, they're good friends."

"I went to see Paul and laid it on the line, asked him about the taskforce and who sat on it."

"And?"

"And he read me the riot act, told me how poking my nose in could destroy my promising career. That the investigation must go through proper channels. That he didn't want to hear any more about it because that would place him in the position of having to take my scalp. But all the while he's jotting names down on a piece of paper. Then he tells me he's had a bout of food poisoning and he needs to run to the restroom, but he expects me to be gone when he gets back."

"And?"

"And before leaving his office, I leaned over and memorized the names he'd written."

"What do you think? Can we trust Speedling?"

"I don't know." Agent Preston shrugged. "His name's on the list."

CHAPTER FOURTEEN

Cady logged into the database for missing persons—the National Crime Information Center's (NCIC) Missing Person File—at 10:30 p.m., after a cold hamburger and a two-hour brainstorming session with Agent Preston. Cady owed Duluth some time and was hoping to calm the police chief by putting Lieutenant Rohr's mind at ease with a quick search, after which he could shift tasks and focus on Roland Jund's predicament. He'd pound away at the NCIC data for a few minutes, maybe a half hour tops...but after thirty minutes of pounding brought forth an interesting array of search-result records, his thoughts of double agents and Soviet-era moles evaporated into the ether. Lieutenant Rohr's mind was going to be put at anything but ease.

Cady began his search by going back an arbitrary three years and including a handful of states in the upper Midwest. He set the age parameters for females between eighteen and twenty-five years of age and hit the search icon. A haystack of results returned in the lower portion of the computer monitor. Cady sighed when he realized that the list spanned a double-digit of screens for him to filter through. After browsing a handful of files, Cady returned to the search screen and set advance parameters to make the task less Sisyphean: brunette, height greater than five feet four inches, age nineteen to twenty-five to get rid of the high school runaways. Cady figured Rohr's perp, if one even existed, would be spotting his prey at adult venues and not tenth-grade swim meets or high-school volleyball tournaments. Then, through some tricks he'd learned over years of database searches, he set up the logic to drop any results in which the females were either tagged as prostitutes or had served time in prison. He clicked the icon again and a more manageable haystack returned, allowing Cady to begin snooping for potential needles.

Cady sorted field headers to bring basic disappearances to the upper portion in his list of search results, as he wasn't interested in females leaving behind abandoned cars or kicked-in doors or traces of blood—all red-flagging foul play. He was looking for strikingly attractive brunettes who appeared to have fallen off the face of the earth.

That's how Cady came across Courtney Andrews of Michigan.

Even though he had pictures of Katrina Mortensen and Nikki Huckle staring up at him from the folder open on the table, Cady almost missed Courtney Andrews, as, quite frankly, her image in the NCIC database did not do her justice. But as Cady began surfing the Chelsea *Standard* and Ann Arbor newspapers regarding Andrews' disappearance, he felt the hair on the back of his neck begin to rise. One word popped into Cady's mind as he pondered the images of Katrina Mortensen of Newton, Iowa, Nikki Huckle of Cloquet, Minnesota, and now Courtney Andrews, late of Chelsea, Michigan. That word was *understudy*. Courtney Andrews looked as though she could be Nikki Huckle's double in a community theater's production of *The Katrina Mortensen Story*, or else Mortensen could be Huckle's alternate in *The Life of Courtney Andrews*, and there would be little need for pancake makeup or stage lighting.

Courtney Andrews was last seen leaving her evening shift as a waitress at Leary's Pub off Main Street in Chelsea, reportedly to make her way all of a two-mile drive back to her apartment in the sleepy berg's north side. As far as anyone could tell, Andrews never made it home. That had been a year ago in July and Ms. Andrews and her car—a beat-up 1994 Saturn—were never seen again.

By the time he decided to call Lieutenant Rohr, Cady had found two more lookalikes.

Heather Klyn, of Belton, Missouri, vanished after leaving night school at a local community college nearly two months ago. Danielle Logan had gone missing after a night of dancing at a club in Bellevue, Nebraska, the previous winter. No signs of foul play, no abandoned cars or emptied bank accounts. Just missing.

It had taken Cady less than an hour to find three missing girls from three different states in the Midwest—and all of them virtually identical.

"I fucking knew it," Rohr said. She had answered on the first ring and sounded more pissed than tired.

"I'll send you what I've got right now, and I'll find a specialist to hammer on both NCIC and ViCAP, to do a more methodical search."

ViCAP stood for the Violent Criminal Apprehension Program, which, in addition to other incidents, compiled data on missing persons where foul play was suspected.

"I fucking knew it the instant I saw that picture of Nikki Huckle."

"At first I had you at thirty percent, with seventy percent just a coincidence. But I'm listening now. And I'm data-dumping this to my guy in Behavioral for the profile."

"Do that," Rohr said. Then repeated, "I fucking knew it."

"This isn't going to cheer you up, Lieutenant," Cady said, "but the Behavioral scientists at the Bureau believe there are upwards of fifty serial killers honing their craft at any given time."

"How delightful," Rohr replied. "What's your point?"

"I believe one of the fifty may now be honing his craft in Duluth."

CHAPTER FIFTEEN

"I don't want to die."

After the blond man cut her ankle and wrist bindings, he loosened the noose about the young woman's throat so she'd have less trouble breathing. He sat behind her on the rock outcropping of the lakeshore, one hand on the rope in case the girl had any fight left in her. It was nearly two in the morning and they both sat in silence, staring out into the cold, dark waters of Lake Superior.

The girl, Taylor Ganser per her Minnesota driver's license, looked young, but not as young as the blond man assumed when he'd first spotted her outside the Papa Murphy's Take 'n' Bake at the strip mall off West Arrowhead. Not counting the large pepperoni and cookie dough she carried to an old Honda before jumping into the driver's seat, Ms. Ganser had been alone. According to her driver's license, which the blond man examined after making his introduction, Ms. Ganser was thirty-two. The night, her neon blue hair, and her variety of face piercings cloaked her in the illusion of rebellious youth. Didn't matter at this point, the blond man thought—Ganser looked young enough.

The blond man had followed Ganser back to a small two-story shack about halfway down the hill from the Papa Murphy's. He parked his car a street over, crossed a sidewalk, then cut behind a pine and disappeared into the backyard shadows. The blond man moved silently, working his way to Ganser's back lot, edging along the side of her detached garage and slipping along the back of her house. A small dog barked from several houses down, but the pooch clearly wasn't all that committed to the cause and threw in the towel after a few yelps. The blond man stood without moving for fifteen minutes, listening, becoming one with the night.

Invisible.

Even though the girl had lights on in the house, which would make it difficult for her to see out into the darkness, the blond man took several peeks from the lower corners of the windowsills as he moved around the back and sides of the house. After each peek, he'd lean back into the darkness and process what he'd seen. The girl was alone. The TV was on in the front room, providing a little noise, which worked for him. The girl was spooning the cookie dough into her mouth while waiting for her fourteen-inch pepperoni to finish baking. The blond man went to the back of the garage and sat on the grass. He had time. He'd let the girl enjoy her last meal.

At midnight, the blond man did another recon. The lights were off now but the girl remained awake, watching cable in her front room. He slipped around to the back. The door was locked, which took him five seconds. Though slight—the girl was maybe an inch over five feet and possibly a hundred and ten pounds—she could really pack the food away. A lone sliver of pizza remained on the kitchen countertop. The blond man picked it up and took a minute, slowly savoring its taste. Then he walked around the corner into the front room and coldcocked the girl as hard as he could in the forehead.

He bound her hands and feet. He put the noose around her neck and pulled the line tight, not lethal but a quick tug from it. He shoved a dishrag into her mouth for added insurance. The blond man ate the rest of the cookie dough batter, as well as a large wedge of cold lasagna out of the fridge. After he finished with her, he still had the drive back to Minneapolis ahead of him and then a flight to D.C. in the morning. Best to eat while he could.

During the day he had scouted a scenic overview north of town. It was really a patch of dirt and a guardrail that allowed for a dozen cars to park. More importantly, there was a nearby series of trails that wound down through the woods to the lake. The blond man assumed the trails had been used by generations of tourists' children running off a long drive and college students hauling down keggers for hidden beer parties.

He had thought it best to use Ganser's Honda for this particular undertaking, even though it meant having to return it to her house and fetch his rental car. It would not do for any errant constable to note the plate number of his rental while he was down at the lake holding court with young Ms. Ganser. He had disabled both the interior and trunk lights while the car was in her garage. At the overlook, the blond man slowly backed into the spot nearest the trails. It took him three seconds to lift the semiconscious girl from the trunk, heave her over his shoulder in a classic fireman's carry, and disappear into the tree line.

The blond man's client at the Federal Bureau of Investigation was dead serious about utilizing *any means necessary* to impede Agent Cady's D.C. inquiry into the Jund affair. The client was easily prone to panic, a classic nervous Nellie…but not without reason. The client had much to lose if Cady changed the *narrative*, if Cady caused the bureaucracy to switch direction midstream.

In fact, the blond man's client had everything to lose.

But dead or missing FBI agents were only a last resort—that's how the game was played. A dead or missing FBI agent could rip open a Pandora's Box of unintended consequences. Consequences not palatable for those soft of heart—or for nervous Nellies.

The blond man had a better idea.

The data provided by his client was limited, as Duluth PD and Agent Cady had kept the modus operandi of their local serial killer close to the vest. The case, as far as he could tell from the newspapers, had more or less to do with a naked dead girl floating in Lake Superior. And if another dead girl floating in the Great Lake would cause Special Agent Drew Cady to drop all things Lynchpin-related, hop a flight, and race back to this high-profile in Minnesota, then Lake Superior would get its dead girl.

"I don't want to die," the girl repeated.

"This isn't me," the blond man said, as if by way of an apology. "But sometimes—*sometimes*—being *this* is what's required."

He drew back the cord with his left hand, his right gripping the noose behind her neck. The girl began choking, twisting, lurching away from him as though reaching the lake would grant her asylum. He let the girl lurch, her blue hair now dipping into the frigid water.

But there was no sanctuary. The blond man never took his eyes off the Great Lake. He'd not prepared but felt a few lines from Longfellow might be apropos.

"'Bright before it beat the water, beat the clear and sunny water,'" the blond man whispered into the dying girl's ear, and then, softer yet, "'beat the shining, big-sea-water.'"

CHAPTER SIXTEEN

Cady was torn in half.

He'd booked a flight back to Minneapolis for the end of the week—yet more pretzels and airline coffee—where he'd pick up the Escape from the airport's long-term parking and hightail it back to northern Minnesota. He'd sent Lieutenant Rohr the files on the Katrina Mortensen lookalikes, as promised, during the wee hours that morning and CCed Chief Weflen in order to grease the skids for the reluctant chief to face the hard fact that there might be more—far more—than met the eye to the Katrina Mortensen case, Duluth politics be damned. He had squeezed in four hours of shuteye at the DoubleTree and then cabbed it back to the Hoover Building.

Cady now shared a conference table with Liz Preston. Cups of ignored coffee towered above folders, notebook pads, loose papers, and ballpoint pens strewn about the tabletop. Each had a copy of Drommerhausen's Benedict Arnold report—a profile done on the sly and hand-delivered to Agent Preston earlier that morning. Drommerhausen's analysis provided insights into the personal characteristics of individuals who had it in them to betray their country. It provided common and contrasting themes amongst traitors from the Cold War era—from Julius and Ethel Rosenberg, George Koval, and Alger Hiss on up to the more contemporary John Anthony Walker, Aldrich Ames, Robert Hanssen, and Kendall and Gwendolyn Myers, among others.

It would be a weighty read, which Cady would save for the DoubleTree that evening—but scanning the summary section with Liz Preston provided a bottom line on the recognizable traits of a traitor: arrogant, egotistical, self-important, and other words indicating that Drommerhausen owned a thesaurus. Other traits included: risk-taking—clearly—extreme narcissism, selfishness, and a vindictive streak of pettiness that allows one to rationalize away sticking a knife into the home team's back over the most trivial of slights, either real or imagined. Motivations often appeared pitiful and flimsy. Ten American agents whose covers were blown by CIA counterintelligence officer Aldrich Ames were all executed just so Ames could keep his Colombian wife in the lap of luxury. Hanssen appeared to desire handfuls of walking-around money. You had to turn the pages back to the early years to find motivations more in line with those of Communist true believers.

"Director Connor Green is the man to whom Agent Parrish ultimately reported," Preston said.

Cady and Preston had been kicking back and forth the individuals representing the Bureau on the joint FBI-CIA "Lynchpin" taskforce.

"But how many layers of bureaucracy? You know how it is—Director Green might not even recognize Agent Parrish to say hello at the urinal. Might not be able to tell Parrish from the Channel 6 weatherman."

"But Green's division—as well as the late Steve Parrish's division—is Counterintelligence."

Cady nodded. He knew the names on the FBI side of the aisle. Roland Jund, obviously. Assistant Director Paul Speedling—Jund's friend from the Cyber Division—Cady knew on a nod and exchange-vague-pleasantries level. He knew of Connor Green but had never met the director. The same held true for the last Bureau name on the joint taskforce. Liz, on the other hand, knew all three of the assistant directors, as well as Director Green.

"What's the story on Assistant Director Litchy?" asked Cady.

"Mike Litchy is from International Operations and, quite frankly, fits Drommerhausen's characteristics snugly. I find him arrogant to the point of pomposity, certainly self-centered and narcissistic, but Roland said, and I quote, 'Litchy's got his head so far up his ass he needs a glass belly button to see where he's walking. He's too goddamned dumb to be a double-agent.' Unquote."

Agent Preston had connected with the on-leave Jund over cold beer and soggy fries the night before at a too-loud bowling alley— not exactly Preston's natural habitat—in order to get Jund's general impression of the names on the taskforce list. Outside of questioning AD Litchy's intelligence quotient, Jund had not been much help with the list; however, he did bowl a 180.

When the two agents had flashed the taskforce names past Eggs Nolte at the end of the previous day's meeting, he'd been similarly little help. "The taskforce had me attend an initial meeting to provide a historical background last year, not unlike what I've done for you today, and though they all seem like decent enough chaps, good conversationalists, what I really know about any of them is next to nothing," Eggs Nolte had informed the agents as he walked them to Preston's car. "I've made a decent living relying on my instincts—my gut-check, that is—and to be honest, my gut has always told me that our Lynchpin was CIA, not FBI."

Cady dropped the file he'd been perusing to rub his tired eyes, then looked over at Preston. "I think we start by org charting the three we know: Green, Speedling, and Litchy. List those in their close orbit." After a moment, Cady added, "And find a way to do the same for the CIA officers on the taskforce. Then we need to figure out a way to ask the right questions of the right people and do so without getting fired."

"That'll be the hard part."

Cady's phone buzzed. He saw it was Rohr and clicked talk. "Hey, Lieutenant."

"You sitting down, Cady?"

"Should I be?"

"There's been another girl. This time a couple of tourists spotted her from one of the hiking paths along the shoreline outside of town."

"A lookalike?" Cady glanced at Preston, who held his eye.

"That's the damnedest thing. She's *youngish*-looking—consid- ering the circumstances—she's been stripped of clothes and dumped in Lake Superior, but she's not one of our lookalikes. She's on the short side and her face and body are full of metal."

"Full of metal?"

"Body piercings," Rohr said. "I'm here at the lake right now with Foeller and there's one other thing."

"What's that?"

"She's been strangled."

"Jesus."

"Look, Cady, the chief wants your ass back in town yesterday. He's having a cow," Rohr said. "Come to think of it, I am too."

"Tell the chief my *ass* is on the next flight out."

"Make it sooner."

Cady stared at Liz Preston, who nodded her head slowly in return.

He'd already shared his late-night discovery with Liz, as well as his sense of dread, his concern that Lieutenant Rohr had been correct and Katrina Mortensen was merely the tip of the iceberg. As gruesome as it appeared to be, this was, after all, their true forte.

"Work it fast," Agent Preston said. "Old Drew would have nailed the UNSUB by now."

Liz was referring to Cady's earlier persona, from years back, when he had acquired quite the reputation for getting the hard jobs done quickly, no matter the cost. Unfortunately, it had indeed cost Cady dearly, as Old Drew's life outside of his chosen profession had become a train wreck.

Cady shrugged. "Old Drew needed a glass belly button."

CHAPTER SEVENTEEN

"I've got your ticket punched, shithead." Lieutenant Rohr entered the interrogation room and tossed a folder at Taylor Ganser's ex-boyfriend. It bounced off his chest and a handful of papers floated to the floor. Agent Cady followed the lieutenant into the room and leaned against a wall.

Kal Hoyer looked to Cady. "Can she talk to me like that?"

Cady shrugged.

Early in the morning after the body had been discovered, as Chief Weflen was making the decision to seek the public's assistance in identifying the Jane Doe by feeding the media a physical description—sex, stature, the blue hair, an age range, and individualizing traits such as the deceased's piercings—a couple approaching retirement age and a younger woman with skin the color of cappuccino entered the Duluth Police Department and asked to see someone about filing a missing-persons report. The older couple turned out to be Taylor Ganser's parents. The younger woman was the day manager at the tanning salon where Taylor Ganser was employed. When Taylor hadn't reported for work the previous morning, or returned the string of messages left by Baja Tanning, the manager eventually contacted Taylor's parents, who, in turn, had begun trying to locate their missing daughter. The reason for this flurry of activity was that both Taylor's parents and the salon manager were worried about Kal Hoyer, whom the Baja Tanning manager referred to as "the ex from hell."

Taylor's malicious ex, Kal Hoyer, evolved at great speed from person of interest to suspect. The unit sent to his home found Hoyer passed out on a mattress that occupied the bulk of the real estate in his efficiency apartment. Drug paraphernalia—a water bong—and half a dime bag of cannabis were sitting on his kitchen table. Another baggie of what appeared to be Oxycontin tablets and speed was stuffed in the back of Hoyer's silverware drawer. The investigators hit pay dirt when they checked his decades-old Skylark. The latch on the Skylark's trunk was broken and Kal Hoyer had been using a strip of rope to tie the hood of the trunk down in order to keep it from flopping up while he was driving. Inside the Skylark's trunk were additional strips of rope, as well as a box cutter stuffed under the driver's seat.

"Do you know what that is?" Rohr sat directly across from Hoyer and pointed at the fallen folder and papers.

Hoyer shook his head, but Cady caught a glimpse of deer-in-the-headlights.

"Funny. If I had a restraining order filed against me," Rohr said, "that's not something I'd soon forget."

The icing on the cake was that a widowed neighbor swore she'd seen Hoyer drive past at dusk on the night of Taylor's disappearance, and even described Hoyer's rust bucket perfectly, right down to his tied-down trunk. And to make Hoyer's future murkier yet, his confiscated mobile phone contained dozens and dozens of pictures of Taylor Ganser, many of which were taken from a distance and time-stamped after their breakup and subsequent restraining order.

Hoyer seemed to have no response.

"I just finished reading the order, shithead," the lieutenant said. "You were a busy little beaver, weren't you? Went a little bat guano after the breakup, huh?"

Hoyer shook his head. "I don't have to say nothing to you."

The kid was a piercer, too, just like his ex. Cady had seen the photos of Taylor Ganser's face taken by the ME. Both she and this Kal Hoyer piece of work had matching septum piercings—the area between the nostrils—with identical circular barbells and silver cones. The lovers likely got their septums pierced at the same time, back in better days.

Taylor Ganser's ears were a smorgasbord—a black rook piercing in the folding cartilage between the inner and outer conch, a wire ring piercing her tragus, a string of helix pierces curving downward along the upper ear, as well as the more traditional, ho-hum lobe piercings. Both eyebrows were pierced with something called a Titanium Micro Bananabell, colored blue to match her hair. Taylor also had what Cady discovered was called a Monroe piercing—that is, a sixteen-gauge labret stud placed to the left-hand side of her upper lip to resemble Marilyn Monroe's beauty mark. Taylor's front teeth were pierced with blue gem stars, also matching her hair. The last bit of face piercing included a center-of-the-tongue barbell with a metal bead. ME Foeller had noted a collection of other piercings on Ganser's body, the least private being in her navel.

Kal Hoyer added balance to his septum piercing by adding a nasal bridge, a surface bar that pierced the skin on the bridge of his nose. Other of Hoyer's accessories included an upper incisor pierced with some kind of ball closure ring that would have looked more natural hanging off a drill press, a pierced lower lip, and two side-by-side horizontal tongue piercings—a style Cady found out was known as a venom bite. Surprisingly, Hoyer had no eyebrows. In their stead were blue and green tattoos of lightning bolts, which, Cady had to admit, showed originality and would look chic on the anti-hero of a bad sci-fi movie insomniacs might watch in the wee hours of the night.

Kal Hoyer's earlobes had also been pierced; however, his had been stretched with tapers and fitted with flesh tunnel jewelry. Staring straight on, Cady could see through the holes in Hoyer's earlobes. It made him relieved he'd only eaten half a bagel for breakfast. Cady figured his lunch would be shot as well if he found out what went on underneath Hoyer's clothing.

"You stalkers really get my goat," Rohr said. "Twenty-four-seven phone calls and drive-bys, the matinees at her place of employment, sucking her coworkers into your psychodrama. And what you did on her stoop—Jesus Christ, that takes the cake."

"That's all bullshit." Hoyer looked off to the side. "Taylor made that up."

"More like Rottweiler shit, if it wasn't yours. But a neighbor spotted you leaping off Taylor's steps and racing to your car. Don't expect to travel incognito if you model your face after a tackle box."

"I didn't do *anything* to Taylor!"

"So you keep saying, but look at it from my point of view. Court-issued restraining orders go to motivation. It's like a roadmap. If anything happens to a poor girl whose life has been turned into a horror story by some shithead stalker, guess who we come for first?"

Hoyer met Rohr's eyes. "Where the hell is my lawyer?"

"Your public defender?" the lieutenant said, looking at her watch. "I think we're a little early." She looked at Kal Hoyer and shrugged. "My bad."

"I'm not saying jack shit to you."

"I'm just making small talk until your PD shows up. Kind of thinking aloud about how the alibi's a bit weak. Playing *Call of Duty* by yourself all night. Hey, do you have the version that lets you shoot civilians?"

Hoyer stared at the table and said nothing. A pinky finger snaked through the flesh tunnel in his left ear and he gave it a little tug.

"Let's see, where were we? You're shit out of luck on both motive and opportunity. As for means…well, we all know about the rope."

"I keep telling you cops—I tie down the trunk so it won't pop up when I drive. And I cut off the knot whenever I need to load shit."

"That's plausible. A lawyer could jury that with a straight face. But a person can get rope anywhere. Even the dollar store sells rope. I mean, it's not as though rope is regulated by the ATF. Isn't that right, Agent Cady?"

Cady nodded.

Hoyer's pinky finger gave another tug at the hole in his left earlobe.

"I read a recent study on the American prison system, and it said that after the first dozen or so *incidents*, it becomes old hat—kind of like everything else in life, I guess—and at that point the new inmates become more concerned about, say, what's for dinner." Using her foot, Rohr slid the papers that had fallen to the floor over to her side of the table, then scooped them up and placed them back into the folder. "So you just need to hang on till double digits, shithead…and then you'll only have to worry about whether it's macaroni or goulash."

Hoyer's chest rose and settled. A single tear began at his nose bridge and slid down past his pierced septum and lip stud. He mumbled something under his breath.

"What?"

"I said I loved her." Hoyer sniffed. "I would never hurt Taylor. I loved her guts out."

"You had a strange way of showing it."

Hoyer wiped his eyes with a forearm. "We were soul mates."

The door to the interrogation room opened. A man in a three-button flannel suit filled the doorway. He looked from Hoyer to Rohr to Cady. And he wasn't wearing his happy face.

Kal Hoyer's public defender had arrived.

"The kid's lying," Cady said. The two investigators were sitting in Rohr's office. "At least about the mess he left on her stoop."

"If I did something like that, I'd lie about it too," Rohr replied. "You know the numbers on r-orders, right?"

"Yes."

"Something happens to a woman and there's a restraining order in play, you follow it straight to the perp. It's a slam dunk—two plus two equals four."

"Strangling is routine where crimes of passion are concerned, even if a rope is brought into play. But there's usually a sense of *immediacy* involved." Cady shook his head. "The field trip to Lake Superior breaks the mode."

"The lake could be symbolic. Could be the place where she first yanked on his ripcord."

"The trip to the lake would indicate intent when it comes to charging."

Rohr nodded. "Hoyer blames Taylor for breaking his heart—she was his *soul mate*, after all. His insides are torn up. Then he hears about a dead girl fished out of Lake Superior and he forms a plan. The kid's not a hundred-watter, so he figures he can do away with the woman who betrayed his love and the police would be too goddamned stupid to figure it out."

Cady shrugged.

Over the past twenty-four hours he'd taken a crash course in body piercing, trying to see if he could dig up a connection as to how Katrina Mortensen, the first in their line of lookalikes, had been drained of blood via an embalming process. Though Taylor Ganser was not a lookalike, not by a long shot—way too short, a decade too old, and wearing a body full of stainless steel—his initial thought was that Ganser and her circle of piercers might be involved with the Mortensen slaying, and that Ganser was killed to keep things quiet. But as they looked into Ganser's lifestyle, her friendships, and her colleagues at the tanning salon where she worked fifty-hour weeks, it became apparent that there was no lethal coven of Duluth piercers who had decided to take body piercing to a heretofore unknown level. Piercing was just something Taylor, and her ex-boyfriend Kal Hoyer, did, either separately or together. It defined who they were. And the discovery of the restraining order against Kal Hoyer pushed them immediately in his direction.

"If it wasn't for our lookalikes, I'd be a hundred percent that Hoyer killed her," Rohr said. "But I'm still ninety percent it's him."

"Eighty percent it's Hoyer. Ten percent Ganser is *somehow* linked to the lookalikes." Cady set his notebook on the lieutenant's desk and leaned back in his chair. "And ten percent unknown."

CHAPTER EIGHTEEN

Cady was heading into Grand Rapids on US-2, and then on to Cohasset and Terri's resort. Three days earlier, Cady'd sped straight to Duluth upon his arrival at the Minneapolis St. Paul Airport preoccupied with the news of another body discovered on the Lake Superior shoreline. He now needed to swap out his luggage, grab a change of clothes, see Terri, and spend a relaxed night in a familiar bed before hightailing it back to Duluth the next morning.

Unfortunately, there hadn't been much progress on the Taylor Ganser killing.

A receipt found in Taylor Ganser's kitchen garbage placed her at a pizza joint right before ten o'clock on the night of her abduction and murder. The employees that handled Taylor's order remembered her coming in and leaving by herself. Both the back door to Taylor's house and her side garage door had been left unlocked, which, according to Taylor's family and friends, was unusual for her. Taylor's purse was found on the kitchen table with thirteen dollars, her checkbook, car keys, and a credit card inside. Her cell phone was left on the couch in the front TV room. These findings led Cady and Rohr to the obvious conclusion that Taylor's abduction had occurred inside her own home.

Surprisingly, there were no fingerprints on the steering wheel, door handles, or the back trunk of her Honda Civic, which indicated that the perpetrator could be anyone who'd ever watched TV.

Cady didn't like playing the percentage game, but at this stage in the Taylor Ganser investigation, he'd now place seventy-five percent on the pierced-faced boy and the other twenty-five percent on the work of an unknown copycat. Perhaps Taylor Ganser ran afoul of some deranged soul in search of a thrill kill that he could pan off on recent headlines. Cady had considered the Papa Murphy's pizza joint and its constant stream of customers, coming and going, while someone sat off in a car watching, waiting, searching for a single female that might meet his twisted need.

Cady had viewed the security camera footage from the pizza shop, which angled down from the ceiling above the cashier. Though Cady was able to observe Taylor Ganser entering, placing her order, waiting for a few minutes, and then leaving with her pizza and cookie dough, he wasn't able to see anything outside the shop. The firm that owned the strip mall had a camera set up outside, but that only covered the front sidewalk and the eight or nine cars lucky enough to acquire the choice parking spots. Cady couldn't see any figures waiting in those parked cars, and none of the cars pulled away in the minutes after Taylor left with her pizza and passed out of the camera's view as she went to her car.

Friends, family members, and colleagues at the tanning salon were unified in pointing the finger at Kal Hoyer, but Hoyer continued to proclaim his innocence through his public defender. The lab was looking at the strips of rope taken from the trunk of his car but, realistically, Cady didn't expect them to come back with anything earth-shattering unless the kid was a real dope or wanted a keepsake. Rope, as Rohr had pointed out, was ubiquitous.

The chief, however, was elated to have a suspect in custody. It gave him shelter from the storm. Rohr reported that Chief Weflen had almost done the two-step when he heard the news about Hoyer's restraining order.

Cady no longer believed it possible that the Taylor Ganser homicide could be the work of the UNSUB responsible for the death of Katrina Mortensen and the disappearance of all the lookalikes. He and Rohr had gone over the differences time and time again. Although Taylor Ganser possessed a youthful appearance, she was nearly a decade older than the women he and Lieutenant Rohr had uncovered. The lookalikes were medium height to the short end of tall, whereas Taylor was diminutive. The lookalikes gave this generic girl-next-door impression that Taylor's neon hair and piercings precluded. Finally, Taylor had been strangled to death, but Katrina Mortensen had been drained of blood and injected with embalming fluids. No minor deviation.

Bryce Drommerhausen, Cady's profiler at NCAVC, had been juggling enough work for five behavioralists, but he'd managed to slip what he could do for Roland Jund—the Benedict Arnold profile—to the head of the class. After that Drommerhausen had to play catchup, but in Cady's mad dash back to northern Minnesota he'd found time to coax Drommerhausen into fast-tracking a report, more an informal collection of thoughts, on the Katrina Mortensen killing. Granted, what Cady provided Drommerhausen from the Mortensen murder file was threadbare, not much for the harried behavioralist to chew on.

Drommerhausen's analysis arrived in Cady's inbox as he was departing for Cohasset and Terri's resort. He forwarded it on to Chief Weflen and Lieutenant Rohr and took a minute to scan through the profile before shutting down his laptop.

Interesting stuff.

Cady's mind wandered toward picking up a bottle of red from the liquor store off Grand Rapids' main drag. He'd just flipped on the right turn signal when his phone began to vibrate. He grabbed it from the front cup holder and saw it was Lieutenant Rohr. She probably had questions about Drommerhausen's report. Cady brought the cell to his ear.

"Another one floated in," Rohr cut off Cady's salutation.

Cady slapped off the turn signal and continued straight ahead.

"Where?"

"About four miles northeast of the city."

Cady felt the hair on the back of his neck begin to rise. "Is she a lookalike?"

"Female, check. Black hair, check. Bloodless…check. Definitely one of ours this time, Cady. Some kid out sailing thought he saw a naked girl sunbathing along the shoreline. A weird spot, but a sunny morning—he thought maybe he'd found a nude beach, so he came in for a closer look. Last I heard he was still throwing up."

"Jesus."

"Roger that," Rohr replied. "The body is with the medical examiner and I'm heading there now. I talked to Doc Foeller for a moment before calling you and it's not good. Think if Katrina Mortensen hadn't been found for another week or so. Decomposition. And some critters got at her."

"Those names I sent you before, of the missing lookalikes: go for dental against the Jane Doe, unless you think you can get a workable photo ID—"

"We'll go for dental," Rohr cut in. "And one other thing you ought to know."

"What's that?"

"Your SAC from Minneapolis is flying in."

"I'm in Grand Rapids. I'll do a U-ie and be back in two." Cady clicked off and restrained from pounding the dashboard.

He was ten minutes from Terri's resort in Cohasset. He made it in five.

Terri was nowhere to be found, likely out running errands. Cady opened his rolling bag and shook it upside down in the laundry room. He knew he'd face blowback from Terri for this maneuver but didn't have time to sort and wash. Cady scooped together underwear and dress socks from his drawer and dumped them into the bag, followed by a pair of jeans and a couple of polo shirts grabbed at random. He emptied his garment bag on the floor next to his side of the bed, leaving an almost-folded pile for dry cleaning. He stripped out of his suit and dress shirt and added those to the mound. More blowback. He did eight seconds with an electric shaver in the master bathroom, six seconds with a toothbrush, and two with a comb. He twisted into dress clothes, jammed his last clean suit jacket in the garment bag, zipped the roller, and carried both pieces of luggage out to the Ford Escape.

Three seconds later he jogged back to the kitchen and scribbled a note for Terri.

Within five minutes of Cady's arrival at Sundown Point Resort, he was on the road again, heading back to Duluth.

CHAPTER NINETEEN

The media had invaded.

The first red flag was that the Duluth PD parking lot was jam-packed full of cars. Cady had to park a block down and two over. The second red flag was the type of cars he caught sight of in the lot. Cady spotted news vans from Channel 3 and Channel 6—network affiliates. He also spotted a truck from PBS, and a couple others he hadn't identified. Plus, gauging from some of the dented beaters that lined the lot, local reporters from both the Duluth and Superior papers were in attendance as well. This second red flag sent Cady rifling through the glove compartment to see if Terri—who often kept Pepto-Bismol on hand for families who rented her cabins—had miraculously left a pink bottle in the car.

Having struck out on the Pepto-Bismol front, Cady hiked back to the police department and paused to peer through the front glass doors at what appeared to be an impromptu press conference taking place in the entrance hall, a dense armada of video cameras and humanoids sitting in folding chairs with their backs to Cady. In front of the crowd, he spotted a red-faced Chief Weflen behind a podium filled with microphones. To his left stood a gloomy-looking Mayor Renquist, and on his other side stood Ron Bergmann, the special agent in charge of the Minneapolis Division of the FBI. Cady had seen death row inmates in their final week look more at ease than Special Agent Bergmann did now. His instincts told him to turn and run, but Cady pushed open the heavy glass door and joined the circus.

"Concurrent jurisdiction," the chief was answering a question that Cady had missed, "exists when a crime violates local, state, and federal law all at the same time. That's what we were looking at until the events of this morning, with the Federal Bureau of Investigation acting in a consulting role. However, the discovery this morning in Lake Superior of the body of a *comparable* victim changes that relationship per," Weflen glanced down at his notes, "...per Title 28 of the U.S. Code, section 540B, detailing the investigational jurisdiction of serial killings."

The crowded room fell silent. Any pins dropped would have echoed for blocks.

The chief continued, "This code grants the FBI special jurisdiction to investigate cases of this nature."

A hand touched Cady's forearm. "Nice of you to make it in time to be tossed to the lions," Rohr whispered in his ear.

"Again, I'm not here to talk specifics about the case." Weflen appeared to be searching for a quick way to wrap up the press conference. "We're here to let the good people of Duluth know that this has officially become an FBI matter."

"So this third murder connects back to your first case?" a voice like gravel spun in a cement truck shouted from the back of the room.

The red-faced chief nodded.

"But the second case from earlier this week—the Taylor Ganser homicide—is not connected to your first or third case?"

"We have a suspect in custody in the Taylor Ganser homicide."

"It's my understanding that Taylor Ganser was strangled by her ex-boyfriend, but you're saying that these two other victims were murdered in a different manner?"

"Correct. The first and the third cases are linked by the exact same M.O."

"About which you won't provide any information."

The chief nodded again.

"My source informs me that these two girls were both drained of blood from wounds in their necks."

Any pins dropped now could have been heard in Minneapolis.

"No comment," the chief said, his face a deeper red.

"I'll take your no comment as validation of my source's information." The voice belonged to a middle-aged man who sat sideways in his folding chair in the back row.

"Mr. Jahnsen," the chief said slowly and cleared his throat, "we had a discussion in your office last week about the *uniqueness* of this investigation and how, with that in mind, you planned to adhere to the standards of journalistic integrity."

So that's the infamous Alan Jahnsen.

"I was also informed, by both you and the mayor at that very same meeting, that an arrest was imminent," Jahnsen replied. "That was a week and two dead girls ago."

The editor of the Duluth daily paper and the Duluth police chief locked eyes for several seconds in which nothing was said, but everything communicated.

"So tell me again, Chief Weflen," Jahnsen said slowly. "Is an arrest imminent?"

"No comment."

"Are there any leads?" a female reporter called out from next to a video camera.

"No comment." The chief looked sunburned from the neck up. "I don't wish to be sidetracked. Again, the purpose of this press conference is to announce that the FBI has taken over the investigation."

Though the chief desperately wanted to call it a wrap and possibly board the space shuttle, the editor of the Duluth *News Herald* was not done with him. "I was a good boy for you, wasn't I? Spending days printing what you and the mayor desired, instead of informing the good people of Duluth that they had better keep a close eye on their daughters, because my source tells me those two poor girls were drained of all their blood and pumped full of formaldehyde."

This time the room erupted. Cameras pivoted toward Alan Jahnsen and Cady backed against the wall with Lieutenant Rohr as reporters pushed each other aside in order to get at the *Duluth Herald's* editor. Through a blur of legs and elbows Cady caught a glimpse of Lucinda Quilling—sitting on a folding chair with her head in her hands—next to her wheelchair-bound brother Evan, who looked more unwell than before, if that were possible, and seemed to be on the verge of tears.

CHAPTER TWENTY

"I should have kicked that scribbling shit-apple's ass!" Chief Weflen bellowed. "And that Dan Wetmore—that goddamned Wetmore—you know he's that shit-apple's source, don't you?"

"The councilman is using this tragedy as a campaign prop," Mayor Renquist answered the chief. "It is now my sworn duty in life to crush that little fucker."

They had assembled in a private conference room upstairs—Cady, Lieutenant Rohr, and a couple of suits from the Violent Crimes Unit, Mayor Renquist, Special Agent Ron Bergmann, and two other agents out of Minneapolis that Cady had yet to meet. Cady exchanged a look with Agent Bergmann. Due to his battlefield promotion to Assistant SAC—Assistant Special Agent-in-Charge—by Bergmann, he was going to have to seize the reins. Now seemed as good a time as any.

"It would have been best to issue a press release and not give Jahnsen a stage to sing from. That said, you two need to walk this off right now, because we have a more pressing matter," said Cady. "Let's talk profile."

The police chief sighed and sat down at the conference table. "Fuck it. I didn't want to be mayor, anyway."

"In Northern California, maybe, but I find it hard to believe that some kind of satanic cult is bleeding out victims here in the land of lutefisk." Lieutenant Rohr volunteered her two cents. "I'm not sure if this profile is of any help."

"Agent Drommerhausen was working off the Mortensen murder file," Cady said. "He's highlighting cases where the perpetrators have bled out their victims, as that's not something you see every day. That's why some of his examples may seem pretty out there."

"But Haitian voodooists?" one of the lieutenant's plainclothes asked. "Voodoo rituals—don't they use animal blood?"

"Aren't a lot of these satanic cults just dumbass kids with too much time on their hands?" Chief Weflen asked. "Goth dipshits cutting the heads off chickens?"

"And this Elizabeth Báthory—Countess Dracula—from five centuries ago? Bathing in the blood of her victims, for Christ's sake," Rohr added, scanning a paragraph from the report. "I for one won't be sleeping tonight."

Cady shrugged. "Look, the key is the blood—that's Drommer-hausen's point. The examples are just to get us thinking. We figure out what the bloodletting means, we're ten steps closer to catching him."

"Permit me to be pretentious for a moment and quote Arthur Conan Doyle." Special Agent Bergmann spoke for the first time after being handed a copy of Drommerhausen's report. "'When you have eliminated all which is impossible, then whatever remains, however improbable, must be the truth.' I recommend we all read this report in its entirety tonight, sleep on it, and see if anything bites us on the ass when we wake in the morning."

"Gentleman," Mayor Renquist stood and addressed the room, "I've a delicate constitution and it's past my nigh-nigh time. I'm going home to a warm wife and a cold dinner."

"Say hi to Rosie for me." Weflen raised a hand at the mayor's departure.

"Can do." The mayor looked back at Weflen. "Chief?"

"Seven a.m."

"With bells on." The mayor shut the conference room door as he headed out.

Cady took a quick glance at his watch. It was past ten in the evening.

"I wouldn't rule out psychotic teens who have seen the *Twilight* movies one too many times," Agent Desrosier, whom Cady had formally met at the meeting's start, began to make his point, "but the tech savviness of the UNSUB in regards to this funeral home pump scares the hell out of me. It's no longer messed-up kids with corn-on-the-cob prongs or razor blades—you know, idiots we would have caught on the first day. This is someone at a higher level who's going to give us one hell of a ride."

"Anything on the mortuary interviews, Lieutenant?" asked Agent Bergmann.

Rohr shook her head. "We're expanding the search radius out to and including Hinckley and have begun performing background checks on those trained in mortuary science in the search area going back twenty-five years." The lieutenant looked at Agent Bergmann. "We could use help."

"Please coordinate with Agent Schultz to make sure there are no redundancies," Bergmann said. Schultz was the second agent in Bergmann's posse that Cady had just met.

"That brings me to the next topic," Cady said. "On the drive from Cohasset, I received a call from an agent at Hoover whom I'd asked to perform a more thorough NCIC search. I also had him rip into ViCAP. Going back ten years, he came up with another nineteen lookalikes."

"Jesus Christ!" Chief Weflen, suddenly drained of his sunburn, now looked pale. "How can this happen? How come no one at the FBI caught this pattern?"

The room was quiet.

"Too many disparities," Cady said, diving in and hoping it didn't sound like he was covering the Bureau's ass. "The shortest girl on the list is five feet four inches and the tallest nearly five eleven. A seven-inch spread. The youngest was nineteen and the oldest a youngish-looking thirty-one, so a twelve-year spread." Cady looked at his notes. "A grab bag of ethnicities—English, Scandinavian, German, Italian, Irish, French, Polish, whatnot—mixed mutts like most of us. And they were taken from nine states around the Midwest, which means we need to have a long chat about transport."

"But their facial features," the chief insisted. "Why didn't you Feds catch that?"

"All were highly attractive but in a generically similar manner. Nearly half had brown eyes, the rest blue or hazel. It went about fifty-

fifty on mid-length versus long hair, and the color was either black or brown. No natural blonds, unless their hair was dyed."

"Too goddamned broad a pattern," Lieutenant Rohr said. "You could probably find one or two in any college bar on a Saturday night. Probably a couple girls from every sorority house fit the description."

"Makes for easy stalking," one of the plainclothes replied.

"Remember, these women went missing and, quite frankly, there was no pattern to sink our teeth into until the second lookalike washed up on shore," Cady said and looked at Agent Bergmann. "Ron, can I unload these NCIC and ViCAP names on your team, have them investigate the circumstances of each disappearance, see if there are any similarities?"

"You've got it. We can also chart the distance from Duluth for each of the missing girls."

"That would be helpful." Cady thought for a second. Something had been gnawing at the back of his mind. "Anybody think I'm crazy to suggest searching the databases for attempted abductions? See if we can find any lookalikes who may have gotten away?"

"I don't think you're crazy," Rohr said. "I think that's smart as hell. I'll put Herriges on it; he's the Rain Man of database queries."

A loud knock caused all heads to turn toward the door. A winded Wallace Foeller peeked inside. He looked from Lieutenant Rohr to Chief Weflen to Agent Cady.

"You wanted dental comparisons from the three missing girls he found?" Foeller said, gesturing at Cady.

The chief and the lieutenant nodded in unison.

"X-rays were taken and sent off for comparison against the dental records of the missing girls, and we got a hit." Foeller took another breath and continued, "The dead girl that washed ashore today is Heather Klyn of Belton, Missouri."

CHAPTER TWENTY-ONE

"Now who is this again?" Terri asked over the phone.

"Your fiancé."

Cady was sacking out on the leather couch at the satellite office in the Federal Building off Duluth's First Street. He had overestimated the length of the sofa and his legs draped over the armrest. It was after midnight, hardly worth checking into the Holiday Inn since he'd be up at first light. Cady figured a shower in the locker room at Duluth PD would suffice for his morning meeting with both the mayor and the chief.

But he had promised Terri he'd call her before he went to bed, no matter the hour.

"Let's see if I can remember," Terri replied. "Tall, dark, and pig-headed."

"I'm not that tall."

"From my angle, everyone plays basketball."

Terri was maybe five one. When they danced—something Terri took great pleasure in while Cady did whatever it took to avoid—he had no one to talk to.

"Did you catch it on TV?"

"What, that new sitcom called *Duluth Press Conference*? I give it three episodes before it gets canned."

"That bad, huh?"

"My favorite part was when they turned the cameras on that editor who commandeered the meeting. I saw you in the background."

"Great."

"Your fly was open."

—

By all rationale, Cady should have been in a dead sleep. He'd been running on fumes for two days straight, but now he had taken his own advice and read Drommerhausen's report. The behavioralist had indeed rattled off documented examples of *bloodletting* in no particular order to alert the investigators to situations authorities had dealt with in the past.

Although he'd heard many stories, Cady was nonetheless startled by the ruthless creativity of the Mexican drug cartels, many of which appeared fixated on decapitations, ending in no small amount of blood loss. The cartels carried out this shock and gore in order to send a message, that being: *Don't even think of crossing us.* But part of the cartel's message was to leave the savagery out in plain sight, easily discoverable, whereas the Duluth UNSUB had attempted to hide his handiwork—his savagery—and had been successful until these most recent victims washed ashore. Also, it was absurd to think that either of these young women from the Midwest had somehow run afoul of Los Zetas or the Juarez cartel.

The report contained a brief historical section on Countess Elizabeth Báthory de Ecsed—the "Blood Countess"—from early 1600s Hungary. Evidently, Elizabeth and a handful of collaborators took it upon themselves to torture and murder hundreds of the fairer sex, often the pubescent daughters of local peasants, lower-class girls sent to Elizabeth to learn etiquette, as well as many others abducted outright. Legend had it that Elizabeth Báthory bathed in her victim's blood in order to preserve her youthful beauty. Although the numbers were debatable, one witness credited Báthory in the killings of over 650 adolescent females, which would make the Blood Countess one of the most industrious serial killers—male or female—in history. Drommerhausen had placed this historical piece in the report in regard to a group of Elizabeth Báthory cultists who had been sought in the death of a young woman named Heidi Rider in Brenner, Arizona, in the late 1960s.

Cady highlighted the entry as something he'd look into further.

Cady ran through the remaining list of cults, occultists, sects, or those into witchcraft who used animal blood in their ceremonies.

He made a note to find out if any of the rituals involving animal blood would somehow up the ante were human blood involved.

CHAPTER TWENTY-TWO

"Sheriff Hofer died fifteen years ago, but when Glen was in hospice—during my last visit—he brought it up," retired Gila County Sheriff Mitchell Diedrick told Cady. "The lung cancer had eaten him down to a nub and he was heavily medicated, but Glen held my hand and cried about that case. I'd reported to Sheriff Hofer as his deputy before I got the baton, and Glen was as close a friend as I've ever had, probably my best if I gave it some thought. And poor Glen went down thinking himself a failure because those two psychopaths got away—that goddamned couple from the south of hell."

"Rosalita and Richard de León," said Cady.

"The sheriff was old school, been around long enough he'd seen it all, and in our last visit Glen was cogent as hell in spite of the pain meds. He told me it cut to his core because he knew those two were only just getting started, just ramping up. Glen felt horrible—not so much for Heidi Rider, because he wasn't clairvoyant, but for all the ones certain to come."

"I've got the file right in front of me," Cady said. He'd been on the phone with the Gila County Sheriff's Department for a half hour, and a deputy had faxed the file to him at Duluth PD. Cady had heard about Sheriff Hofer's death, but was given a phone number for the retired Sheriff Mitchell Diedrick, who now lived in a suburb outside of Scottsdale to be near his grandkids. Diedrick had been a Gila County deputy in 1969, at the time of the Heidi Rider killing.

"A lot of years have passed but it'll take Alzheimer's to pry what I saw at Pinal Flats out of my mind," Diedrick said. "I expect you want me to walk you through it."

—

The gist was this:

The two blew into the central Arizona town of Brenner like a scorching desert breeze that summer, arriving in a beat-to-shit VW Hippie van that was all the vogue in the late 1960s. They registered as Rosalita and Richard de León, according to the file at the KOA campground a few miles south of Brenner, and claimed to be from Tucson. They told the KOA clerk they were there to celebrate the 4th of July but paid enough in cash to keep a spot through August.

To their followers, a handful of needy and disaffected teens they'd rounded up from the periphery of outdoor rock concerts and lower town parks where the scent of marijuana was more pungent than the odor of fried chicken, they were known as Mom and Dad. Mom and Dad spent July plying these kids with peyote, high-end cannabis, mushrooms, and endless vats of red wine. They'd drive to Pinal Flats to get lost in a sea of sand and cactus, where they'd lay out blankets and copulate under the stars, switching partners until exhaustion set in. They'd then take shrooms and lie staring up into space as Mom and Dad talked of being descendants of Ponce de León, famed Spanish explorer and seeker of the Fountain of Youth. Mom and Dad talked of how they'd succeeded where their forefather had failed, how the Fountain was not a location but something far more vital that would serve to keep them eternal.

Heidi Rider worked at the Brenner diner. She was nearly twenty, still living at home and squirreling her tips away in the hope of moving to Los Angeles and taking modeling classes. It wasn't a pipe dream, as Rider, according to retired Sheriff Diedrick, who had always filled up his coffee mug at the diner and knew Heidi by sight, said she would have been on the higher end of any rating scale, with long black hair, brown eyes, cream-white skin, and curves in all the right places.

Rosalita and Richard ate breakfast at the diner, eventually requesting to sit in Heidi's section where Rosalita, a looker herself, made small talk with Heidi and spoke of a cousin who was making a living as a model in L.A., how she could connect the two of them and how Heidi might even be able to stay with her cousin until she got a gig of her own. The de Leóns always left Heidi tips larger than the cost of their meals. This went on for weeks until one Friday night Rosalita asked Heidi if she'd care to join them at Pinal Flats—smoke some good weed, drink a little wine, listen to music…groove and be mellow. Heidi Rider accepted.

Rosalita drove with Heidi in the old station wagon her parents had given her for high school graduation. Richard drove the van bearing three of their teenage disciples. He informed them that tonight would be special, that he and Rosalita had a big surprise in store. Heidi was afraid of puncturing an already bald tire, so she and Rosalita left the station wagon roadside and jumped in the van, let Richard navigate off the road onto the packed dirt and sand, slowly creeping along, beams on high, a hundred yards or so before the sand loosened and going on became impractical.

They spread the blankets and Richard was able to make Simon and Garfunkel come in on a transistor radio from a pop station out of downtown Brenner without too much static. Then Richard poured red wine into paper cups for the kids and Heidi and joked about this being communion. Richard and Rosalita shared a joint while the others sipped away. Then Richard passed shrooms around to the kids while Rosalita practically had to carry Heidi over to the VW to show her the "gypsy clothes" she'd sewn together.

Richard started a little fire, more for light than for hotdogs or s'mores. He sipped beer from a can of Coors until Rosalita called to him from the back of the van. A minute later he rolled a newish-looking wheelbarrow across the fire from where the kids sat and set it down, tip pointing toward the disciples. Then he disappeared.

According to the statement he gave later, Tony Kittermen, the youngest disciple at age fifteen, had been having the greatest summer of his life. He'd gotten laid, repeatedly, mostly by the two chicks on either side of him, but a couple of times by Mom herself. After Rosalita, it was hard to get excited about these other two, but tonight Heidi Rider had joined them. Heidi used to hang with his older sister, and Kittermen had fantasized about Heidi for some time.

But now Kittermen could barely move, even though the radio had turned to static eons ago. Although he had trouble forming words, when Richard returned Kittermen would find a way to ask him to fix the reception. Not that the static bothered him. He'd never been this mellow before, content to just stare into the fire; Kittermen didn't even care that he might not be able to get it up for Heidi tonight. Man, that Richard had really given them some powerful shit.

After another eternity, the three came out from behind the VW, none wearing a stitch of clothes, and an aroused Richard guided an unsteady Heidi Rider over to the wheelbarrow. Richard leaned Heidi forward until her palms touched down on metal. Rosalita was out front, licking at Heidi's neck and kissing at her lips as Richard entered her from behind, beginning to thrust as Heidi's eyes drooped, betraying neither pleasure nor pain. Rosalita circled the fire, kneeling before each disciple, taking time to kiss each full on the mouth, her tongue penetrating deeply, before moving on to the next.

When Rosalita finished with the kids, she returned to her spot beside the wheelbarrow as Richard reached forward and grasped a handful of Heidi's hair, pulling it backward, stretching her neck. Richard continued thrusting as Rosalita's hand disappeared inside the wheelbarrow and returned with something shiny. By the time it registered in Kittermen's mind that she was holding a scalpel, the woman he knew as Rosalita de León had begun her perverse surgery, slicing deep across Heidi's throat, opening her left-side carotid artery. The blood sprayed across the fire, showering them before Richard lowered Heidi's head, blood now gushing into the basin of the barrow. Rosalita danced backward, a quick two-step before dropping the scalpel and shoving her face under the steady flow of Heidi's crimson essence. The half of her face spattered with blood looked so dark she might have dipped it in ink.

Rosalita couldn't control herself. She danced backward, giddy, tongue darting in and out like a snake, and issuing squeals of delight that even as sluggish and frozen from whatever Richard had slipped him, Kittermen could not believe was human.

Richard pulled out of Heidi and slung her lifeless body aside as though it were nothing. The husband and wife then dipped their hands deep into the wheelbarrow and began smearing the warm blood over one another, animalistic, repeating the ritual, faster and faster still, before falling to the ground and not making anything remotely close to love, as Kittermen had later informed the authorities, but fucking like dogs in heat, rapidly twisting and changing positions, pausing, recharging, and starting again.

Later, Rosalita came around with a wineskin, squirting something into each of the disciples' mouths.

Kittermen awoke to sobbing from one of the girls who had woken first. The boy had hoped it had been a dream, a bad trip—but there lay Heidi Rider, crumpled and chalk white beside the wheelbarrow, marble brown eyes sightless.

Fearing for their own lives, the disciples looked around, but the VW van and the two de Leóns were long gone...

"Nothing came of the fingerprints, and we didn't do DNA like today," retired Sheriff Diedrick told Cady. "Anything we had would be in boxes and bags in the evidence locker, rotting away."

"Did you ever find the van?"

"Sheriff Hofer chased the VW down to a parking lot in Phoenix, where it had been abandoned after the murder. Turned out Richard de León, or whoever the hell he really was, had bought it for cash off a student at the University of Tucson, but, of course, de León never followed through on the title change."

"Killing like that must have made a huge splash in the papers. You get any tips on the couple?"

"The sheriff and I tracked down each and every sighting—all dead ends. Glen played the media, figuring we'd get them that way, but it all got dropped from the headlines a few days later."

"Why?"

"The Tate and LaBianca murders took place. Similar savagery, but celebrity names with a higher body count. And if that wasn't enough, the Hollywood angle got the media all-out salivating. It stole our thunder. When they started arresting the Manson clan in November, the sheriff got to thinking, especially when he heard one of the crazed Mansonite chicks admit to tasting Sharon Tate's blood. He had the kids and the student who sold the VW page through mug shots of the Manson family members. Glen figured that maybe the de Leóns were part of that crazy Helter Skelter shit."

"That would make sense."

JEFFREY B. BURTON   103

"Sadly, it was another dead end. Those sick fuckers got seriously lucky about timing—the Manson clan stole their notoriety."

Cady flipped through the faxed documents. "You got good descriptions."

"That Kittermen boy was a big help. Said Richard looked like a tall Jim Morrison. Although we figured from some of the hair on the blankets that Richard was probably wearing a wig. The sheriff chased that angle as well," Diedrick said. "As for Rosalita, Kittermen told us that if Heidi Rider had an older sister, she'd look like Rosalita."

Cady felt as though he'd been slapped in the face. As Diedrick spoke, he had been going through the murder file, which contained old statements, timelines, and autopsy photos that Hofer and Diedrick had compiled, when he came across a black-and-white photo of Heidi Rider that had been taken from her high school yearbook. He stared at Heidi in her cheerleader outfit, and even though her hairstyle was four decades out of date, Cady knew in his gut that he'd found another understudy—and, quite possibly, the first of the lookalikes.

"You still there, Agent Cady?"

"Yes."

"You know, rehashing all of this, I think I'm going to pour myself a stiff drink."

"Wish I could join you, sir."

"Can I ask a favor?"

"Anything," promised Cady.

"If something comes of this, especially if you catch these warped fucks, you'll let me know, right?"

"You'll be the first one I call."

CHAPTER TWENTY-THREE

"Freezer burn?"

Cady was in Chief Weflen's office, being debriefed on the autopsy results by the medical examiner. The chief, Lieutenant Rohr, and a couple of her people stood on one side of the police chief's desk while Dr. Wallace Foeller sat in the hot seat, being peppered with questions. Cady stood on the other side of the chief's throne while his new staff, Agent Schultz and Agent Desrosier, hovered near the wall of windows, taking constant peeks out at Lake Superior as if to confirm the great lake hadn't disappeared since their last glimpse.

"So sayeth the tissue samples," Duluth's ME answered. "It explains the epidermal discoloration."

"Storage," Rohr replied, and heads about the room began to nod. "Wouldn't be the first time a perp used something like that."

"Heather Klyn disappeared two months ago. So after the—I don't know, *draining*—Klyn was placed in a freezer," Cady said, establishing a timeline, "which means the UNSUB hung onto her until he finished with Katrina Mortensen before dumping both of them into Superior."

"Are you thinking the guy froze all these other girls?" Weflen asked.

"That's pretty incriminating, even if you have a large freezer or a walk-in on your premises," said Agent Schultz.

"Once the thrills are done, don't these pricks switch over to get-rid-of-the-evidence mode?" the lieutenant asked.

"John Wayne Gacy—the Killer Clown, if you remember him—buried his victims in his own crawlspace," Agent Desrosier answered.

"Isn't that the exception that proves the rule?"

"Jeffrey Dahmer kept victim parts in his freezer."

Rohr shrugged.

"I'm thinking Lake Superior was a mistake. The killer or killers," Cady said, thinking of "Mom" and "Dad" de León of Brenner, Arizona, "didn't go out far enough, didn't puncture the bodies to keep them from rising, and didn't weigh them down."

"Killers?" The chief caught Cady's eye. "As in multiple serial killers?"

"It's something we need to consider."

Weflen shook his head. "This just keeps getting better and better."

"I have a question." One of Deb Rohr's plainclothes spoke up. "Why would he or they take them out during a squall?"

The lieutenant looked at her detective. "Might have thought a storm would work in their favor, provide added cover, but realized how big a fuck-me it was once they got in the middle of it."

"So suddenly there's a need to dump the two recent kills, and one of these kills had been stored in a freezer for a couple months. What does that tell us?" Cady asked the room.

"That they ran out of storage space."

"A system existed—based upon the number of lookalikes, even if not all are a part of this case—that worked. And the system worked until, as the lieutenant put it, they ran out of space."

Rohr pulled a vibrating phone off her belt clip, crossed the room and left the chief's office.

"So he or they were tossing these girls down a well, but the well filled up so he or they turned to freezers and Lake Superior?" Weflen asked.

Cady shrugged.

The chief cleared his throat and addressed the investigators, "I'm not sure if I'd call it good news, but we've got the Coast Guard checking the coast line. They're up past Two Harbors and nothing to report so far."

Lieutenant Rohr returned to the room, eyes on Cady.

"Herriges found a lookalike that escaped."

Lieutenant Rohr led Cady downstairs, into a shared office space, and over to a beige cube marginally bigger than a deck of cards.

"This is Rain Man," Rohr said, pointing to a young man working at a PC with dual monitors.

"Steve Herriges." The search genius swiveled his chair and held out a hand to Cady. "She calls me that because I look like Tom Cruise."

"Right, in the second half of *Born on the Fourth of July*," Rohr said.

Herriges looked like he'd never seen the sun. He had a long neck that arched forward, likely seeking the desired Vitamin D off the glare of his monitors.

"What have you got for us?" Cady asked.

"A girl fitting your description, Ashley Hill, dodged the bullet a year ago summer when someone tried to grab her outside a bar in La Crosse, Wisconsin."

"You got the police report?"

"Yup." Herriges reached for a handful of pages sitting in the printer. "Hot off the press."

"I'm going to need to talk to her. Can La Crosse PD contact her for us?"

"Better yet, they're picking her up. We can Skype in ten minutes."

"I got slammed against the side of a van." Ashley Hill spoke through the Skype feed on Herriges' computer, her image filling one of the screens. "One second the old lady in the driver's seat is asking me which way to Western Avenue, and the next thing I know I'm smashed against the van and the side of my face is splashed with something wet."

Cady pegged Ashley Hill as a lookalike at first sight. Ms. Hill had finished running them through the assault that summer night in La Crosse, but now Cady wanted to walk her through it again, slowly, to see if there was anything additional to glean.

"Can you describe what the old woman look like?"

"It was hard to see her and everything happened so quickly, but… short hair, either gray or white. She also wore glasses that I think were plastic rims, real wide. I remember they covered a good part of her face."

"You said she pulled the van up next to you?"

"Look, it's a bit embarrassing to talk about, Mr. Cady. Hanky's—

the nightclub I was at—had Circus Life playing. They're a crappy local band, but the bar was packed and the line to the ladies room was nearly all the way to the entrance. So I snuck out the back."

"The back of the bar?"

"Yes. I had a couple of margaritas in me and really had to pee. No way could I wait for the bathroom. There's a hill behind Hanky's with some bushes, plus it's dark outside. Girls who know have been using that area as a restroom for years whenever the line backs up."

"So when you finished you came street side?"

"I had my hand stamped so Hanky's would let me back in. Even though I left through the back, the door locks automatically and they aren't supposed to let anyone enter through there. The staff could get in trouble."

"That's when the van pulled up," Cady prompted.

"Yes," Ashley Hill answered. "Startled me. It came out of nowhere. But then this sweet old lady—well, seemingly sweet old lady—asked me how to get to Western Avenue. I turned my head to look at her, and that's when he hit me. My ribs hurt for a week."

"Did you see him?"

"No, I didn't get a chance. I was turned toward the van when I was hit."

"And the attacker smeared the side of your face with something wet?"

"I screamed bloody murder and went all dead weight, you know, like they tell you to. I saw a shadow leap into the passenger door and the van peeled out. At first I thought it was some drunken asshole from the bar with whiskey or something on his hand, but the cops thought it was something else. What do you think?"

Rather than answer that, Cady said, "Tell me about the van."

"It happened so fast, but it was white, or at least a light gray."

"Did you see any part of the license plate?"

"There was a second when they peeled out, when I was lying on the ground still screaming, when Jake—the bouncer—came running out, that I actually tried to get the plate number. It was clear, the moon was out, but I couldn't read anything. I found that odd."

"You think they covered it up, smeared it with mud or something?"

"Yeah, maybe mud."

"Was it a full-size van or a minivan?"

"Wasn't a minivan," Hill said. "But that's another thing; it wasn't a normal full-size like they sing about in that Chevy Van song, either. I don't know vehicles and, like I said, it all happened so fast, but being pressed against the side of it sticks with me. It had a bit of an odd shape, you know, different. Maybe like the kind they use for deliveries when they don't need a big truck, for groceries or something."

CHAPTER TWENTY-FOUR

"He told me to call off the bloodhound."

It was getting late, nearly eleven, but Cady answered Agent Liz Preston on the first ring. He'd planned on touching base with her first thing in the morning, not only to get a status update on Roland Jund's situation, but to pick her brain about the eerie nature of current affairs in Duluth, Minnesota…and his fear that it might stretch back some decades to a parched piece of desert near Brenner, Arizona.

"Bloodhound?"

"He means you, Drew."

"But I'm not even in D.C."

"He knows you were here and suspects you'll be back."

Assistant Director Mike Litchy from International Operations, one of the three ADs on the joint FBI and CIA taskforce, had appeared in Agent Preston's office full of wide grins and *aw shucks.*

"Litchy told me he found it impossible to believe his *dear friend* Roland Jund would be involved in anything—*anything at all*—of a seditious nature. He recalled being invited to a soirée at Jund's home for some beers over a Nationals game, and how Roland stood, even though it was on TV, and put his hand on his heart and sang along with the national anthem."

"Sounds like Jund."

"Yes, but then Litchy goes on to say that although he's *certainly not referring to Roland*, that double agents, historically, adapt affectations to throw trackers off the scent."

"Thus calling Jund a traitor."

"Pretty much," Agent Preston replied. "He goes on to state that it makes *perfect sense* for someone like me to be concerned about the recent turn of events, about Jund's ties to Steve and Dayna Parrish, who are looking more and more a part of a Russian cell operating inside the FBI, and how we need to leave the investigation to the *counterintelligence boys* in the National Security Branch to *do their job and sort this mess out.* The AD emphasized twice that I need to let the investigation go through the proper channels."

"How did he know to come to you?"

"I've been talking to people, Drew," Preston answered. "Putting out feelers."

"Is that wise?"

"Like Litchy said, it makes perfect sense for me to be curious and ask questions about Roland's situation. The AD I've hitched my wagon to is suddenly on involuntary leave and being investigated for breaching national security—it would be suspicious for me *not* to question what the hell is going on. Since providing the list of the taskforce members, Assistant Director Speedling has kept me at arm's length, not returning my calls or e-mails. Same with Director Green; I can't get past his receptionist. As for the CIA reps, I get answering services, but no calls are ever returned. It's like I'm speaking into a black hole."

"I don't think this is safe, Liz."

"Don't worry. I don't have anything beyond reasonable questions and righteous indignation. I'm making a little noise, but it's all smoke without fire. I'm pushing out some waves to see what washes back in."

"And what washed back was Assistant Director Litchy."

"Yes. And there's one more thing. Litchy said I needed to stay out of the inquiry, not only because I have a major conflict of interest and can't be objective, but because my proximity to Roland Jund has already placed me under the microscope and the last thing I need is to raise additional red flags by interfering in a Bureau investigation."

"A thinly veiled threat."

"Very thinly veiled. And even though he said a lot of pro forma pleasantries about Roland, I got the distinct impression Litchy already had Jund tagged as the Lynchpin."

"And through you and Jund, Litchy spots me in the background."

"You're a known commodity after the Chessman investigation, Drew. You should be honored. They know you're fiercely loyal to Jund," Agent Preston said. "Either that or—"

"Or what?"

"Or I'm under surveillance."

CHAPTER TWENTY-FIVE

"It's a bit hard to study with you staring at my boobs," Hannah Erickson whispered across the table at Brad Schussler.

"Now you're knocking my hobby?"

"Shhh." Hannah held a finger to her lips. "It's a library."

"You're the one who said boobs," Brad whispered back.

"And what is it with you? I thought we took care of all that before coming here?"

Hannah Erickson and Bradley Schussler were on a study date, parked at a table on the third floor of the campus library at the University of South Dakota in Vermillion.

"Hey, I'm twenty-one. I can be taken care of, but then five minutes will pass."

"I've got to make it through chapter seven," Hannah said, tapping the open page of her chemistry textbook with her yellow highlighter for emphasis. Although school had begun a month earlier, Hannah appeared to be the only one at the table concerned about that. "And not just read it—I've got to understand what it means."

"Grog's party is starting any minute now."

Dave "Grog" Sackett was the U's answer to John Belushi in *Animal House*. Though Hannah despised him, Grog was one of Brad's best friends and a permanent fixture among the perpetually revolving wingmen and assorted flunkies who shared a dilapidated three-bedroom shack that should have been torn down about the time the meteors did in the dinosaurs. It was miles off campus; the only thing it had going for it was its proximity to the Missouri River, a mere stone's throw away from a site that Grog hadn't yet been able to tarnish—but, Hannah figured, give him time.

"You've said that five times already," she said.

"I just figure maybe I could help them out."

"Yes, all those keggers won't drink themselves."

Brad looked pained.

"Go already."

"Really?"

"You don't need my permission."

"I just don't want you mad at me for breaking our study date."

"Goodness, you're not doing any studying anyway."

Brad smiled.

"What?"

"You said goodness."

They both cracked up.

"You okay with walking back?"

"I think I can make the two blocks." Hannah shared a university-affiliated apartment with a roommate.

"So I can go?"

"Go."

"And you're not mad?"

"Go already," Hannah replied. "Your boyfriend misses you."

"Can I swing by later?"

"I don't want a drunk pawing at me in the middle of the night. You're already over so much you make Anna nervous."

Anna had been Hannah's roommate in a variety of dorms and apartments since freshman year. Anna and Hannah—BFFs.

"But I might have things to tell you."

"What things?"

"Issues. Feelings," Brad said. "I'm very deep and sensitive."

"Beat it."

Hannah finished chapter seven and decided to begin chapter eight in the comfort of home, especially since the entire purpose of studying in the library had been to get Brad out of the apartment and give Anna some privacy. She'd been making noises lately about Brad being there so often he should kick in rent, how uncomfortable she felt with the paper-thin walls leaving nothing to the imagination, and how she'd break the lease and move out if *that Grog guy* ever darkened their step again. Anna just didn't have it in her to forgive Grog for ferreting through a hamper of dirty wash, coming up with some of her underwear, and using them in a suggestive puppet show that had put Brad in stitches and, Hannah hated to admit, nearly had her in tears, she'd been laughing so hard.

"Anna needs to get laid" was Brad's response every time Hannah broached the subject.

Hannah typed out a text to Anna on her way out of the library and then cut across the parking lot to the adjacent sidewalk, books shuffling in her backpack. She was checking her phone for a reply when the white van pulled up next to her and the passenger window rolled down.

"Excuse me, sweetie, but that's the U library, isn't it?"

Hannah saw the driver was a smiling elderly woman, her gray hair in a bun and a scarf shawl wrapped about her neck.

"That's it."

"Is it still open?"

"For another hour."

"Do you know Welch Flowers?"

"Yes," Hannah replied, smiling back at the grandmother-like woman. Hannah had gotten many a rose from Welch Flowers over the past few years and, truth be told, not all from Brad.

"Could you do me a big favor, sweetheart?"

"What?"

"I'm Les Welch's aunt, and he and the boys have got the stomach flu."

"Oh no."

"So a bunch of us gals are running deliveries and running so far behind, dear heart, I'm afraid we're making a botch of it." The woman held up what looked to be a small lavender plant with a red card taped to the paper about the base. "Do you know a Vicki Lynn Smith?"

Hannah shook her head.

The woman looked at a slip of paper. "She works at the library's main desk. If I drove you back, sweetie, could you run it in for me so I could zip off to my next stop?"

"You'd trust me with that beautiful thing?"

"Someone as beautiful as you, dear heart, of course I would."

Maybe it was the night shadows, or the warnings from parents to never get into cars with strangers, or a lifetime of being hit on by horny guys. More likely it was the saccharine manner in which the old woman kept calling her *sweetie* and *dear heart* that creeped Hannah out, but Hannah knew she would not be getting into the van—good cause for Welch Flowers or not.

"I'll walk it back for you."

"You sure, sweetie?"

Hannah nodded.

"I can't thank you enough." The old woman leaned across the front seat and held out the plant.

Hannah opened the passenger door and two things struck her as odd. First, the interior light did not turn on; the only light came from the dashboard and the streetlamp down the block. Second, there was something a little off about the woman's face—perhaps a trick of the light, but from Hannah's angle it appeared somehow artificial, like those aging Hollywood actresses who've seen the surgeon one too many times.

The elderly woman pulled the lavender plant back to her chest and inhaled deeply. Hannah stepped up into the cab and leaned across the passenger seat to collect the flower delivery for Vicki Lynn Smith.

"You've got to smell this, Hannah."

Her heart froze. "How did you know my—"

A hand shot from the darkness behind her, covering Hannah's mouth with something wet—a feeling of being lifted—and then nothing.

CHAPTER TWENTY-SIX

Cady couldn't do the couch at the satellite office for a second night in a row, so he beelined it from Duluth PD to the Holiday Inn. It was after midnight, and the gallon of caffeine he'd drunk throughout the day had worn off, leaving him exhausted. The events of the past few days had caught up with him. He needed sleep.

"You're already checked in, Mr. Cady," the clerk at the front desk informed him.

"How can that be?"

The clerk poked about on the computer for a few seconds.

"It shows your wife checked in at six o'clock."

A sluggish Terri pushed herself up in bed with the palms of her hands when Cady entered the room and flicked on the light. She was wearing one of his t-shirts, and she squinted against the brightness.

"I wore Saran Wrap until ten o'clock, then said screw it and went to bed."

"Why didn't you let me know you were coming?"

"I wanted to surprise you," Terri answered. "I brought you clean laundry and lunch-ticket money."

Cady leaned in for a kiss and then sat next to her on the bed, holding her hand.

"I can't tell you how glad I am to see you, Ter," Cady said after an eternity.

Terri smiled. "The things a girl's got to do to get some romance in northern Minnesota."

—

"Drew." Terri touched his shoulder.

"Arglesnug," Cady said, or something to that effect.

"Wake up, Drew." Terri gently rubbed his arm.

Cady opened his eyes. It took a few seconds to focus on the digits on the clock that faced him on the bedside table.

5:50 a.m.

"What's up?"

"Your phone. It keeps buzzing."

Cady rolled over, fumbled for it.

"This is Cady."

Terri watched his profile from the bed as the seconds ticked past.

"I'll be right in," Cady said and clicked off his cell phone.

"What is it?"

"A girl disappeared at a university in South Dakota last night... another lookalike."

CHAPTER TWENTY-SEVEN

Her name was Hannah Erickson.

She had last been seen exiting a campus library around ten p.m. the previous evening, right after she texted her roommate to let her know she was on her way home and to start popping the corn. When Hannah didn't arrive at the apartment after a reasonable amount of time, her roommate began calling and texting Hannah's smartphone. Repeatedly. At midnight the roommate drove over to Hannah's boyfriend's house, pulled the boyfriend out of drunken revelry, only to discover that Hannah was not at the party and had never been. At that point the roommate and Hannah's boyfriend went to the police.

Duluth PD had issued a soft APB—all points bulletin—to police departments around the Midwest requesting they let Duluth know if any females broadly fitting their lookalike description—young, thin in stature, mid-to-lengthy dark hair, brown eyes, mid-height or taller, highly attractive—were reported missing, and *not* to wait twenty-four hours for it to turn into a missing-person's case.

Hannah Erickson was another lookalike. Her picture told the story. If Hannah Erickson had been grabbed by Cady's UNSUB, and if that UNSUB was still following the pattern from Katrina Mortensen, then Hannah had less than a day to live.

Cady looked at the other adjectives he and Lieutenant Deb Rohr had scribbled down on notebook paper—more personality traits than physical characteristics: vivacious, outgoing, sociable, fun-loving, alluring, a sense of fashion, trendy, and on it went. So their appearance and personality would make the lookalikes stand out in a crowded room like beacons, with young men flocking to them like ants to sugar. Meantime, a pair of killers lurked somewhere in the shadows, silently watching.

A pair of killers?

Husband and wife de León had seemingly fallen off the edge of the earth after Brenner, Arizona. Had they worked their urges out of their system, cleaned up their act, and gone on to have children and coach Little League, bake cookies for the PTA, and volunteer at the soup kitchen on Sunday mornings?

Cady, like the late Sheriff Hofer of Gila County, feared not.

More realistically, the de Leóns—or whoever the hell they really were—had laid low after Brenner, astonished at what they'd gotten away with and sweating every knock of room service on their motel door. They must have been ecstatic—must have thanked their lucky stars—when the Manson Family killings knocked them from the headlines.

And they also would have learned. In the future, they'd have to enjoy limited, private engagements rather than flaunt their bloodlust in front of groupies. They recalibrated their tactics, settled for a more personal ritual, more private in nature, just a husband and wife and— if Cady's hunch about the case was correct—a desired lookalike.

A Hannah Erickson.

Or am I the crazy one?

Sure, these lookalikes could easily understudy for one another in a theater production, but so what? Serial rapists and killers often preyed on certain types. What was it about these girls that turned these particular killers' crank? Was it the other, more essential trait that connected these lookalikes? Not the eye-catching looks and social-butterfly-cheerleader/bubbly-girl-next-door personalities of each victim…but their *youth*?

Cady thought again about Rosalita and Richard de León's line of shit about being descendants of Ponce de León, the explorer and conquistador famed for his quest for the Fountain of Youth. Sheriff Hofer had followed that genealogical red herring to its proper dead end decades earlier. But Rosalita and Richard had informed their disciples that they had, in fact, discovered the Fountain of Youth, and that it was not a location, per se, but something *far more vital in nature* that would serve to keep the couple eternally young.

Hence newer victims, such as Katrina Mortensen and Heather Klyn, found drained of their life's essence, pumped full of poison, and tossed into Lake Superior?

Cady shook his head. He had to stop fixating on the de Leóns. His hunch about them operating out of northern Minnesota was likely nonsense. For all he knew, the twosome known as Rosalita and Richard de León had been dead for years or, likelier yet, incarcerated decades back—convicted for other crimes—which Cady knew from previous cases was not that uncommon an event.

The blood remained the key to everything.

And what exactly was it that Countess Elizabeth Báthory de Ecsed believed the blood of young virgins gave her?

Jesus Christ, Cady thought, I'm insane. Hannah Erickson had less than a day to live and he was burning time ruminating about the "Blood Countess" from the sixteenth century. What was it Liz Preston had said to him at their last meeting, deep in the bowels of the Hoover Building in Washington, D.C.?

Old Drew would have nailed the UNSUB by now.

New Drew sat in front of the stacks of files that made up the case. He pushed the folder on Taylor Ganser/Kal Hoyer over to the far side of the conference table. He didn't believe Taylor Ganser was related to the lookalikes and didn't want to waste time falling down that rabbit hole. On top of the first stack were his notes from the interview with the lookalike that had gotten away—Ashley Hill—and Ashley's tale of escape from the odd-shaped van in La Crosse, Wisconsin. Everything Miss Hill had told him about that night in La Crosse Cady had read, and read again, and highlighted in blue.

Several times he had worked his way through the stack of files in a chronological order. After a long moment, Cady rearranged the pages around the conference room table and began to reread them, only this time out of order, to see if any patterns would emerge, if anything in the documents would scream out at him.

Three hours later Cady was scanning the list of embalming equipment and supply companies that Lieutenant Rohr had handed him what now seemed a lifetime ago. The names of the various pump manufacturers meant nothing to him, but something on Rohr's list nibbled away in the back of his mind. Cady read each name aloud, oblivious to any foot traffic passing outside the open conference room door, and then he read the names of their corresponding parent companies, if they existed.

That's when he saw it.

Embalmatic Company was the arterial pump manufacturer. The name was meaningless to Cady. However, it was a subsidiary, and Cady had most certainly heard of its parent company—RobustEquip Incorporated. RobustEquip was a major player in the health care industry, a market leader in durable medical equipment. And Cady had seen their logo recently.

On the wheelchair of a crippled man at a Duluth City Council meeting.

CHAPTER TWENTY-EIGHT

"Fuck you," Rohr said. "I'd toss you out of my office if I wasn't so goddamned tired."

"Just hear me out."

"I didn't picture you as a joker, Cady. And I assure you the chief will toss you out on your ear."

Cady stared silently at the lieutenant.

"For Christ's sake," Rohr said. "You can't be serious."

"Ten minutes."

"Clock's ticking, but you know how flimsy the wheelchair thing is, don't you? Rich guy has a stroke and has the bookoo bucks to buy a motorized wheelchair made by this RoboFuck Corporation—"

"RobustEquip Incorporated," Cady interrupted.

"Whatever." Rohr took an earring off and dropped it on her mousepad. "So *RobustEquip* owns a subsidiary company that makes embalming pumps. That's grasping at lame-ass straws, Cady."

"Grasping at straws, *Rohr*, got me thinking of what Ashley Hill said about the white van she almost got shoved into last summer. Odd-shaped, not a normal van. Perhaps like the ones used by handicapped drivers."

It was Rohr's turn to stare at Cady.

"Are all handicapped vans white?"

Cady shrugged. "You know with handicapped plates and room enough to hide most anything, it's not the worst vehicle for sneaking someone from here to there."

"Have a seat, Agent Cady." The lieutenant took her second earring off. "You make me nervous standing there."

Cady sat.

"Interesting tie-in," Rohr continued, "but a guy in a wheelchair buys a van. Nothing earthshaking there."

"I contacted DVS." DVS stood for Driver and Vehicle Services, a division of the Minnesota Department of Public Safety. "The Quillings bought that van eight years ago. Awful smart of Evan Quilling to get his ducks in a row seven years before he actually had a stroke."

Rohr sat upright. "You *are* shitting me?"

"And they owned another one for eight years before that."

"I've never seen Evan or Lucinda drive a handicapped van until his illness."

"Probably stashed them at a rental garage in Askov or Finlayson. Pine County's a big place."

"They own that huge spread on Superior. Probably get ten vehicles in their chauffeur garage out there. Could have stashed them there, tarp it up or something."

Cady knew he was making inroads, and he was just getting started.

"Remember Lucinda's story at the council meeting about the antique dolls Elisabeth Congdon brought her from Amsterdam?"

Rohr nodded.

"I did some digging. Elisabeth Congdon never went to Amsterdam, not even once."

"But I can't run with that," the lieutenant said. "The mixed-up memories of a little girl? Congdon could have bought her a Barbie at Penney's and told her it was Anne Frank."

"I'll spare you the Latin," Cady said, "but false in one thing, false in all."

"Fuck that." Rohr's eyes zigzagged about her cluttered desktop before stopping on Cady. "This is nuts. For Christ's sake, Lucinda's a friend of mine."

"You ever go on a trip with her?"

"She's not gay."

"That's not what I'm saying." Cady sighed. "You ever see some great acting in a high school production where the leads knock it out of the park in a drama like *Driving Miss Daisy* or *Flowers for Algernon*?"

"So what?"

"So you're completely sucked in, and after the play, out in the lobby, you go to congratulate the stars and you see them acting all squirrelly with their high school friends and you suddenly realize that they're just kids."

"So what?" Rohr said again

"That's what it's like with sociopaths. They can be *on* and stay in character for bits at a time, and even be charming. But if you hang around long enough, you'll begin to see the cracks in the veneer, and, eventually, the mask comes off. Have you ever been around the Quillings for lengthy periods of time, or just for council meetings or coffee at Starbucks or cake at a retirement party?"

"A lot of short periods over the years, I guess."

"Did you know Lucinda attended Berkeley in the late sixties and graduated in 1971 with a degree in sociology? She and Evan bought a duplex near the university."

"She might have mentioned Berkeley."

"Ask me what Evan Quilling studied there."

"Cough it up."

"Evan Quilling never graduated, but he did nearly four years of pre-med." Cady read *arterial pump* in the lieutenant's eyes.

"Fuck me."

The two investigators sat unmoving for several seconds, and Cady knew he had her.

"But I thought the shitbags in Arizona—the couple that called themselves Rosalita and Richard de León—were married?"

Cady shrugged. "So they said."

"That's just fucking gross."

"Here's the topper—and I had a devil of a time getting this from St. Mary's, had to tear an administrator away from her *nightly sherbet* to open the high school and get me this. Checkout Lucinda's senior picture on the page with the Post-it note."

Cady handed the old yearbook to Rohr, who opened it to the page where Cady had placed the yellow Post-it. The lieutenant scanned the rows of pictures.

"Fuck me," Rohr said. "She's a lookalike."

"Are my ten minutes up?"

—

"Their mother died of leukemia when Lucinda was a toddler."

"The dad's not still around, is he?" Cady asked.

"The Quillings own a chateau in Switzerland, somewhere near Lake Geneva—the Alps or somewhere," Rohr said. "Lucinda told me her father would go for daily hikes and one day he took a tumble. When he didn't return, Lucinda and Evan got concerned and went looking, but couldn't find hide nor hair. They went to the village for help, but by the time the search party found Evan Quilling Sr. the next day, it was too late and…and stop looking at me with that fucking smirk, Cady. I'm just telling you what I heard."

"How old was Lucinda at the time?"

"I think mid-twenties. Evan a bit older."

"The dad may have walked in on something or the two may have decided their *lifestyle* would be less complicated with Evan Sr. out of the picture."

"Good God."

"And there's another thing that occurred to me." Cady glanced at his watch. "If I'm uber-wealthy, sure, I'll kick some back to the hometown. Show up at parades, cut ribbons. Makes good sense. But this network the Quillings have is a bit excessive—this pipeline of theirs. It drills right into city hall. They're privy to everything in real time."

"Why didn't you run to the chief with all this?" Rohr asked. "Why me?"

"You know why."

"Politics."

"He's in bed with the Quillings over the election. So is the mayor."

"I get the dynamics, but ultimately Chief Weflen is a good man. If you walk him through it, just like you did me, he'll come around."

"He'll kick it to the lawyers and by then Hannah Erickson will be dead."

Rohr nodded once. "We'll take my car."

CHAPTER TWENTY-NINE

It was half past eleven when Cady and Rohr arrived in the lieutenant's Mazda3. The Quillings' hilltop mansion was several miles north of town. They owned sixty acres of choice lakefront property, which included a boathouse big enough for a small navy destroyer. The manor house itself was tucked half a football field back from the water and built into the side of the hill in order to offer the Quillings a million-dollar view of Superior, the lake the Ojibwe called Gichigami.

The first line of defense for Cady and Rohr to ponder were the wrought-iron arms of a gate that swung shut from brick posts on either side of the driveway. It was more decorative than anything else, but the arms had been swung shut—and padlocked accordingly—in order to block the driveway leading to the Quilling manor.

"We were going to do this silent alarm anyway," Rohr said, her point being that they were approaching the Quilling compound like squad cars answering a silent alarm, with no blaring sirens, so as to catch the perpetrators in the act.

Cady pointed at the two signs, one posted on each arm of the closed gate. One read *No Trespassing* and the other read *Protected by Pro-Tek Home Security System 24/7 Police Dispatch*.

"I imagine the prosecuting attorney will bring that one up in our hearing," Rohr said, pointing at the trespassing sign. "That other one I'll go check on."

Rohr went back to her Mazda, which she'd pulled onto the grass off the access road servicing the handful of designer mansions that dotted this section of the Great Lake. Cady walked around one of the redbrick posts that tethered a gate bar and headed into the tree line.

It was a clear night, chilly in the final week of September. A night that let Duluthians know that summer was, in no uncertain terms, over, and it would be best to gird your loins, as the white stuff wasn't far off. Cady wore his FBI windbreaker and kept his penlight aimed at his feet until the trees thinned out, and then he flicked it off. He stood beside a tree and looked down on the Quillings' compound, trying to glean a sense of what he and the lieutenant were in for.

My God, Cady thought, as the moon's reflection off Lake Superior framed the siblings' mansion in an unnerving silhouette. The place looked like some sort of medieval keep.

"The sign's a decoy," Rohr said. "I had one of mine check with Pro-Tek, and there's no account registered at this address."

"Wouldn't want to have police show up every time a bird flies into a window." Cady had returned from his brief reconnaissance and now sat in the Mazda3's passenger seat. "Have they got staff down there? Chauffeurs or maids?"

"The Quillings don't toss their wealth in your face. No chauffeurs or maids or other servants. Lucinda once told me a cleaning service comes in every month, mostly because she'd go insane if she had to vacuum every room,"

Cady nodded. "That fits. No one around to bump into anything."

"Look, if it turns out that we're fucked in the head on this, just follow my lead. You came to me with this data and I went all cavalry and dragged you out here as backup."

"You don't have to do that."

"I'm a dyke in a city job," Rohr said. "No one can fire me."

"I wouldn't be so sure."

"I've got Deets and Monroe on call."

Deets and Monroe were detectives in the lieutenant's Violent Crimes Unit.

"They know anything?"

"Just that we're here."

"Good."

—

"Jesus Christ," Rohr said when she saw the Quilling mansion from the tree line. "It looks like something from those Hammer horror films I watched as a kid."

"That's because of the shadows," Cady replied. "And what we suspect has been happening here."

Rohr sighed. "You want to be Van Helsing or Jonathan Harker?"

"Who's Jonathan Harker?"

"The boyfriend of the girl Dracula's got the hots for. Keanu Reeves played him in the movie."

"You can be him."

"You see anything?" Rohr whispered.

The two had worked their way along the far side of the property, keeping the hill between themselves and the Quilling residence until they were even with the chauffeur's garage, a structure the dimension of a mid-sized rambler that, like the mansion, was also dug into the hillside. There were four double sliding garage doors facing the lake. A serpentine cement driveway wound its way down from the access road at the top of the estate, curved a wide circle about a fountain in front of the manor's double-wide entry doors, and then stretched sideways another forty yards to form a small parking lot. A smaller stretch of paved blacktop slanted down to connect with the backside of the boathouse.

"No." Cady knew the lieutenant was asking if he'd caught a glimpse of Evan Quilling's white van. "The windows are opaque, tinted or something."

They were on the side of the garage opposite the house and Cady had done a pull-up—penlight in mouth with the bulk of his weight on the toes of his shoes, his good left hand, and his right elbow—to peek into a window that stood a good eight feet off the ground.

Cady dropped down. "Is that normal?"

"You think you'd want natural light."

"What about this?" Cady pointed at the side garage door. It looked heavy, like a fire door in a high-rise stairwell. Instead of a window, the door had a peephole at eye level.

"I've only seen that once before, when a mechanic was playing games with the city and running an auto repair shop out of his home garage."

The doorknob was locked. A half foot above the handle was a deadbolt. Cady leaned against the door. Solid.

"Something tells me I could kick at this all night and it wouldn't budge," Cady said. "Have you got an expandable baton?"

"Yes."

"I'll use that to break the window and slide in."

"Won't that make a little noise?"

"You got a better idea?"

"I suppose I could use this," Rohr said, shining a light on a small leather case she'd pulled from a back pocket. She flipped it open and Cady saw a handful of picks and a couple of stainless-steel tension tools.

"The Fourth Amendment deemed optional in Duluth?"

"Means a lot coming from Mister 'let's bust the window and break-and-enter.'"

"I need a little more tension." Rohr had been working the handle lock with a pick and the tension rod for several minutes as Cady held the light.

"I don't suppose you've got a pick gun on you?"

"You're lucky I took this off a nine-year-old house thief."

"A nine-year-old?"

"Yeah, and if the little juvie shit were here right now, we'd already be in," Rohr replied. "I've only played with bullshit locks at my desk, but I'm trying not to scratch the hell out of its face so at least that won't come up at our hearing."

A minute later the lock on the handle clicked open. Rohr began working the upper deadbolt, using the same pick and tension rod.

"I've got a drill in the trunk as a last resort," Rohr said. "Though I'm not an attorney, I feel safe speaking on behalf of the bar association when I say that we're royally screwed if we go that route."

Three minutes later the deadbolt gave way.

The lieutenant withdrew her picks and shoved open the door. "The point of no return, Special Agent Cady."

Terri gave Cady no end of banter over his *tenacious* moral code; of course, if Terri had her druthers, they'd hang thieves from the village square like Christmas ornaments, so Cady tended to take her lighthearted ribbing with a grain of salt.

But when it came to the wholesale slaughter of young women, Cady's moral code blinked like a neon sign on a dark Vegas night... and the sign flashed: *It Ends Now.*

Special Agent Drew Cady stepped into the garage.

CHAPTER THIRTY

Gray.

Cady and Rohr shined their lights about the dark garage. Everything was gray: floors, walls, cupboards, ceiling. And when Cady nudged open a cupboard, the inside was empty and gray.

"I don't think they use this area for anything beyond parking," Rohr said. "I'm sure mechanics do all the maintenance."

"Not many cars here."

A silver ML550 Mercedes-Benz SUV sat ignored in the far corner, waiting, likely in anticipation of winter. Parked next to it was a black Porsche Boxster.

"The Porsche is what Evan used to tool around town in," the lieutenant informed him, and then pointed her flashlight. "That's her ride."

A blue ES 300h Hybrid sat facing out in front of one of the center garage doors.

"What's that over there?" Cady aimed his penlight toward a structure of metal frames along the opposite wall.

"I think that's a car elevator to a lower level, and if Evan's wheelchair van isn't down there, Cady, we're shit out of luck."

They weren't shit out of luck.

The car elevator was more a simple lift, and when the investigators peered down through a maze of metal grates, they saw what appeared to be the ceiling of Evan Quilling's ambulette. They crisscrossed lights as they scrutinized the lower level of the parking garage, one flight below.

"Van's in the lift," Cady whispered.

"Another door," Rohr replied, gesturing toward the wall right outside the elevator.

Behind the lift, they found a metal staircase slanting down a dozen steps. Cady pulled his Glock 22 from his shoulder holster as he began the descent. Rohr followed suit with her Beretta 92FS, making sure to keep the barrel aimed at the floor. The lower level, gray as well, had a walkway wide enough for one person to maneuver about the side of the lift with about ten feet between the car elevator and the door that likely tunneled back to the Quilling mansion. The sliding metal gate to the lift had been left open, and Cady slid around the van to the driver's side window and peered in. He did the same on the passenger's side. Cady couldn't see into the back; a divider or blackout curtain blocked his view.

"Handicapped accessible," Rohr said, looking at the sliding side door.

"Something accessible."

Cady understood why Ashley Hill of La Crosse, Wisconsin—the lookalike that broke free—had said it was no ordinary van. This was a full-size white van with a raised roof, raised lift doors, and dark red stripes running across the length of both sides. It had been converted into a wheelchair van, or ambulette, for non-emergency medical transportation, the kind often used by nursing homes or long-term care facilities. Not a terrible way to transport a most unusual cargo from point A to point B—that is, for sneaking human contraband across state lines. The vehicle's outward appearance and handicapped plates made it unlikely for a state trooper to pull over except in cases of the most egregious driving.

Cady checked the handle on the sliding side door. Unlocked. He motioned at Rohr, who stepped back and assumed a classic Weaver shooting stance, aiming her Beretta at the side of the van. Cady slid the door back.

No one was inside.

Though the side door was open, no interior light came on and their flashlights cut paths through the darkness of the ambulette's interior, revealing stretcher mounts, oxygen storage containers, wheelchair

JEFFREY B. BURTON   133

storage brackets, a cushioned bench along the length of one side, and
the hydraulic lift for lowering wheelchair patrons.

"Isn't that Evan's?" Rohr shined her flashlight at a wheelchair that
sat secured to the floor in back of the driver's seat.

"Evan Quilling needs a wheelchair about as much as you do."

Cady stepped up into the van, slipping about the hydraulic lift,
and knelt down in front of the cushioned bench.

"You thinking what I'm thinking?" Rohr said, peering in from the
side, now aiming her light at the white bench.

The bench was coffin length, hard vinyl, and must have been
part of the van's retrofit, as it was secured to the flooring and wall.
A couple of seatbelts were strapped tight together on the cushioned
top, though Cady couldn't imagine that making for a comfortable
journey of any distance. It didn't look out of place, Cady thought, and
most would assume its worth as a storage compartment for, perhaps,
medical supplies or wheelchair accessories. He tried pulling up the
top rim, but it didn't budge. He gave a solid knock on the plastic
panel in front of his knee.

"Hollow."

"Run your hands along the top lip, under the cushion," Rohr said.
"There might be a keyhole or latch or something."

Penlight back in his mouth, Cady began in the middle—the
obvious place to center a locking mechanism—and ran his thumb
along the top edge, working his way toward the rear of the container
seat. When he reached the rear of the ambulette, Cady leaned his
right shoulder against the back door and shined his light down the
side of the storage bin. A flash of metal caught his eye.

"I see two small grates or vents along the bottom."

"Same here," Rohr said, checking her side and looking up. "Air holes."

As Cady brought his thumb around the back edge he felt an indent
in the smooth plastic, a button that had some give to it. He pressed
with a finger and tried to raise the lid. Again, no movement.

"I've got some kind of release latch on this end. See if you have one
on that side. I figure they had this box custom rigged, so they may
have designed it to take both of them to open."

"So if a cop ever stops them and wants to look inside, this is just
for seating as far as anyone can tell." The lieutenant crawled inside

and ran her fingers along her end where Cady had directed. Rohr found the matching release and looked at Cady. They both pressed and lifted the lid.

The two aimed their lights inside the open bench. Cady pressed his hand down on the bottom, which felt like the wrestling mats used in a high school gym. He saw a lump of shadows in the corner, grabbed at it and held it up for the lieutenant to see.

A short gray wig, a handful of scarves...and duct tape.

CHAPTER THIRTY-ONE

"Fuck is that noise?"

Lieutenant Rohr had worked her magic on the tunnel door, no longer caring about scratching up the lock faces on this entryway—at this point the two investigators were beyond legal niceties and into speed. When the fire door swung inward there were two things that became apparent.

One was a dank scent, clammy and humid, overpowering as though they had entered a long-forgotten vegetable cellar. Cady figured the central air and dehumidifier system from the main house hadn't been retrofitted to service this subterranean level—this sepulcher—that the Quillings had cut into the hillside above Lake Superior.

The second was a sporadic cackling that danced on the periphery—on the edge of their consciousness—and registered somewhere between gleeful hysterics and rapturous squeals. Cady felt the hair rise on the back of his neck as he recalled the police report on the dark ritual that had occurred decades ago in Arizona, and on the most alarming behavior of a young woman who called herself Rosalita de León.

"We've got to hurry," Cady said.

"What's that?" Rohr pointed at the wall near Cady's shoe.

A square-inch cube of plastic was attached to the lower part of the wall—at trim level if there had been any trim—about a foot inside the entryway. A red dot glowed in the cube's center. Cady swung the door back and saw an identical cube on the opposite wall, also glowing red in the center. A sensor of some kind.

Cady looked at Rohr. "They know we're here."

—

The hallway-slash-tunnel was barren, painted gray like the garage behind them. It swerved back toward the mansion, so it was difficult to see more than the bend right in front of them. The hysterical squeals became more pronounced the closer they got to its source. Cady hugged the right wall, penlight and Glock in front of him; Rohr stayed left, her Beretta as divining rod. She held both flashlight and cell phone in her other hand and kept checking for reception, but couldn't get a bar in the subterranean passageway.

Before tackling the tunnel door, the lieutenant had run up the steps to the upper garage level to make a quick call. Cady had listened as Rohr shouted at Detective Deets that he and Monroe had better get their *asses in gear* and *get over here with some paramedics.* She had ordered Deets to *cut the padlock on the entry gate or just drive through the goddamned thing* as well as *arrest anyone trying to leave.* Detective Deets obviously knew who the Quillings were, and there must have been some pushback, as Cady had heard Rohr scream, "On my say so!" followed by "You can call the goddamned chief after you get here!"

"That fucking voice is creeping me out," Rohr said. "It's like a bad soundtrack to a haunted house."

"And it's getting louder." Cady gestured with his chin. "Up ahead."

The two investigators were coming around what Cady thought had to be a final curve and had hit a straight passageway that appeared to burrow its way toward Quilling manor. Dim light shone out from a crevice in the wall ahead of them, adding to the murk and shadows.

"A staircase going down," Cady whispered.

"It's where the voice is coming from," Rohr whispered back. "This is where it happens, Cady. It's their fucking lair."

The voice had reached a fever pitch—grinding giggles to husky squeals of delight, bouncing off the gray walls, now coming from every direction. As they approached the light from the stairwell, they noticed that if they skipped the stairway going down and continued forward perhaps fifteen yards, another stairwell ascended up. The wall next to the upward stairwell contained a service elevator, old fashioned, the upper and lower doors shut tight.

"Leads to the house," Cady mouthed at Rohr.

The lieutenant assumed a firing stance as Cady pressed against the corner and peered down into the staircase. About twenty concrete steps leading down to an eight-by-six landing. That was all he could see. The light and the voice came from whatever subterranean hell was at the bottom.

Cady motioned the lieutenant over and stuffed his penlight in a pocket. Rohr stepped into close proximity so they could speak over the madness of the voice as they huddled at the top of the stairs. Her face was void of color, her eyes wide.

"You good to take it from here, Cady?" the lieutenant spoke in a hush. "It really is federal jurisdiction."

"We hit the room fast," Cady said into Rohr's ear. "Anything that moves—threatening or not—gets knocked on its ass."

Rohr nodded and lifted her cell phone for a last look. "Still no fucking bars—"

And then Evan Quilling was on her, slicing upward. Something cut into Rohr's wrist and the side of her face, and down she went. Cady had no time to think so he simply threw himself into Quilling, then latched onto the wrist holding the scalpel with his good left hand before it began its lethal downward arc. The two battered against the wall. Quilling was naked, had what appeared to be dark paint across his face, like a tribal warrior, but at this intimate distance, Cady could smell warm blood.

Cady swept his Glock sideways, but Evan seized his pistol hand—his gimp hand—in a vice grip, shaking and smashing the flesh against the wall. Cady's hand went numb, the Glock falling to the floor. Evan Quilling went on the attack with his free hand, raining blows against Cady's face and chest, forcing him backward toward a cliff of cement steps. Cady brought up a knee, but Evan jerked back, and then shoved Cady back again.

Evan Quilling was no longer the withered man bound to a wheelchair. He had to be into his sixties, but he looked decades younger—his body wiry, chiseled with muscle—and he was using his innate strength to batter Cady backward, inch by inch.

Then Cady did the unexpected.

He tightened his grip on Evan's scalpel wrist with his good hand, the one that had compensated over the years for his ruined one, and wedged his numbed hand into the cranny of Quilling's armpit. Cady bent away from Quilling's jostling, pulling Evan with him. He brought his knee down, angled back on the lip of the top step, and leaped backward for all he was worth, launching them both into the air. Cady saw the shock register in Evan's eyes. Brother Quilling hadn't expected to be copiloting this downward flight.

Cady tucked his head forward and took the first bounce on his shoulder blades. A piercing pain spiked through his body as he lost his hold on Quilling and the two continued ass-over-teakettle down the steps. Cady was on his heels near the bottom landing for the shortest of instants before his tailbone cracked into the basement concrete and his head snapped back with a sickening thud.

CHAPTER THIRTY-TWO

Stunned, like a bird bouncing off a window, Cady lay on the cement landing.

He watched the scene unfold before him as though he were a detached observer—viewing a play and observing actors that he felt he should somehow know. As a disinterested bystander, Cady witnessed the steps down which he'd flown. He saw legs tangled atop his. He saw Evan Quilling lying next to him. He watched as Quilling sat himself up, shook his head, rubbed at his elbow, and then pushed himself up, streaks of red running diagonally across his hairless body, someone's warped idea of a human barber pole. He watched as Evan Quilling looked down on him, eyes afire. He watched as Quilling kicked at his face with the heel of his foot.

Cady's head whipped sideways and then back as he watched Quilling bend and reach for something shiny that lay on one of the lower steps. Quilling stood over him, the scalpel at home in his hand, and it sunk into Cady's disassociated mind that the frenzied voice had returned. In fact, the voice had never left, but it now reached a crescendo—a fever pitch—in giddy anticipation of what Brother Evan was about to do. Cady couldn't move a muscle. His brain had disconnected from his body, leaving him to witness his own death.

A vaguely familiar popping sound trumped the voice, and Evan Quilling spun around. Crimson droplets rained against the wall above Cady's head. Cady spotted a nickel-sized hole in Quilling's right shoulder blade. A bullet wound, Cady recognized, as three more pops drove Brother Quilling against the landing wall. The scalpel hit the floor, followed a moment later by Quilling himself, his blood leaking out of fresh wounds in the center of his already scarlet-striped chest. The voice switched from euphoric giddiness to undistilled fury, a rabid animal.

I can move, Cady thought as he lifted his head sideways and saw the source of the cackling rage for the first time—Lucinda Quilling inside the hidden basement room. She too was naked. Blood matted her hair, coated half her face, her neck, and nearly all of her breasts, with streaks across her stomach. She advanced on Cady, her mouth wide and howling, guttural—an inhuman sound defining her existence. A whirling dervish in a blood frenzy. Sister Quilling snatched the scalpel and darted toward the injured agent to finish what Brother Quilling had begun. Cady raised an arm, a simple act that caused his head to pound like a hammer. Grimacing, he dropped his head back to the floor.

Lucinda leapt over her brother, snatched a fistful of Cady's hair, and yanked his head a foot off the ground. Lucinda wound up, but before she could lay open the agent's throat a Beretta 92FS was pistol-whipping into her mouth, shredding cheek and shattering teeth, sending Lucinda backward over her fallen brother and down onto the cement. At long last, the screech came to an end. In a flash, Lieutenant Rohr was on Lucinda, stomping on her hand until she dropped the scalpel, kicking the blade across the room. The lieutenant cuffed Lucinda's hands behind her and then to the leg of a sink in the adjacent room.

Rohr took a second to pace the room, then came over to Cady and stared in his eyes. Blood was streaming down a cut in the side of her face, and she kept her left arm—her sleeve a sponge of blood—crimped to her body.

"Jesus, Cady," Rohr said. "Can you sit up?"

Cady grimaced again and nodded. The lieutenant put down the gun and volunteered her good arm, and the two fought to get Cady into a sitting position, his back against the landing wall. Rohr disappeared up the steps and returned seconds later, breathing hard. She placed the Glock in his lap.

"I'm going to get help. Anything else pops up—go center mass."

Rohr jogged back up the steps and was gone.

CHAPTER THIRTY-THREE

Cady stared into the basement hideaway, begging his head to stop throbbing.

Lucinda Quilling sat tethered with her back to the sink and her face down, strands of blood hanging from her broken mouth and stretching to the floor. The room was a forty-by-sixty rectangle, and gray, just like everything else since they'd entered the chauffeur's garage. In the far corner of the hideaway were about ten sections of wrestling mats, clean and scuff free, similar to the one they'd found inside the hidden bench of the wheelchair van.

Jesus Christ. An epiphany broke through Cady's still-dazed mind as he stared at the wrestling mats. *We interrupted their mating cycle.*

Also disrupting the gray of the walls and ceiling was the contrasting white of the cement floor and a freezer Cady prayed was empty. He also noted an abundance of stainless steel, countertops and sinks—like the one Lucinda was cuffed to—and cupboards and gurneys and…

That's when Cady saw her. A pallid, nude body lay motionless atop a stainless-steel gurney along the far wall.

Hannah Erickson.

An Embalmatic arterial pump sat on a countertop next to her.

Cady pushed himself up the wall. Head spinning like a top, he stepped over Evan Quilling and stumbled his way to steady himself on the nearest table. He felt dizzy, nauseated, as if he were on a carnival ride that a deranged barker had no intention of bringing to a halt. Cady vomited on the tabletop and then continued his journey. He thought he heard noises coming from above, doors slamming, but couldn't be sure of anything at this point. Somehow he made it to the gurney, to Hannah Erickson, but he didn't have it in him to look at her.

He took off his windbreaker and laid it over her face and as much of her body as possible.

Cady made it back to his little corner by the stair landing, sat down, and threw up again.

"You've lived up to your billing, Agent Cady." Lucinda Quilling spoke for the first time, a lisp now apparent, likely due to her wounded mouth. "You're to be congratulated."

Cady didn't look up. He put his palm on the backside of his head, felt a goose egg growing quickly. The upper part of his spine also hurt like hell. His jaw, right eye, and temple throbbed, and it took a moment to remember being punched multiple times by Brother Evan. But his aching face had nothing on his head or spine.

"I wish Lieutenant Rohr hadn't killed Evan, though. I'm going to miss him no end."

Cady heard footsteps and spotted Rohr at the top of the steps.

"Stay the fuck awake, Cady," the lieutenant shouted down. "The paramedics just arrived. I'll bring them down through the house."

Cady wanted to yell back that the paramedics should tend to her cuts first, but shouting at this juncture was right up there with scaling Mount Everest, and Rohr had already disappeared anyway.

"Ev and I tried to stop," Sister Quilling said. "On several occasions, actually. We even made it two years once."

Cady didn't listen as Lucinda prattled on. He thought of Terri, of how Lieutenant Rohr had saved his life, and of Hannah Erickson, lying alone on the stainless-steel gurney on the other side of the basement room.

"...potency...in the blood that—"

"You need to stop talking," Cady said, cutting her off, sickened to be in the same room with her.

He didn't look up but could feel her staring at him.

"I shall respect your wishes," Lucinda Quilling said finally.

Together, they sat and waited.

CHAPTER THIRTY-FOUR

"You shouldn't have put your jacket over her," one of the detectives said.

"Fuck you, Deets," Lieutenant Rohr responded, and then turned back to Cady. "I stole this ice pack from the medics. Keep it on the back of your head."

Cady did as instructed, grimacing now becoming a way of life.

"Quick thinking to take Evan down with you," Rohr said. "He'd have gutted me like a fish if you hadn't."

"Where the hell did he come from?" Cady asked.

"That service elevator up there has a frame that juts out about ten inches. The fucker must have squished himself into the corner, with the frame blocking so we couldn't see him." The lieutenant turned her attention to the other Quilling. "Hey, Lucinda, it looks like Glensheen Mansion's going to have a run for its money."

Quilling ignored the taunt, keeping her face down.

Cady heard footsteps coming down the staircase.

"The medics are going to check you out and then we'll get you to St. Luke's pronto."

Cady gestured toward Rohr's face.

"Yeah, yeah. Me too."

A paramedic with a kit stooped in front of Cady, shined a light in his eyes, checked the back of his head, and instructed him to keep the ice pack on. He asked Cady a few questions to gauge how cognizant he was. After a heated discussion with Detective Monroe, something about how Rohr had to stop bleeding all over the crime scene, a different paramedic led the lieutenant back upstairs.

After five more minutes of the paramedic's poking and prodding and sneaking peeks at dead Evan and deflated Lucinda, Cady heard footsteps on the stairs.

The chief had arrived.

Chief Weflen's eyes moved from Cady to the body of Evan Quilling to Lucinda, who continued to look intently at the floor, and finally settled on the body of Hannah Erickson. From Cady's angle, he saw the fingers on Weflen's left hand begin to tremble.

"I had to see it myself to believe it," Weflen said softly, more to himself than to the room.

Lucinda Quilling raised her head at the sound of the police chief's voice, her face a gothic horror of crimson and snot.

"Deets, I need you upstairs to meet the forensics team," Weflen commanded, and then turned to address the paramedic next to Cady. "He good to go?"

"Yes, sir."

"Then what are you waiting for? Get the man to the hospital." Weflen turned back to Quilling as Deets maneuvered around them and headed up the steps.

As the paramedic helped him to his feet, Cady's eyes stayed glued to the Duluth police chief, Weflen's hand hanging near his sidearm, like a marshal in the Wild West. Then Cady remembered what the chief had said that first day in the ME's office as he looked over the body of Katrina Mortensen: *I'm going to kill whoever did this to that pretty young girl.*

Lucinda Quilling must have picked up a similar vibe as Cady watched her broken mouth turn to a jack-o-lantern smirk.

"Chief," Cady whispered. His throat was raw and it pained him to talk.

Weflen turned a cheek in Cady's direction, still focused on Lucinda Quilling.

"Would now be an inappropriate time to discuss fundraising?" Quilling said, goading the chief. "Let me go get my checkbook."

Weflen unsnapped his sidearm holster with a forefinger.

"Chief," Cady repeated. "Families are going to have a lot of questions, and she's the only one who has any answers."

What Cady didn't point out were the different shades of the white concrete that covered the basement floor. Cady suspected most of the answers had been buried in slabs of cement over the years in this subterranean hellhole before it had become too full, forcing the Quillings to turn to Lake Superior. He didn't think it wise to share that information with the police chief. Not now.

Chief Weflen turned toward Cady, eyes moist and a tear swimming down the side of his nose. He took hold of Cady's free arm.

"Let's get you the hell out of here, son."

CHAPTER THIRTY-FIVE

"You shot the door?" Even with pain meds, ice packs, and smiling nurses, Cady's head throbbed with each heartbeat and his shoulder blades felt like a designated hitter had taken a baseball bat to them.

"Shut up and listen," Rohr said, leaning over the hospital bed. "What we did was righteous, but needs a little tweaking."

The lieutenant had a narrow bandage down the left side of her face, and her left arm was in a blue sling, her sleeve cut off at the shoulder. Rohr had come to see him after being stitched up, and she only had a minute. She had waited until the RN left before approaching the bed.

"This is too big for the court to fuck us with that poison tree crap. The public would hang the judge from the lift bridge. But just in case any bullshit runs downhill, here's how it played out. You came to me with your findings. I was highly skeptical; after all, these were the Quillings we were talking about, but because Hannah Erickson's life was on the line, we took a drive. Pretty much the truth so far."

Cady nodded.

"No one answered at the front door, so we went to the garage and found the outer door unlocked. Once inside, we saw the van with Evan's wheelchair still in it, as well as the hidden wig in that creepy storage bin. We were wondering about the tunnel door when we heard that inhuman screeching, so I shot open the door to gain access." The lieutenant began to count her fingers and rattle off talking points. "Good faith. Probable cause up the ass. A girl's life on the line. Rinse and repeat, got it?"

Cady nodded again. "They'll bring up the scratching on the locks on the outer door."

"The concussion must not be too bad since you're able to collude," Rohr replied. "Her lawyers will bring up the kitchen sink, but for Christ's sake, they're going to dig up the floor and you and I know what they'll find. And the chief is contacting the Swiss about their chateau. Lucinda's fucked."

"They'll go NGRI." Not guilty by reason of insanity. "Push M'Naghten, the Durham standard, or the ALI test."

"The nature of these killings, she probably is fucked in the head. Either way, she'll never see the light of day."

"How are you doing?" Cady pointed at her face.

"There's a plastic surgeon in my future. Maybe I'll get the boobs done as well. Listen, Drew, I've got to run."

It was the first time she'd used Cady's first name, he realized, as she headed for the door.

"I'll stop by later with a balloon."

"Lieutenant." Cady's voice was still hoarse. "All that and we couldn't save her anyway."

Rohr did a slow about-face in the doorway.

"I know. That's why I've got to keep moving. If I slow down or stop, that's going to fucking haunt me."

"They contacted your wife," an RN with a beehive said.

"We're not married yet."

Cady was a little groggy. He'd recently returned from a promising CT scan. No evidence of bleeding under the skull.

"I'm sorry. It must be your fiancée," Beehive replied. "She's on her way over."

"Terri's coming here?"

"I can only imagine how happy she'll be to see you."

"Terri's coming here?" Cady asked again.

"Yes."

"Where are my shoes?" Cady sat forward in the hospital bed, off the ice packs. He pushed the movable tray with the Jell-O and TV clicker aside.

"What are you doing?"

"You don't understand," Cady answered. "Are my clothes in that closet?"

"You are on bed rest, Mr. Cady," Beehive said, palms up and voice stern. "You are going nowhere."

"Look, Terri will not be *happy* seeing me in the hospital again," Cady insisted. "I need to get my suit on. Stat."

"If you don't lie back down this instant, I'm going to call the doctor."

"Listen to me—a hundred bucks if you get my clothes. I can tell her I'm here visiting the lieutenant and writing up reports. I'll sit with her in the cafeteria until she goes away and be back in an hour…tops."

A throat was cleared and both Cady and Beehive turned to look at the new arrival.

"You're too late, buster."

Terri Ingram stood in the doorway, arms crossed, looking much like a vice-principal proctoring detention hall.

CHAPTER THIRTY-SIX

Cady slipped out from underneath the comforter and tiptoed from the room, hoping not to disturb Terri. At least one of them deserved a night's sleep.

Six days had passed since the night at Quilling manor. He'd spent the first three at St. Luke's Hospital on acetaminophen and ice while the doctors monitored his concussion. Between being poked and prodded and gaped at, Cady spent those days answering an array of questions from Chief Weflen and the detectives in the Violent Crimes Unit. The case had taken on a life of its own, with media from halfway around the world flying into the city on Lake Superior in order to cover the story. If it bleeds, it leads—and the peculiar case of the Quilling siblings had led the headlines for the past week, with no sign of letting up any time soon.

That first morning at St. Luke's, his head still throbbing like a cranked-up boom box, Cady placed a call to retired Gila County Sheriff Mitchell Diedrick in Scottsdale, Arizona, as per his promise. He knew it wouldn't be a cheerful conversation, but Cady felt Sheriff Diedrick needed to hear about the capture of Lucinda Quilling and the death of Evan Quilling—alias Rosalita and Richard de León—directly from him and not from the parasites on TV. Although the retired sheriff had been grateful, and thanked Cady for letting him know, there was no getting around what the Quillings had been up to since falling off the radar in Arizona all those years earlier. And although Cady's reassuring words about trails going cold were heartfelt, he could tell they fell on deaf ears.

On Cady's last day at St. Luke's, Lieutenant Rohr stopped by to let him know that Gila County had tracked down Tony Kittermen, the ex–de León disciple who'd told the story of what happened in Brenner. He was a minister now, living in L.A., spending his days working with disadvantaged youth. When a deputy showed Kittermen the yearbook photograph of Lucinda Quilling, there had been no hesitation.

"Kittermen told the cop that's been the face of his nightmares for the last four decades," Rohr told Cady. "He said he'd go anywhere, even Timbuktu, to testify against her."

They didn't need forensic geophysics using GPR—Ground Penetrating Radar—to determine what the Quillings had been up to all these years. Duluth PD simply dug up the sections of concrete in the hideaway basement room. The authorities in Switzerland followed suit, digging up the basement in what the Swiss media had labeled *Chateau Hell*.

The families of the missing would finally get their answers, but there would be no happy endings for any of them.

Cady trudged to the kitchen and thought about making coffee, but it was only three in the morning, and he played along with the delusion that he might fall back asleep. Cady wasn't hungry and had, in fact, lost nearly ten pounds since his plunge down the flight of stairs with Evan Quilling. Mostly he swallowed a banana or toast to keep the pain reliever from making his stomach ache, but he'd already begun to taper off the acetaminophen. St. Luke's had given him a clean bill of health, advising him to take it easy until the bruising healed. His own doctor in Grand Rapids had concurred. And Cady had already had three physical therapy sessions for his ruined hand.

Cady walked out onto the deck, oblivious to the chill of the early October night, though he was dressed only in boxers and a t-shirt. He stared out at the darkness of Bass Lake, at yard lights across the way, at nothing.

"Drew." Terri stood in a bathrobe in the frame of the sliding-glass door he'd left open. "Come back to bed."

Cady turned around.

"I couldn't save her, Terri," he said. "I couldn't save her."

PART TWO

The Lynchpin

CHAPTER THIRTY-SEVEN

The letter began:

Special Agent Elizabeth Preston,
RE: The Lynchpin Files (Conception)

"This was sent anonymously?" Cady asked. He'd driven the rental straight from Reagan National to Preston's townhome off Crittenden Street in Washington, D.C. Immediately upon his arrival, Liz had handed him the letter.

Preston nodded. "It came in today's mail, in an envelope that appeared to be from the Department of Motor Vehicles."

"The envelope was probably lifted from the DMV. Whoever sent it would know it's a piece of mail you wouldn't ignore or toss without opening."

"Read on."

In June of 2010, the FBI arrested ten Russian Foreign Intelligence Service (SVR) operatives in an operation the Bureau dubbed "Ghost Story."

Question: What are illegals?

Answer: Russian spies who are either native-born American citizens or pretend to be.

The history of Russian illegals stretches back to the heyday of Soviet espionage—the twenties and thirties—when Soviet agents recruited the ill-famed "Cambridge Five," Kim Philby, Guy Burgess, and that U.K. lot. American George Koval, who died in Moscow in 2006, was one of history's most infamous illegals. Koval was awarded, posthumously, the Hero of the Russian Federation medal from no less than Vladimir Putin himself, as Koval's pilfering of atomic secrets accelerated the Soviet development of the atomic bomb. Koval, born in Iowa, had initially been recruited by Russian Military intelligence, and he then went on to infiltrate the top-secret labs of the Manhattan Project.

The Ghost Story illegals of 2010 were swapped for several of our Russian double agents and, upon their return to Mother Russia, these SVR operatives were praised as heroes. This story of the Russian operatives was, at the time, released for public consumption, but our story of intrigue does not end there. Not by a long shot.

Hidden from public consumption is the unequivocal fact that the Ghost Story illegals were but the tip of the iceberg, so our overseas assets—our double agents—continue to inform us. Our best intel, based on the interrogations of more recently detained SVR operatives, points toward an orchestrator—in deep cover—manipulating actions per old-fashioned dead drops and drop boxes, notes under windshield wipers, postcard messages, even the briefest of phone calls from an unknown entity utilizing a voice changer, and on it goes, which led our joint intelligence services, the CIA and the FBI, to believe that a modern-day Lynchpin was in play, directing a wide-spread penetration—coordinating activity, placing individuals in lucrative positions, running agents, compiling information from multiple sources and multiple cells.

Also hidden from public consumption is the escalating number of our overseas assets who have gone missing without a trace over the course of the past decade.

Question: What do present-day Russian illegals, hidden amongst us, hope to accomplish in the new century?

Answer: Core motives have changed since the end of the Cold War, as ardent ideological convictions relating to the collapse of democracy and capitalism are no longer front burner, but the Russian ruling class, many of which are past members of the KGB, desire to tilt our institutions—our banking systems, our media, our bureaucracies—to make our country more to their liking, that is, more welcoming for themselves. There are, without a doubt, SVR operatives in places of influence in the government, in the military-industrial complex, in think tanks, and, of course, in the media and academia, and these agents are continually on the prowl for others to identify, recruit, and train. "Spotting and assessing" is the phrase utilized, meaning to collect data and send it back to Russia. Russian illegals identify friends and colleagues and vulnerable targets that one day may hold positions of power.

In other words, Russia plays the long game.

The above is by way of an explanation into the formation of the Lynchpin taskforce. Weary of the recurrent house cleanings, the taskforce decided to change the game; it decided to go after the Lynchpin himself...and the leaks of such measures have, unmistakably, come to the Lynchpin's attention.

Suddenly, the unusual case of the Russian cell of Mr. and Mrs. Steve Parrish is dropped upon us—a cell perhaps led by Assistant Director Roland Jund, or perhaps not. Special Agent Steve Parrish has penetrated the Counterintelligence Division of the Federal Bureau of Investigation. No small undertaking. His late wife Dayna Parrish appears a classic "swallow"—that is, a highly sexualized female undercover agent, used commonly for seduction, a honey trap for blackmail. Jund's story, if believed, makes the most sense in that his death by natural causes combined with certain red flags—planted by Parrish and/or others at the Bureau—would have pointed to AD Jund being the highest-ranking Russian agent in a generation, which would have led to the joint CIA and FBI taskforce patting each other on the back, disbanding, and wondering whether Clooney or Damon would portray them in the film adaptation.

All the while the Lynchpin lurks in the weeds...and the cycle continues.

Had Jund died of a heart attack and classified materials known only to the Lynchpin been found on his home PC, it would have appeared to onlookers as a plausibly wrapped gift. As the circumstances now stand, with national security secrets implicating Assistant Director Roland Jund appearing only on the Parrish home PC, the gift wrap begins to unravel.

However, it is where the evidence currently leads and where our intelligence resources will continue to focus their pursuit unless something new should arise...

—

"Who do you think sent this?" Cady asked.

"An F.O.R."

"F.O.R.?"

"A Friend of Roland. Someone on the taskforce who would rather leak helpful background info to us than talk directly with us."

"Assistant Director Speedling?"

Paul Speedling, from the FBI's Cyber Division, and Jund's longtime friend and colleague, had slyly provided Agent Preston with the list of members on the Lynchpin taskforce.

"Speedling or Connor Green," Preston answered. Connor Green, the director of the Counterintelligence Division, was the highest ranking of the four Bureau executives on the taskforce. "Doubtful it's AD Litchy."

Assistant Director Mike Litchy from International Operations, who had not so subtly demanded Preston and her *bloodhound* back off. Jund, whose instincts Cady trusted, had a disdainful view of AD Litchy and thought the man a pompous ass of limited ability. Jund had tagged Litchy as the Dunning-Kruger effect personified—a blowhard ignoramus who vastly overestimated his skill set while failing to recognize his own inadequacies or any genuine skills in others.

Cady circled Preston's kitchen before filling a cup with tap water. He took a sip and then emptied the rest of his cup into the sink.

"You sure I can't get you something to eat?" Preston asked.

"No thanks."

"They didn't feed you on the plane, did they?"

"Those days are long gone."

"Can I ask you something, Drew?" Preston said. "It's off topic, and somewhat of a personal nature."

Cady turned to Liz. "Go ahead."

"I know what you went through in Duluth. I know it was traumatic, and I'm willing to blame the weight loss on hospital food, but you're not acting like yourself. You seem a little drained and distant."

Cady shrugged. "Long flight."

"How's Terri?"

"It's not that."

"If it's not that," Preston said, "what is it?"

"You can't be serious?"

"You said it yourself at our last meeting," Cady pressed. "*Old Drew would have nailed the UNSUB by now.*"

Agent Preston stared at Cady as though he were the crossword puzzle she worked with her Special K and orange juice every morning.

"I said that in jest and in part, frankly, to prod you along for a purely selfish reason: to get you back to working on Jund's situation ASAP."

"Doesn't matter, Liz. What you said was true. I kept building a case for hours after I knew in my marrow it was the Quillings, and then I dumped it in the lap of the best cop I've ever worked with and had her do all the heavy lifting." Cady crossed into the living room to look out at the coming twilight. "*Old Drew* would have kicked in that door three hours earlier...and Hannah Erickson would be among the living."

Preston sighed. "Just stop for a second and think of that scenario's more likely outcomes: First, the Quillings call 911 and *Old Drew* is stopped in his tracks without getting close to their dungeon of horror. Second, the Quillings have been on a spree for decades—they've become experts at this task—so *Old Drew* gets put down on the Quillings' home turf without rescuing Hannah Erickson."

Cady shook his head at the window.

"The Quillings were certifiable. They weren't about to stop until they *got stopped*. If you're going to take on the blame, you need to cut yourself some slack. What about the future Hannah Ericksons you and the lieutenant saved?"

Cady stood still while Preston remained seated at the dining room table, both absorbing the silence.

"Drew," Agent Preston said finally. "I have a confession to make that you're not going to like."

Cady pivoted, his turn to stare at Preston as though she were a puzzle.

"A few years back—during the reign of *Old Drew*—I met with
Roland and did everything in my power to convince him to put you
on leave pending a…psych eval."

"I was never crazy…"

"You were burnt out, stressed to the breaking point—a frayed
rubber band."

Cady began to shake his head.

"I don't want to argue about this, Drew. I think you know it's true.
I felt strongly—back then—that you needed, at minimum, some
counseling. You were taking chances. Someone was bound to get
hurt, it was just a matter of time…and the person who got hurt the
worst was you."

Cady digested this piece of information. He had only one question.
"What did Jund say?"

"That's not my point. What I'm sharing with you are my *true*
feelings about the *Old Drew*," Preston insisted. "And I want you to
know I don't feel that way anymore."

"And Jund said?" Cady prompted again.

"You know how Roland loves to hear himself talk. It was just
another one of his sayings, that's all."

"Liz."

"I pleaded with Roland, but he wouldn't budge. He called you his
'hot knife through cold butter,' and he said, 'No one touches my hot
knife.'"

CHAPTER THIRTY-EIGHT

"So what do they call the sex-change operation where they make a chick into a guy?"

Cady looked at the chubby redhead who'd dropped into the empty chair across the wobbly table that held Cady's beer—a Heineken he'd been nursing for most of the past hour, much to the disapproval of the bikini-clad, bleach-blond waitress working his section at the rear of the strip club.

Cady shook his head.

"An addadicktome." The redhead laughed at his own joke, waved at the roaming bikini and pointed at his empty shot glass and chaser. "Get it?" He guffawed again. "An add-a-dick-to-me."

The man stunk of the Jack Daniel's he'd been drinking. Cady'd heard the commotion behind him and turned in time to see the buffoon stumble forward into this table, splashing a dollop of beer onto Cady's suit. After a vaudeville of apologies and a fistful of napkins commandeered from a table of innocent bystanders, the man settled in at Cady's table like a grizzly readying himself for hibernation. Though it lacked the prerequisite length in back, his thick mop of red hair screamed mullet—you knew it was just a matter of time. And though he didn't introduce himself, Red, as Cady had internally knighted the drunk, acted as though the two of them were the oldest of friends and provided a running commentary on the different pole dancers plying their trade on the front stage.

"Fake!" Red screamed, pointing at the current dancer, and then turned to Cady. "A couple of beach balls with a body behind them. That's an insult to our intelligence."

Cady thought about asking Red to move it along, but figured the barfly bought him cover, as opposed to Cady sitting alone at a dark table in the back of Humdinger's, an establishment whose sign boasted fifty exotic dancers and a hundred humdingers.

Cady did the math.

He'd been tailing Assistant Director of International Operations Mike Litchy for the past two days, which had been exceptionally easy as the AD's full days were spent in the Hoover Building. Liz Preston had provided Cady a dossier on AD Litchy, more a short curriculum vitae than anything else, containing background information, years of service at the Bureau, positions held, board seats, education, etc.

It turned out Litchy had received his BA in Political Science at Penn State and his J.D. at Penn State Law. Litchy had started out practicing contract law at a mid-level D.C. firm for a handful of years out of law school and, if you listened to Jund, Litchy was part of the ninety-nine percent of attorneys that gave the other one percent a bad name. Soon after, Litchy left the firm and found his true home at the Federal Bureau of Investigation. He'd been with the FBI for the past twenty-two years, the last five in his current position. Litchy had been married for a six-year stint to a lobbyist in the renewable energy industry, but irreconcilable differences had shredded that union three years back.

"Don't get me wrong. I love fake tits. *Hustler*'s not had a real tit in it since the '80s. But Wendy up there, she's pushed the fucking envelope. And don't get me wrong," Red continued, now slurring his speech, "I'd do Wendy in a heartbeat. Hell, Wendy's seen more ceilings than Michelangelo, but not one guy ever bought them beach balls were real."

The bleach-blond bikini showed up with Red's Jack Daniel's and Bud chaser and asked if Cady wanted a refill.

"Fuck yeah!" Red shouted, accepting for Cady as he tucked a twenty in the waitress's bikini bottom, which was really little more than a g-string. "When are you up, darlin'?"

"I'm on in two."

"Blow us a kiss."

The bleach blond gave Red a smile as counterfeit as some of her other appendages and walked away into the burgeoning crowd.

"You a regular?" Cady asked after a quick peek at Litchy, who still sat at a side table near the front stage, sipping what appeared to be a Scotch and soda.

"Just Christmas and Easter." Red cackled again. "I was so messed up the other night, Jasmine and Delilah had to pour me into a cab. You know them bodily humors? Blood and bile and phlegm?"

Cady nodded.

"It all came out. I was at my high school weight by the time it was done."

Cady found that last statement a little hard to accept, as Red's dress shirt, besides looking generally unwashed, seemed at least two sizes too small. The fabric was pulled so tight between the buttons that Cady was able to see card-sized splotches of the man's belly. Red was everything Cady expected in a strip joint called Humdinger's: unshaven face, untied tennis shoes—the whole nine yards. His thoughts drifted from keeping tabs on AD Litchy to how it might be possible to talk Red into renting one of Terri's cabins for a long weekend. The first smirk to grace Cady's face in the past month stemmed not from the drink-spilling buffoon's off-color musings in regard to the fairer sex, but the thought of how Terri would react toward said drink-spilling buffoon. It would be worth all the hell he paid later to bear witness to that particular culture clash.

Cady and Agent Preston had decided to focus their attention on Mike Litchy. With his security clearance as Assistant Director of International Operations, Litchy had an abundance of national security data working its way cross his desk. Were Litchy an "illegal," he was in a perfect position to hemorrhage top-secret information. Additionally, of the four FBI executives on the joint taskforce, Litchy was the snuggest fit for Bryce Drommerhausen's Benedict Arnold profile—arrogant and egotistical, narcissistic and petty, etc. Granted, this was loose guesswork, conjecture at its weakest. But the kicker was that AD Litchy was the only taskforce member who had taken Agent Preston's bait. Litchy had shown up in Preston's office full of pretense and thinly veiled threats, apparently taking an active role in selling his fellow assistant director and dear colleague Roland Jund down the river.

Cady had spent time driving around Mike Litchy's neck of the woods, a swank part of Belle Haven, south of Old Town Alexandria in Fairfax County, Virginia. He was getting the lay of Litchy's land. The AD lived in a colonial two-story brick-and-stone front, five bedrooms and nearly five thousand square feet—Liz Preston had done her homework—that was all of two country blocks away from the Belle Haven Country Club, where Litchy was an esteemed member and could rub elbows with the Washington elite. The colonial was conceivably doable on an AD's salary, but he and his then future ex, the green lobbyist, had purchased the home together in bygone days. In the divorce settlement, Litchy got the house... his ex got out.

Red threw back his whiskey in one gulp and then burped or farted or both.

Cady re-evaluated his flight of whimsy and figured Red wouldn't last an hour at Sundown Point Resort before Terri tossed the drunken swine out on his well-padded ass.

Cady had been following Litchy—who was presumably heading home from a long day's work at the Hoover Building—south on US-1 when Litchy cut across two lanes of traffic, made the jump onto I-495, and began heading northwest on the interstate highway known as the Capital Beltway. Litchy was driving his midlife, a Jaguar XF, which lived on the low end of the Jaguar spectrum but still had a sticker price that could induce cardiac arrest. Minutes later, the Jaguar took a North Springfield exit and began creeping up and down the blocks intersecting the frontage road as though trying to spot or shake a tail.

Being Litchy's tail, Cady got paranoid and began checking his rear and side views to see if someone had come up behind his rental car. Nothing in Litchy's background indicated he'd been trained in evasive tactics. Cady pulled over and double-parked on the frontage road, which fed back onto 495. He pulled his smartphone and was about to speed-dial Liz Preston to noodle out who AD Litchy might be visiting in North Springfield when the AD's blue Jaguar turned onto the frontage road two blocks in front of Cady and headed back up 495. Cady let a couple cars slip past him before he followed suit. Now extra vigilant, Cady followed at a respectable distance, figuring he'd hit pay dirt now that he'd outlasted the assistant director's escape maneuvers. But then Litchy exited the Capital Beltway again and followed another frontage road, finally turning into Humdinger's parking lot. He slid his Jaguar between a couple of pickup trucks, stepped out of his car, looked left and right, and headed into the club.

Bikini dropped off Cady's second Heineken and nodded as Red pointed at his empty shot glass. Cady peeled his last twenty from his wallet, handed it to the waitress, and watched as Litchy worked his way toward the restroom.

"I'm up when Candy Beth is done," the blond announced to the table with about as much excitement as a comatose patient.

In response, Red aimed two fingers at his eyes and then pointed them at her chest. He repeated the pantomime as Bikini walked away, now indicating her derriere.

Red was on a roll.

A minute later Litchy exited the bathroom and returned to his table.

"Excuse me," Cady said and stood up.

"Leak that lizard!" Cady heard Red bellow as he headed for Humdinger's men's room.

Thankfully, the lavatory was empty. Cady did a quick lean down, but didn't spot any feet in the back stall. Then he checked the stall, peeked behind the toilet, under the tank cover, and even jiggled the toilet paper rolls. Nothing. He pulled on the towel dispensers. Locked. He wrapped a hand in several towels and swirled it about the garbage bin. Also nothing.

After spending time with Red, Cady felt he needed a shower. He washed his hands instead, hoping that would suffice.

The first thing Cady noticed when he came out was Litchy's empty table. Cady scanned the club as he neared the exit, but still saw no Assistant Director of International Operations.

"Hey!" Red yelled from the table they'd been sharing, a confused look on an intoxicated face. "Your brewski?"

"It's yours," Cady replied.

Red picked up the bottle of Heineken and made an obscene gesture with it.

CHAPTER THIRTY-NINE

Cady felt like a peeping Tom. About the only thing he had left to do was comb through the AD's banana peels and eggshells once the man brought his trash curbside, like a celebrity reporter for tabloid television.

He'd followed Assistant Director Mike Litchy for the remainder of the week, to and from work, about Market Square in Old Town, to grocery shopping and restaurants, the library, the liquor store, evenings at the Belle Haven Country Club, another stop at Humdinger's, and a Texaco to fill up his gas tank, among other spots of high intrigue. Although Agent Preston was unable to access the assistant director's online calendar, she was able to browse it as though she were scheduling a meeting with Litchy in order to see what blocks of time were filled and what hours were free. It was during the AD's busy hours, with Litchy likely tied up in meetings, that Cady switched cars from his original rental Camry to a Subaru Outback to his current Ford Taurus, just in case having the same vehicle poking about in his rearview mirror worked its way into the AD's consciousness.

Cady was impressed with the local gendarmes. The first evening he trailed Litchy home to Belle Haven, he found a nice perch to park his rental car that was halfway between two neighboring estates, out of view of either and a full country block from Litchy's colonial. Within an hour Alexandria PD had pulled in behind him. Cady badged the two officers and mumbled about being on surveillance duty, albeit an extremely boring duty that he was not at liberty to discuss. They chatted for a bit and one of them suggested Cady roost in the driveway of a residence that been through foreclosure and was now up for sale by the bank. Cady followed the officers to the home in question and quickly realized it was a perfect pinch point: AD Litchy had to pass it to get on any of the county's main drags. Cady thanked the two officers profusely, hoping they'd not feel the need to scratch beyond the surface of his cover story.

Surveillance such as this consisted mostly of downtime, endless stretches of waiting that gave one pause to think. And Cady didn't want to think. He didn't want his mind to wander down dark and desolate roads, as no matter what twists and turns were taken, they all led back to Hannah Erickson…and how Hannah Erickson would have turned twenty-two in January and how Hannah Erickson had consistently made the Dean's List at the University of South Dakota in Vermillion and how Hannah Erickson would have graduated next spring with a Bachelor of Science degree in Biology and how Hannah Erickson had a promising future all laid out in front of her.

Yes, Hannah Erickson had an entire life to live…if someone had done his job.

Cady did what he could to keep busy, to keep his mind from drifting toward places best left unexplored. He read the past two months' worth of *Sports Illustrated* cover to cover, including a puff piece on badminton. He got familiar with a dozen smartphone applications he'd never use. He studied the maps in the rental's glove compartment as though he were Christopher Columbus in search of the New World. He examined every license, card, or expired pizza coupon in his wallet as though it contained the mysteries of the human genome. He called Terri for long chats and then would pester her again an hour later under the guise of wedding plans.

On Saturday evening, while sitting in his car at the Belle Haven Country Club, Cady had voiced his concern to Liz. Perhaps Blowhard Mike Litchy's trek across Agent Preston's radar with veiled threats of ending careers and votes of no confidence in Roland Jund was because Litchy was nothing more than a blowhard. Yet even blowhards deserved their privacy. Sure, it wasn't in best judgment for an assistant director of the Federal Bureau of Investigation to stop by an off-the-beaten-path strip club on the way home from work for a drink or two, but it was more symptomatic of a man passing through the middle years of his life with no one at home to go home to. If anything, it was pathetic.

And more pathetic yet was Cady pursuing Litchy into the club and then auditing the man's potty breaks to see if the AD could possibly have met anyone while he stood at the urinal.

Agent Preston grudgingly agreed—grudgingly, because there was not an abundance of options left on the table. And, granted, cloak and dagger was hardly Cady's or her forte. Plus, Cady reminded her, Roland Jund himself would have been the first person to assert that Assistant Director of International Operations Mike Litchy lacked the prerequisite gray matter to be the Lynchpin.

No, Cady argued, now was the time for Jund to call in any markers held by people higher on the Bureau totem pole. The process would be glacially and nerve-wrackingly slow, but Cady had to believe that in the end the innocent man would prevail, as had Agent Brian Kelley over the traitorous Robert Hanssen. Unfortunately, in this scenario the Lynchpin would almost certainly dance away, scot-free.

In the end, Cady and Preston agreed to continue in their efforts but to meet with Assistant Director Jund next week to report their dead end and beg advice, which, as stubborn an SOB as Jund was, would not likely be forthcoming.

But Sunday was a game changer.

CHAPTER FORTY

It began at the pinch point, where Cady had parked sideways in the roundabout driveway of the foreclosed estate. He was listening to the Redskins lose on the radio when AD Litchy's Jaguar—heedless to any posted speeds—shot past. Cady followed several cars behind Litchy on his hurried journey into Alexandria. When Litchy drove into the entrance of Oronoco Bay Park, Cady pulled over on Pendleton Street. He counted to sixty before following the Jag into the park.

He spotted Litchy's midlife parked on the outer rim of Oronoco Bay's first parking lot, the AD's sports car's front tires planted against the curb and facing Pendleton. Fortuitously for Cady, what appeared to be a couple of grade-school-age soccer teams were having a joint picnic, with children in blue and green t-shirts and tennis shoes running rampant and a half-dozen other kids banging on playground equipment while harried adults grilled hotdogs and tore open bags of potato chips. Cady entered the parking lot and steered his rental to a spot among the soccer moms' vehicles. With a black SUV blocking his park side and a Mini Cooper on his right, Cady could keep tabs on Litchy, who remained seated in his Jaguar some forty yards away. Cady put on a Nationals baseball cap, scanned in every direction to see if he'd tripped anyone's radar, and then brought a miniature pair of binoculars up to his eyes.

He had a perfect view of Litchy's left profile, perhaps not the AD's best side. Litchy had a jaw and nose that jutted outward in sharp contrast to a hairline that had begun the long march backward in retreat. Litchy looked to be in an animated discussion, and since he wasn't wearing a headset, Cady assumed the AD was holding a cell phone to his right ear. Though it was a bright fall afternoon, the windows on the Jaguar remained closed. The AD appeared frustrated with the direction the conversation was taking—outright angry to be more accurate—and Cady wished he could read lips.

Cady peered about the park a second time, relieved that all nearby adults had their hands full herding a rambunctious platoon of little tikes toward the eating tables. He brought the binocs back to his eyes. The AD was silent now, listening, his face a chiseled grimace. Then it was Litchy's turn to bark a few more words before holding the cell phone in front of him. He stared at the phone for several seconds as though expecting a written apology from the inanimate object before flipping it onto the passenger seat. Then the AD exploded, hammering at the top of his dashboard with his fist. Even with the dull roar of the soccer kids chomping hotdogs in the background, with the Jag's windows tightly shut, and with more than a hundred feet between them, Cady could hear the hushed thumps of Litchy's blows.

Cady felt sorry for the Jag. As an adult, he'd never had a telephone call tip him over the edge into physical violence—not even the final calls from his ex-wife. Cady did remember putting a dent in the basement sheetrock when Sherry Dordell dumped his heartsick ass unexpectedly by phone during the waning days of senior high, but he highly doubted AD Litchy had been on the phone with Sherry Dordell.

Cady dropped the binocs into his lap and leaned back in his seats so as not to be visible when the assistant director came to his senses and started glancing about the commons to see if anyone had witnessed his outburst. To Cady's surprise, the AD stepped from his Jag, spun a three-sixty with a prefab smile glued to his mug—just another well-adjusted person out for a walk on a pleasant day—and headed for the walking trail. Cady didn't want to leave the sanctuary of his rental car and give the AD a chance to spot him, even behind the Nationals cap and sunglasses—AD Litchy had referred to Special Agent Cady as a "Bloodhound" in a conversation in Agent Preston's office, and if he knew *of* Cady, he might very well be able to recognize him.

Screw it.

His hand was on the door latch when AD Litchy stopped, playacted another *ain't we all having fun in the sun* scene as he took a quick peek in each and every direction, and then dropped the village idiot grin as he walked onto the grass near a tree and stuffed a McDonald's bag into one of the park's waste receptacles. The AD did a quick pivot, returned directly to his waiting Jaguar, reversed onto Pendleton Street, and exited Oronoco Bay Park.

Cady peeled a banana he'd brought along and began to eat. He wanted to let time pass to make sure Litchy didn't come back, or to see if anyone unexpected made a beeline to the garbage container. Cady figured it could be trash, perhaps a half-eaten Big Mac, but that didn't seem likely. It could be a drop, like the kind Eggs Nolte had told them were used at the height of the Cold War, but the smart money was on the prepaid cell phone AD Litchy had picked up when Cady had followed him into a Walmart that morning.

If it were more than a disposable phone or half-eaten dinner— say, for example, a Memory Stick or compact disc—Cady would put it back, immediately call Liz Preston, and they'd be forced to shove this *unauthorized* venture up the chain of command. It was too bad Cady hadn't snapped some pictures with his smartphone, but the AD's move was unexpected and he had not been ready.

Cady climbed out of his rental car and headed for the trash receptacle. When he reached it, he found himself scanning the park, much like Litchy had done, and thought for a moment about the irony were he to yank the bag out of the trash only to be surrounded by a flock of agents from Counterintelligence. In one fell swoop Cady popped the dome lid, reached down and snatched the McDonald's bag, and was back in his car a minute later. The soccer kids were now sucking on popsicles and spilling Orange Crush. The soccer parents were off at their picnic tables, looking much relieved and catching up on the day's gossip. Cady opened the McDonald's bag.

Sure enough, a prepaid cell phone. Cady shook the phone from the crumpled bag onto the console between the driver and passenger seats and examined it. He hoped the AD hadn't wiped it down. He hoped the AD had used his credit card, but Cady had been too far away to catch the specifics of Litchy's transaction with the Walmart cashier.

Who does a prepaid talk to?

Another prepaid, Cady answered his own question. Also likely not long for this world. Cheap prepaids did not have a wealth of functionality, but Cady poked at a couple buttons and arrows with the cover of his BIC pen until a number displayed. He jotted the phone number down on his notepad. He could find no other numbers.

Cady glanced about the park for what seemed like the hundredth time, and then closed his eyes for a moment. When he opened them, he rolled down the driver's side window, as the soccer kids were now back at play. He picked up the cell phone with a Kleenex and two fingers of his left hand. He punched in the number with the BIC pen and then pressed the green dial button.

The call was answered on the first ring.

"What now?"

No light bulb went on over Cady's head; he did not recognize the male voice at the other end of the phone line. He focused on AD Litchy's obvious annoyance when he had been talking to the man who owned the prepaid with this phone number.

"We need to talk in person," Cady snapped into the mouthpiece. Though he'd never heard Mike Litchy speak, he hoped that keeping it short and intense would afford him an adequate impersonation of the assistant director. And he hoped the park noises in the background would buy him additional cover.

A pregnant pause.

"Who's speaking?" the voice at the other end of the phone line was now a whisper.

Cady knew in an instant that he had failed, but swung again for the fences.

"You know damn well who this is," Cady snapped again, hoping a pinch of pomposity and a huge dash of impatience would carry the day. "We need to meet."

A longer silence. Cady squinted his eyes as though that would somehow offer him a glimpse through the phone line at the caller on the other side. Cady got the impression the unknown voice was doing much the same. The soccer kids continued to play. The soccer parents had begun to pack. But Cady sat still, frozen.

Finally: "You have the wrong number."

Click.

Even without his old high school flame involved, it was all Cady could do to keep from smacking the dashboard.

The blond man stared at his disposable cell phone as though it could explain exactly what the hell had just occurred—fill him in on the joke.

The voice pretending to be that supreme braggart of the *vaunted* Federal Bureau of Investigation was not sufficiently whiny to be Assistant Director Litchy, yet it originated from the same phone number that, minutes earlier, the legitimate Litchy had used from per their arrangement.

Had Litchy been detained?

If that were the case, why tip their hand with this charade? Wouldn't they rather turn Litchy—which the blond man figured would take seconds at most—and use the Bureau executive to reel in some of the other fish, himself included, that moved around the assistant director's orb?

The blond man grimaced. He had been slated to go home. He longed to go home.

And now he could not.

CHAPTER FORTY-ONE

Assistant FBI Director Entangled in
Manslaughter/Murder Investigation
By E. Duranty Walters, The New York Times

As reported in the New York Times on September 15, Assistant
Director Roland Jund, of the Criminal Investigative Division of the
Federal Bureau of Investigation, claimed self-defense in the strangulation
death of an at-the-time unidentified intruder who Mr. Jund alleged broke
into his home in Leesburg, Virginia, in the early hours of September 14.
When it was later reported that the intruder was identified as fellow FBI
Agent Steve Parrish of the Counterintelligence Division, who, like Mr.
Jund, worked out of the J. Edgar Hoover Building in Washington, D.C.,
attorneys for Mr. Jund provided a statement to the press that "Assistant
Director Jund had never met Agent Parrish through either work or
social events until the night in question," and that they would make no
additional comment on the matter at that time.

Another twist involving the case was the suicide by hanging on
September 17 of Dayna Parrish, widow of Agent Steve Parrish, at the
couple's home in Kings Park, Virginia. Sources close to the investigation
have informed this reporter of two significant developments in the
tragic saga of Dayna and Steve Parrish. First, Assistant Director Jund,
who is married, has admitted to having an affair with Mrs. Dayna
Parrish, with liaisons as recent as late August. Mr. Jund's admission
has led investigators to re-evaluate the events in Leesburg, Virginia, in
the early hours of September 14 as potentially more complex than the
home invasion alleged by Assistant Director Jund.

The second major case development, again according to a source inside the investigation, is that forensic evidence at the scene indicates Dayna Parrish was likely murdered by a person or persons unknown and was then made to appear a suicide by hanging. Forensic tests reveal that Mrs. Parrish's fingerprints were only on the noose fastened about her neck and not on other areas of the rope or on the rafter beam about which it was fastened. In addition, no footprints or indentations appeared on the hood of Parrish's Jeep Grand Cherokee, indicating the impossibility of Dayna Parrish having committed the act herself. As a result, Mrs. Parrish's death is now listed as a homicide.

On September 18, the day following Mrs. Parrish's death, FBI agents removed all computer hardware and software as well as additional items from the Parrish household. The FBI has yet to release any findings on the seized contents from the Parrish home.

Calls for comments to Roland Jund's attorney have gone unreturned.

"What did Jund say about this?" Cady asked.

Liz Preston had just gotten off the phone with the assistant director when Cady arrived, and she flipped the *New York Times* article his way.

"I'd tell you, but I make it a point not to use that kind of language," Preston answered. "The gist of the matter is that the narrative of Roland Jund as multiple murderer is being planted so when the other boot—the national security boot—comes down on Roland's head from this quote, 'dogshit reporter,' unquote, it's no great leap to accept Roland Jund as the quote, 'top-secret oozing Lynchpin,' unquote."

"As much as it pains me to say this, Jund is right."

Agent Preston briefed Cady on her meeting—this time at a pie shop—with Jund the night before. She'd shared with Jund Cady's discovery of Litchy's throwaway cell phone in a trash bin at Oronoco Bay Park. Per the mounting paranoia she found herself now sharing with Jund, Preston had typed this update in a short paragraph in an unsaved Pages document on her iPad and slid the tablet around the AD's French apple a la mode for his review. While making idle chitchat, Jund typed his thoughts over her paragraph and returned the iPad next to Preston's carrot cake.

Weak smoking gun, Jund had entered, *based on unauthorized surveillance of a sitting assistant director of the FBI by agents closely associated with and rumored to be part of Jund's Russian cell.* The AD had shaken his head at Preston while asking about the weather.

Blowing whistles with evidence as flimsy as this would place them in hot water from which they could possibly not extract themselves. Even if AD Litchy denied, denied, denied, there would be the minor issue of their having stalked the assistant director at both home and play. Plus, were Litchy ever seriously asked to explain the cell phone, a smart thing would be to say he suspected he was being followed—likely by Jund's agents—and wanted to draw them out into the light, so he purchased a couple of cheap prepaids, made a call in a public place, and tossed one in a garbage can to see who floated to the surface.

Agent Preston had used Bureau resources—another no-no—to track down the other cell phone, which AD Litchy had called from Oronoco. It had been purchased the week before at an electronics shop in Tysons Corner Center, just outside the nation's capital. The prepaid was impossible to track since it wasn't turned on, its battery likely removed—and, quite frankly, both battery and unit probably had a new home at the bottom of the Potomac.

Cady agreed. It might be a *weak smoking gun,* as Jund had typed into Preston's iPad before she closed out of the never saved document. But that wasn't necessarily the point of Cady's discovery, as it confirmed in his mind that they were barking up the right tree. Whether AD Litchy himself was the Lynchpin or merely one of the Lynchpin's assets, Litchy was most certainly *involved.* And if they did latch onto a smoking gun of some substance, they could then arm wrestle over which federal agent, Cady or Preston, wished to jettison a promising career in order to blow that whistle long and hard. Cady figured it should be him, as he was currently on quasi-medical leave, which at the end of the week would flip over to vacation time and, if Jund's frame-up dragged on, would turn into a temporary leave, which, following the Duluth case, he reckoned Special Agent-in-Charge Ron Bergmann of the Minneapolis field office would approve in a heartbeat. Though he knew a career at the Bureau wouldn't survive any potential Litchy blowback, Cady didn't anticipate jail time—he'd only go so far for Roland Jund—unless the FBI got exceptionally creative in their vindictiveness. After all, he'd only broken a half-dozen Bureau protocols and the spirit of a half-dozen more, stalked a private citizen, lied to officers of the law, and trespassed on private property…all in a day's work.

If he could somehow find a way to prove what he suspected—that Assistant Director Litchy was not the valued employee he appeared to be and that, in fact, he was the very breach the FBI and the CIA were looking for—perhaps the Bureau could be persuaded to look the other way. Hell, if he caught them on a good day, they might even let him keep his pension.

"Jund have anything else to say?" Cady asked.

"He typed a short note saying you shouldn't have made that call back."

Cady thought about the voice on the other end of Litchy's prepaid for the thousandth time. Had he spoken with the Lynchpin?

He was about to defend his actions when he was interrupted by loud steps in the hallway. A half second later, Assistant Director Mike Litchy poked his head into Agent Preston's office.

CHAPTER FORTY-TWO

"I hate to blindside you, Elizabeth," Assistant Director Litchy said, "but there's been a reassignment of roles in lieu of, well, you know, and we need to talk."

Cady realized then that he'd not even been in the ballpark of imitating Litchy on the cell phone at Oronoco Bay Park. Litchy had a higher pitch than Cady had guessed.

Rather than respond to Litchy's announcement, Preston kept her eyes on Cady until Litchy followed her gaze and acknowledged his presence in her office.

"Assistant Director," Preston said, "have you met Special Agent Drew Cady?"

Litchy looked as though he'd been served a soiled diaper at a five-star restaurant. There was an awkward pause, and then his face lit up in a reception-line smile as he approached Cady, arm outstretched.

"Don't think we've ever formally met, but I've read a lot about you in the paper lately."

"Don't believe a word of it, sir."

Cady stood and held out his gimp hand. He hated this part but had given up the social clumsiness of sticking out his left hand. Unfortunately, the AD's grasp lived up to Cady's expectations. Litchy shook Cady's hand as if he were squeezing a pair of pliers. Cady did his best not to grimace.

"Aren't you based out of Minnesota?"

"I work out of Grand Rapids for the Minneapolis field office."

Assistant Director Mike Litchy had lost the faux smile and stared at Cady. "Then what in hell, Agent Cady, are you doing here in D.C.?"

"I'm here on medical leave," Cady replied, holding up the hand that Litchy had just clutched, the top of which was crisscrossed with scar tissue. "I'm getting a second opinion at George Washington, from my original surgeon there, to see if I need additional surgery."

And that was to some extent the truth, just in case the AD made it his business to check up on Cady's medical-treatment-slash-alibi. Cady had stopped at the university's hospital for all of a ten-minute consult with Mitch Corrigan, the doctor who had previously performed a string of surgeries on his hand. Corrigan had, of course, agreed with St. Luke's in Duluth as well as his current guy in Grand Rapids that there was nothing more surgery could accomplish and it was all up to the physical therapy sessions to recoup whatever percentage loss of use had occurred after Cady's recent grapple with Evan Quilling. Cady made a mental note to set up some PT appointments at a nearby clinic in case Litchy cared to push it.

"You really dive down the steps with that crazy asshole?"

Cady nodded. "Backward, even."

"Doesn't sound too bright."

"You had to be there."

The AD continued to look at Cady, his stare transformed into an open glare. Cady glared back at Litchy, but noticed Liz Preston, behind the AD, bring a forefinger to her lips. He got the point.

"I've already informed Agent Preston of this unfortunate reality, but I want to make certain you understand the gravity of the situation as well, Agent Cady. The Roland Jund investigation is now a matter of national security." Litchy pointed at Cady. "As such, it's off limits, meaning you cannot and you will not interfere in the investigation."

Cady said nothing.

"Just so you and I are crystal clear: your fifteen minutes of fame will not save you if I find out you're messing around in matters of national security," Litchy said. "*Comprende?*"

Cady nodded again, but kept quiet. He feared that once he started talking, no amount of pantomiming from Agent Preston would save him from getting his ticket pulled, which was likely what Litchy was attempting to provoke.

"This isn't some low-rent nutbar carving up coeds in the garden shed, so it's got nothing to do with you." Litchy continued, pointing at Cady's chest as though there might be confusion over who he was addressing. "Consider yourself forewarned. I don't give two shits if the press calls you and that beat cop the fearless vampire killers."

Lieutenant Deb Rohr had made the TV circuit, and in an interview on *The Today Show* mentioned that if she had to do it over again, she'd remember to bring her garlic and crucifix. Within a day, the media began referring to Special Agent Drew Cady and Lieutenant Deb Rohr as "the fearless vampire killers." Fortunately for Cady, he'd been able to remain "an undisclosed FBI agent" in the media for the first several days, and by the time his name leaked out, Cady was already out of Duluth. The Minneapolis field office, which was handling all press inquiries for the Bureau, did not provide Cady's contact information to any inquiring reporters. And Cady's absolute refusal to comment on the Quilling case had kept him hidden in the background, out of the glare of publicity, long enough for the world to move on to the next big story. Cady dodged media coverage with the same vim and vigor that he anticipated he'd be dodging colonoscopies in another ten years' time.

"No worries, sir," Cady lied to the AD. "I'm just in D.C. to get my paw to work."

"Thanks for stopping by," Litchy said, dismissing Cady with a wave toward the door. "Good to see you're on the mend. I hope you don't mind, but it's important I bend Agent Preston's ear. ASAP and in private."

Cady took the hint and left.

CHAPTER FORTY-THREE

The bartendress had tits out to Montana.

Mike Litchy loved the perks that his membership in the Belle Haven Country Club provided him, playing eighteen holes with a federal court of appeals judge on Saturday morning or a senior senator from Delaware on Sunday afternoon or a committee chairman before dinner on Tuesday evening. He loved how Belle Haven let the occasional date who accompanied him to the club know that they were in the presence of someone of great consequence—as if the various women he spent time with were not already aware. Litchy loved sipping his Scotch and soda in the club's pub, sitting in the leather armrest, conversing with captains of industry, and watching whatever game was playing on ESPN.

But tonight was quiet, just a handful of patrons peppered about the bar, and Litchy found himself glancing over at Bambi or Becky or whatever in hell the buxom bimbo's name was. He wondered if they were real, as she wore a blouse that didn't allow for peeks of cleavage. He'd been up to the bar a couple of times already to get his drink refreshed or to grab the pretzel bowl, and once he'd flashed open his wallet to remove a ten-spot for the tip jar and left his badge on display while Bambi or Becky poured his Scotch. Sadly, she failed to comment, and Litchy began to wonder if the girl was a bit dim. The final time Litchy had ventured over, the tendress had started mumbling about her Navy SEAL boyfriend who was currently home on leave. Talk about throwing a damper on a budding romance. Bambi or Becky might not have personality, but did that really matter if you sported a pair of headlights like that? A rhetorical question that deserved contemplation, Litchy chuckled to himself, feeling the effects of the Scotch begin to take hold.

He normally didn't come to the club on Monday evenings, but it had been a long day and he needed a drink. Seeing Agent Cady in Agent Preston's office had thrown him for a hell of a loop. The man made him jittery. Preston was a problem—a desk jockey that could be dealt with—but Cady was the real threat. Litchy looked around the near-empty bar and snuck another glance at the frigid bartender. He should have stopped by Humdinger's. He knew visits there should be few and far between, but, in addition to requiring a drink, tonight he was celebrating. That above-the-fold article in the *New York Times* would go a long way toward putting this entire Lynchpin debacle to rest. The piece all but stated Roland Jund had killed Parrish because he was schtupping the man's wife, and then went on to kill the wife to cover his tracks. Gee, how could the *New York Times* have gotten their greasy little fingers on that story?

Litchy chuckled out loud and then glanced at Bar Tits to see if she'd heard him.

Sure, it would have been much cleaner had Plan A succeeded, had Jund been fed to the Lynchpin taskforce, had Steve Parrish not fucked up so badly to the point of getting his own self killed. Jesus Christ, Litchy thought, how fucking incompetent could one man be? If Parrish hadn't managed to stomp on his own nuts, Roland Jund would have, posthumously, gone down in history as the country's biggest traitor since Robert Hanssen. And the pressure would be off and life could go back to status quo.

But Plan B was working and the story leaked to the *Times* would help hustle it along, and Roland Jund's friends at the Bureau would peel off one by one, like rats abandoning a sinking ship, until all he had left was that dry-hump Liz Preston and that goddamned showboat Drew Cady. To think he had been so angry yesterday when, along with the ongoing financial difference of opinion, his *connection* refused to even contemplate taking that Preston twat out of the equation. Especially after the man had no qualms about taking out Dayna Parrish in order to sever any loose ends and frame Jund.

Dayna Parrish was how Litchy had gotten onboard this crazy gravy train to begin with, and even though they'd not done the nasty in ages, and even though there'd been a needless whiff of blackmail at the very beginning, he still loved the woman. Hell, with Steve assuming room temperature, he'd thought maybe they might pick up again...alas, it wasn't meant to be.

And that fiscal sticking point? The information he continued to provide them, especially this past year with his ass—*his ass!*—way out on the chopping block, the correct answer from his connection was not, "I'll have to get back to you on that." No, far from it—the correct answer was, "Anything you want, boss. Anything you want."

Litchy went to take a piss. He washed his hands in the black marble sink, dried them, turned to head back for a final drink from Bar Tits and...Litchy's connection leaned against the bathroom door, arms crossed, staring at the assistant director.

"Jesus Christ. You scared the shit out of me."

"Appropriate place for that, I suppose," the blond man replied.

"What the hell are you doing here?" Litchy asked. He did his best to avoid gaping at the blond man's missing eyebrow, as the scar tissue glistened in the unnatural lighting of the restroom. "I thought you were leaving the country."

"There can be no more leaking to the newspapers."

"What are you talking about?"

"The *New York Times* article."

"Wasn't me," Litchy said. "But whoever leaked that did us a big favor, in my opinion."

The blond man sighed.

"How did Special Agent Drew Cady get hold of your phone?"

Litchy looked as though he had just seen a Martian, and tapped his breast pocket. "He doesn't have my phone."

"The cell phone you called me from yesterday."

"Bullshit," Litchy said. "I dropped it in a toilet tank at a park restroom."

The blond man didn't move a muscle as he stared at the assistant director. Litchy's complexion took on a lighter shade of pale.

"Okay, all right. There was some kind of picnic going on by the restrooms, a horde of people and a bunch of little shits running around, so I threw it away."

"Where?"

Litchy thought about lying again, but reconsidered. "In one of the park garbage cans."

The blond man shook his head.

"We talked in euphemisms, like we've done for years," AD Litchy said, switching into damage control mode. "No names were used. Just a couple of random businessmen discussing a business project."

"I don't think it was recorded."

"Well, then, my iPhone's on the blink and I've picked up a couple of cheap prepaid cell phones until I get that sorted out. I tossed one when the minutes were up." Litchy worked through an explanation that would cut the mustard. "Now what's all this shit about Agent Cady?"

"We could ask him," the blond man said and gestured sideways with his head. "He's sitting in the parking lot."

"What?"

"I could have put two in his head on my way in. I believe he's been following you for much of the past week, and you confirmed his suspicions with that phone move."

"I'll take care of that right fucking now."

Litchy took two steps toward the door, but the blond man didn't budge.

"You will not talk to Agent Cady," he said. "You will not acknowledge his existence."

"That son of a bitch was in Agent Preston's office this morning," Litchy whispered.

"Which is why Cady's camped out in his car. Too easy for you to spot him in here. But you can bet he's running plates."

"You should go out there and—"

"You will not talk to Agent Cady," the blond man repeated. "You will not acknowledge his existence."

"Seriously? Just let him run free? I warned you about Cady, didn't I? But you knew so much better, you were going to handle it with kid gloves."

The blond man smirked.

"It's not funny," Litchy continued. "Now they got me with the throwaway—like the fucking terrorists use. No way Cady walks away now."

"You will not acknowledge his existence," the blond man repeated as he stood away from the restroom door. "You will not use library computers to check the message board or draft folder. That's too dangerous now. And you will certainly not buy any more cell phones." The blond man motioned for Litchy to exit. "As for Special Agent Cady—let me worry about him."

CHAPTER FORTY-FOUR

Cady sat in his rental du jour, an Acura TSX, jotting down the license plates of the vehicles in the Belle Haven Country Club. He cross-checked the plates against the ones he'd previously fed Liz from AD Litchy's prior evenings at Belle Haven and crossed out any duplicates. Having met Litchy in Preston's office earlier that day, it would be too risky for him to peek about the country club as he'd done on previous occasions. Litchy was already locked and loaded, and the last thing Cady needed was to bump into the AD at his own club.

Cady chewed on a vending-machine sandwich for a second or two, long enough to realize that it was all but impossible to tell the difference between the ham and cheese and the wrapper the sandwich came in. He tossed the uneaten remains into his plastic garbage bag full of other rejects. The other bag—a brown paper bag—was stuffed full of cans of pop, beef jerky, mini donuts, candy bars, and assorted bags of assorted chips. Liz popped up at odd moments to hand off a fresh bag of goodies for Cady's Litchy stakeouts as though she were sending her son off to grade school with a bag lunch.

He had assumed Agent Preston to be a health food fanatic—and Liz did pack the prerequisite apples and oranges and bananas and vitamin water, which Cady consumed contentedly—but he was amazed at all the zero-nutrition junk she shoved his way. He imagined Agent Preston was under the impression that this was what the male of the species desired. If this went on much longer, he'd need to have a word with Liz about the daily donuts, but, for now, he didn't want her to think him an ingrate. Already, Cady caught himself peeking over his shoulder in break rooms at the Hoover Building as he unloaded Preston's smorgasbord of snacks for other agents to enjoy.

But now he had bigger concerns. In fact, he was beginning to worry. He hadn't heard from Agent Preston or spoken to her since he'd been given the bum's rush from her office by Litchy. He had called her cell several times throughout the day, gotten her answering machine, but left no message. He knew she'd recognize his number in her call log and contact him. Cady was ten minutes away from bagging it at Belle Haven and heading over to Preston's D.C. townhome when his phone vibrated.

"It's about time."

"It's been a crazy day, Drew," Agent Preston replied. "Had a late meeting with Connor Green and just got home."

Director Connor Green of the Counterintelligence Division was another of the Bureau executives on the Lynchpin joint taskforce.

"And?"

"I can fill you in on that, but there's something else. I just got home and brought in the mail," Preston said. "There's another letter from the DMV."

CHAPTER FORTY-FIVE

Special Agent Elizabeth Preston,
RE: The Lynchpin Files (Haystack)

The first action plan of the joint FBI-CIA Lynchpin taskforce called for the creation of a—for lack of a better term—spycatcher database. This database, referred to by taskforce members as Haystack, would—to borrow a legal phrase—compile a chain of custody for all known breaches of national security data. The Haystack database would include the names, departments, timeframes, as well as the corresponding organizational charts of the infected areas where compromised data had passed through—that is, a listing of all individuals who had access to the classified data, even if they were an arm's length away. This data would then be mined, filtered down for recurring names and places in both the Federal Bureau of Investigation and the Central Intelligence Agency so that a listing could be created, thus triggering the immediate polygraphs of any agents appearing in the Haystack DB search results.

In other words, Haystack would digest a massive data dump, cull through the intelligence in search of patterns and sequences, and, ultimately, spit out results of said patterns and sequences. In previous generations, a Haystack DB would have kicked the Robert Hanssens and the Aldrich Ameses to the head of the class before their mischief could amass to DEFCON 1 levels.

The creation of the Haystack DB has taken a great deal of time. The database contains user interfaces set up to facilitate the interactions between the multiple systems involved—that is, to facilitate our systems

speaking to one another. As you can imagine, taskforce members and
their team of developers were sworn to strict secrecy, with more than
their careers in the balance.

This database has great potential for separating the needle—or in
our case, the Lynchpin—from the haystack...

"Remember what Eggs Nolte told us?" Liz Preston asked Cady.

The two had commandeered a secluded corner of a first-floor bar in the Embassy Suites Convention Center hotel downtown.

"How they did their damnedest to find the data leaks, but the process was so overloaded that the Lynchpin had them chasing their own tails?"

Preston nodded. "Imagine how much easier Eggs' life would have been had this technology existed at the height of the Cold War. The mainframes from the sixties and seventies didn't quite cut it."

"Eggs would have needed a thousand employees abstracting documents for a dozen years. No secrecy there."

"This Friend of Roland is tossing us some tasty morsels, but I don't know what to make of them."

"Mike Litchy is dirty." Cady voiced what he'd known since Oronoco Bay Park. "He gets placed, or gets himself placed, on the joint taskforce. It turns out the taskforce is not the joke he anticipated it to be. The taskforce has some teeth to it. The FBI and CIA are cooperating, setting aside the customary turf war, and this new database scares the hell out of him, so he sets up Roland."

"I agree with everything you said." Despite that, Preston sounded exhausted and looked defeated.

"What is it, Liz?" Cady asked. "What happened after I left your office?"

"I now work for Assistant Director Mike Litchy, Drew. How's that for ironic?"

"But Litchy's not in the Criminal Investigative Division." Cady was puzzled. Roland Jund reported directly to Allan Hartwick, the Director of the Criminal Investigative Division. Director Hartwick's response to the events of the past several weeks was not only to keep a low profile, but rather a nonexistent one, and acquiesce any and all responsibilities to the investigating authorities. Not having Jund's back, at this juncture, made for wise politics.

"It doesn't matter. Jund's investigation has taken on a head of steam; it's snowballing with its own momentum. And people are jumping left and right to get of the way. When colleagues look at me, Drew, they see Roland Jund. Litchy is using the Jund investigation and his position on the taskforce to put me in a box."

"What's he got you doing?"

"Some light filing here, some clerical over there, but just until the housecleaning of Roland's fiefdom has been completed. Until Roland's show trial is over."

"Jesus, Liz."

"I've been instructed that every e-mail I send, even to order supplies, must be copied to both Litchy and Director Green."

"I was hoping Green was our secret friend," Cady said, pointing at the letter from the DMV. "How was your meeting with him?"

"We walked through the protocol of my new assignment. He seemed distant and depressed, which is the opposite of his normal behavior, but these are trying times. I want to believe Litchy is using Director Green for cover, but who on earth knows at this point."

The two agents sat in silence. Cady didn't like seeing Preston despondent; of the two, Liz had always been the optimist.

"I think Litchy hoped I'd quit, get fed up, and hand in my resignation."

"That would make it easier for him."

Preston shrugged. "One last thing. Litchy was not happy to see you this morning, and that's an understatement. It threw him for a loop. Now that he's got me boxed in, I can guarantee he'll do whatever it takes to box you in as well."

CHAPTER FORTY-SIX

"Special Agent Cady."

Cady turned and spotted a heavyset man in a black Armani, or a reasonable knockoff, stepping out of the passenger door of a Lincoln Town Car and heading towards him. Armani was cleanly shaven with a thick head of hair slicked back in the latest *GQ* fashion.

Two days had passed since Litchy's impromptu meeting in Agent Preston's office. Cady had continued following the assistant director, but at a distance and with no more peek-a-boos when Litchy ventured into shops or restaurants. The AD had been in a holding pattern, circling from home to work to the Belle Haven Country Club to home again. A holding pattern that wasn't yielding anything new.

Cady had trailed Litchy to the Hoover Building that morning, dumped off Preston's latest bag of snacks in an empty break room, and, after Preston confirmed Litchy's calendar was blocked for meetings, scampered to locate a physical therapist who could walk him through the range-of-motion exercises Cady already knew by heart. He'd made the appointment immediately after meeting Litchy, just in case the AD pressed his alibi. The PT office was a ten-minute walk from Hoover.

"Do I know you?" Cady asked as Armani approached.

"I think we're on your radar. I'm an analyst and I work for Peter Gallion's group."

Peter Gallion led the Counterintelligence Center Analysis Group inside the Directorate of Intelligence for the Central Intelligence Agency. Gallion was also one of the four CIA members on the joint

FBI-CIA Lynchpin taskforce that Liz Preston had tried to contact,
to no avail.

Armani held out a hand. "My name's David Davidson."

Cady shook the man's hand. "David Davidson?"

"Don't ask. My parents had issues."

The man had a familiar look that Cady strained to place, but came
up blank.

"Want to jump in the car? We can go grab a bite to eat."

Cady looked at the sedan. The driver was a statue of muscle. He
looked as though he could bench press the Lincoln.

"I'd prefer not to."

"If you need a code word, would Lynchpin suffice?"

Cady stared at the heavyset man. "How do I know you?"

"Well, hell, Agent Cady, after all that quality time we spent together
the other night, I feel kind of insulted," Davidson said. "You even
bought me a Heineken."

"I thought I put too much Chris Farley into it."

"But your hair?" Cady asked.

"This slicked-back goop helps hide the fact that I'm a red-headed
stepchild." Davidson smiled at Cady. "I can sing, too. I owned my
high school theater department."

"You seemed heavier."

"You skinny jokers like to stick your guts out for shits and grins
at parties. You ought to let a fat guy show you how it's really done."

The two sat at a quiet table in the back of Kramerbooks &
Afterwords, a nearby café and bookstore. Cady had rescheduled his
PT appointment and Davidson's driver had vanished in the haze.
Cady stabbed at a salad while Davidson worked on peach cobbler
pie. Both had ice teas.

"I gotta tell you," said Davidson, "all that stuff that went down in
Duluth—that was unreal. I saw the pictures of that dungeon in the
Enquirer. Dude, you're like *Kolchak: The Night Stalker*."

"I'm like something, all right." Cady didn't want to talk about
Duluth. "So the CIA is following Mike Litchy?"

"I was on and off Litchy for a short while. Got off him since you took over. Gallion's got us on all the taskforce Feebs. No offense, Agent Cady, but *this* go-round, the turncoat's on you—whether it's Roland Jund or one of the other Hoovers."

So much for the turf war being on hold. But then again, after his tenure serving as Assistant Director Litchy's shadow, it was hard to quibble the point with Davidson.

"What do you mean by 'since I took over'?"

"We're spread paper thin, but Eggs Nolte informed us you were poking about and that you were—in Eggs' words—*on the up and up*."

"Eggs vouched for me?"

"I love Eggs, and what he says is gospel, but let's face it, Agent Cady: you hunt serial killers, which is pretty freaking cool if you ask me. But you don't have—and aren't in a position to receive—the kind of intel the other side salivates over."

"So I'm clean?"

"Squeaky. That's why Gallion yanked me off Litchy and put me on AD Speedling of Cyber Division, a detail which, quite frankly, is boredom personified. Work. Home. Ailing mother in assisted living. Repeat ad nauseam. Enough to make a man miss Humdinger's."

Cady laughed despite himself. "You got someone on Connor Green?"

Davidson nodded. "That one's a cake walk. Director Green practically lives at Hoover."

Cady opted for the blunt route. "Why are we having this meeting?"

"That leak to the New York Times has stuck in Gallion's craw. The info that reporter got crucifies Jund, and it's more than the droppings of a street cop hoping for a handjob from some pretty in the press. Gallion would like to find out if you're interested in a business arrangement—a limited partnership with the CIC Analysis Group."

"Meaning?"

"Bear with me while I walk you through a little background information, some of which you already know, some of which you absolutely don't." Davidson glanced around the bookstore and then focused his attention on Cady. "In the wee hours of September 14, Assistant Director Roland Jund strangled an intruder in his Leesburg, Virginia, home. Late in the evening on September 15, an antique collector named Sanford Gilreath flew into JFK from Budapest on a ticket that had been purchased that very morning. Only the man arriving at JFK does not collect antiques and his name most certainly is not Sanford Gilreath. The gentleman's real name—well, at least per our files, however reliable they are—is Stepan Volkov. He's an SVR intelligence officer known as the Wolf, and not only because the word *wolf* is derived from the word *Volk*. He's dangerous. Seriously dangerous. Ex-military, fluent in English and a bunch of other languages. An assassin, basically...and now he's in our country."

"How do you know this?"

"Facial recognition technology."

"I've heard that's not all that reliable."

"It's been more effective since it went 3D with geometric face scanning. Plus," Davidson said, "Volkov's got a tell."

"Which is?"

"Some kind of facial wound he got from his time in Bosnia. It's a shame whoever poked him didn't finish the job."

"And you got this off video at JFK?"

"I can neither confirm nor deny that we get a feed on the international flights passing through that terminal," Davidson said with a straight face, "and I can neither confirm nor deny that we run the feed through our FRT software."

"Why didn't you grab him?"

"Would that any of this worked in real time, Agent Cady. But the travel reservations for Sanford Gilreath, a.k.a. Stepan Volkov, indicate he's on a flight out of JFK tomorrow morning, heading to Estonia. We'll have a team on site there to take him into custody."

"Back to my original question," Cady said. "What does Gallion want from me?"

"Any intel you've got. You've been squatting on Litchy for over a week, so anything you've got on him, as well as what's driving you in his direction."

Cady sipped his ice tea. He intuited that he could trust Davidson, at least to a point. The man had been on Litchy before Cady joined the game. Davidson's tale made sense and Peter Gallion, head of the CIA's Counterintelligence Center Analysis Group, was most definitely on his and Agent Preston's radar. Cady wished Liz were here. He felt as though he needed to bounce this off her, get her buy-in, but then he thought about the voice on the other end of the phone he had picked out of the trashcan at Oronoco Bay Park.

"You have the wrong number."

Had that voice belonged to Stepan Volkov, a.k.a. the Wolf?

CHAPTER FORTY-SEVEN

November was Terri's month and it couldn't come soon enough.

October, with just a handful of diehard renters wrapping up the season, was surprisingly her busiest time of year. Outside of the plug-in space heaters in each unit to combat the periodic summer chill or fall bitterness, Terri's cabins were not heated and Sundown Point Resort was closed for ice fishing. Her string of fourteen units on Bass Lake needed to be winterized: the water shut off, full inspections of any and all damage that had been done to the units over the course of an eventful summer and wave after wave of visitors. And Terri needed to prioritize the never-ending list of repairs required by early next April.

She had put it off long enough. Cabins five through eight were in dire need of full carpet replacement with the indoor-outdoor brand she got a fairly good deal on, due to bulk, from a Grand Rapids' vendor. The rotted windows in cabins thirteen and fourteen would have to be addressed. And the rotting floorboards and antiquated appliances in cabin ten could no longer be ignored. Ten would be the big-ticket item for the offseason. Terri shook her head. Life would be a lot easier, not to mention cheaper, if she could burn down cabin ten and collect the insurance. Of course, that might be a little hard to pull off, Terri smiled, considering who she was engaged to.

But November was Terri's month. November was when she said screw it and took a much-needed siesta.

By December, she'd grow bored, catch her second wind, and begin sorting out the little stuff. She'd pick through the dishes in each of the units and junk anything that was broken or had seen better days. She did the same with any furniture that might, literally, be on its last leg. Her secret was to cruise the local Goodwill store for deals on dishware, replacement chairs, tables, or bed frames. Her clientele of hardcore fishermen and family vacationers weren't exactly expecting, or paying for, the Ritz-Carlton, but Terri did her darnedest to make Sundown Point Resort as hospitable as possible.

Nope. November could not come soon enough.

Terri sat in her porch office, which faced Bass Lake off the back deck of her two-story. The office was where her visitors came to settle up, kids came to buy candy bars, and fisherman came for nightcrawlers. She was poring over the previous week's earnings, her fingers tap-dancing on her calculator. The revenue had expectedly tapered off since the boom times of May through early September. This past season had been one of her most profitable, which—considering the economy—was counterintuitive. Terri liked to think it was on account of her hard work and keen business acumen, but she knew the facts of the matter. Collectively, families were, due to the difficult times, downsizing their vacation plans. Trips to Hawaii or Disney World or European holidays were scaled back to a cost-effective week or two at a rustic lake cabin.

Terri hoped to share November with Drew, even if she had to fly out to Washington, D.C. She was worried about her G-Man. He had yet to recover from what had taken place in the Quilling mansion. Drew, Terri felt, was irrationally blaming himself for the last of the Quillings' victims, and there was no magic word she could say to make his guilt go away. It broke her heart. The poor guy had been lucky to walk away from Duluth with just a concussion, shoulder blades more black than blue, and his hand smashed up again.

Agent Liz Preston had called shortly after Drew's arrival in Washington to voice her concern. After a frank conversation about Drew's well-being, in which they pledged to keep in touch, Agent Preston mentioned that Drew was currently on some kind of ad hoc surveillance detail. Preston said she'd make sure Drew would go out daily with a full bag of sandwiches, fruits, and vegetables, and the junkiest of junk food to help the agent to regain his recently lost weight. Perhaps it was not the healthiest of diets, but, on these details, Preston said, agents often ate out of sheer boredom.

Terri knew Drew had a love-hate relationship with Assistant Director Roland Jund; he had admitted as much. She also knew that her fiancé was doggedly loyal and would not leave Jund in a bind if there were anything at all he could do to help. And based on an article that had appeared in the *New York Times* and the small blips of information Drew had shared, Jund was in an extraordinary bind…one that would take more than her crippled G-Man to extricate him from.

Lost as she was in thought, the knock on the screen door caught Terri off guard. She looked up expecting to see one of the diehards wanting to purchase more bait. Instead a man in an American flag cap, a leather jacket and green t-shirt, and a pair of Levi's smiled at her through the door.

"I'm sorry to startle you," the man said.

"Come on in," Terri said, pointing to the chair on the side of her desk. "I'm just crunching numbers—my least favorite job."

The man came in and sat in the guest chair, his wallet in his hand.

"I'm hoping you've got a vacancy I can steal for the rest of October."

"I don't know about stealing, but I can rent you one."

"Excellent," the man said. "My name is Bob Jarvis."

She shook the gentleman's hand. "I'm Terri Ingram, the owner of Sundown Point."

Jarvis glanced out at the lake and then back at Terri. "You've got a lovely place."

"We try to keep it that way," Terri said. "You here to fish?"

"Maybe a little. I was supposed to close on a townhouse in St. Paul, but the couple I'm buying it from hit a snag and it got pushed out two weeks."

"St. Paul? What brings you up here?"

"My grandparents lived in Grand Rapids and we'd come visit when I was a kid. It's been decades, but I have great memories," Jarvis said. "Your resort was recommended in town."

"So you need to kill a couple weeks before the move?"

"I do contract work for IT departments around the country. I'll be gone half the time and working out of the library or Caribou Coffee the other half." Jarvis looked at Terri for a moment and shrugged. "To be honest, I'm going through a divorce and needed to remove myself from a bit of an uncomfortable situation until my new home is ready."

"I'm sorry to hear that," Terri said. "I didn't mean to pry."

"No worries. When everything is said and done, it's for the best. In the long run, anyway." Jarvis crossed a leg. "The short run kind of sucks."

Terri nodded. "Hopefully some fishing or hiking will take your mind off things."

"It'll work out. The kids are all grown and in college." He looked at the lake again. "Is there any way I can get the cabin farthest down? The one next to the woods?"

"Let me check." Terri pointed up at her wooden key rack, which had only two keys missing. "As you can see, we're incredibly swamped, but I think we can finagle you into cabin five."

"Excellent," Jarvis replied. "I'm hoping to *Walden Pond* it when I'm not at work."

"Henry David Thoreau."

Jarvis nodded. "You read Thoreau?"

"I did a term paper on *Walden* in college, but that was a lifetime ago. A couple years back I bought a plaque at a garage sale that had his fish quote carved on it."

Jarvis's face lit up. "'Many men go fishing all of their lives without knowing that it is not fish they are after.'"

"That's the one. I hung it up over the door, but took it down after the tenth guest shook a finger at it and informed me they sure as hell knew they were after walleye."

"They didn't appreciate the nuanced transcendentalism."

"No, they did not," Terri said, looking out over Bass Lake. She hoped Jarvis hadn't caught her staring at his deformity. She'd detected something unusual about his face at first glance, but now noticed that underneath his flag cap a chunk of one eyebrow was missing, with scar tissue in its stead.

"My copy of Henry David's book is dog-eared beyond redemption."

Terri chuckled and handed Jarvis the key to cabin five. "Feel free to *Walden* away. You'll have the woods on one side and the lake in front."

The blond man smiled. "Most excellent indeed."

CHAPTER FORTY-EIGHT

"You should not have called that number back."

"I thought I might recognize a voice or get something I could use before the cell phone Litchy called got tossed," Cady said and shook his head. "I messed up, I know."

"It's not your world, Agent Cady," Davidson replied. "We'll have to be extremely careful. We're talking about an Assistant Director of International Operations, for crying out loud. I hear Litchy's had his home and office swept weekly for bugs since the Roland Jund blow-up, so he's hiding himself behind that. What you've shared will be of great interest to Gallion." Davidson looked at Cady. "Hell, you may have some company at Belle Haven tonight."

Davidson got up to leave, but hesitated long enough to drop an envelope next to Cady's unfinished salad.

"What's this?"

"An act of good faith," Davidson replied.

To Whom It May Concern,

I, Dayna Parrish, resident in the City of Kings Park, County of Fairfax, State of Virginia, being of sound mind and not acting under duress or undue influence, do hereby declare this to be my last testament in case I am met with a suspicious or untimely demise.

What I am about to write—about to confess—will not paint me in anything remotely considered the best of light. For that I have no excuses. Or apologies. It is what it is. If this testament is ever to see the light of day, it means that I am dead and beyond caring about my reputation. *And the purpose of this testament is to aid the authorities in their efforts to resolve my murder.*

My late husband, Steve Parrish, was a special agent for the Federal Bureau of Investigation in their Counterintelligence Division. Unbeknownst to the FBI, my husband and I were also SVR operatives in the employ of another nation. Much of the data that fell within my husband's purview in Counterintelligence has been copied in one format or another and hand-delivered to courier. I can speak directly to this as, over the years, I have taken on the role of "information mule," with most exchanges occurring via the passing off of a shopping bag at the food court at Tysons Corner Center shopping mall.

Assistant Director Roland Jund of the Criminal Investigative Division has been our controlling agent—providing both leadership and counsel—in these affairs for over the past decade. And on numerous occasions, Assistant Director Jund has added USB flash drives and compact disks to Steve's materials for my "muling" trips to Tysons Corner.

Events, culminating in the murder of my husband at the hands of Roland Jund, began over the course of this past spring and summer. In a handful of meetings between my husband, myself, and Roland Jund, held mostly at dive bars outside of the Capital Beltway, the Assistant Director appeared apprehensive, beside himself with worry over actions undertaken by a joint FBI-CIA taskforce looking into the source of multiple security breaches, as well the development of a database that, according to Jund, spelled "End Times for the lot of us."

Whenever Steve and I suggested we work out an exit strategy, Jund would become increasingly agitated and—though Jund would later apologize and blame it on "the drink talking"—he threatened to have us both killed and informed us that there was nowhere we could possibly hide from him or his "wetwork agents." Unfortunately, this scenario repeated itself nearly verbatim any time we tried to recommend plans to alleviate the situation. And as these meetings progressed, Jund appeared, if possible, more riddled with stress and anxiety. The man also appeared to be drinking more, and Steve and I wondered if Jund might be self-medicating with some form of drug, and whether that could explain these mood swings.

In early summer, Jund contacted me individually to meet for lunch in order to discuss the situation. Although I felt improper about meeting without my husband, I felt that refusing the AD's invite was not an option. Far from discussing current Lynchpin proceedings, Jund spent our lunch at Fiola chomping on Sardinian Cavatelli and telling me about his separation from his wife JoAnne and how a man in his position has "certain needs that must be met"—especially considering "the pressure" he'd been living under, and how he had "always held an eye out" for me. It was excruciating, and though I kept repeating "No" and "No, I can't," Jund leaned forward and said in a hushed voice that he wouldn't take no for an answer. He said we were already "in the business of betrayal" and that "Steve never need know."

In the end we drove to his home in Leesburg, Virginia, and had intimate relations. Quite frankly, to say I was terrified by the man at this time would not be an exaggeration. I thought it could be managed. I was dead wrong and, though we had relations on two other occasions, I could not do it anymore and avoided his phone calls. To my horror, Jund stopped by in person on the morning of Steve's death, after Steve had left for the office. Jund told me he'd tell Steve if I didn't "fulfill" his "needs." I couldn't, and told him so.

That evening, when Steve arrived home from work, I told him everything—how sorry I was, how I had been coerced into the liaisons out of fear of what an unstable Roland Jund would do, how we needed to plot our own exit strategy, how Jund was unhinged and would take us all down with him. Steve took it as the dear heart he has always been, told me not to worry, told me he would make it end that night.

I begged Steve not to go. I begged him. But he wouldn't listen.

The call came hours later, on the cell phone we used to arrange our secret meetings with the assistant director. I thought it would be Steve. I prayed it would.

I answered.

"Your monkey failed." It was Jund. "If you wish to survive the next few days," Jund told me, "you'd best play your cards right, Dayna Parrish. You'd best play your cards right."

"All this time and it turns out Jund has 'wetwork agents,'" Cady said.

"I assumed that part referred to you," said Liz Preston. "The note spins a provocative tale, and Roland's real-life affair with the late Dayna Parrish certainly doesn't help his cause, even though he'd never met Steve Parrish or known Dayna Parrish was married."

"The note doesn't square with the Dayna Parrish I met, and it gives Jund an emotional depth that—let's face it, Liz—we both know he lacks."

"Someday, I shall make Roland aware of this conversation," Preston replied. "The note puts it on Jund, and the classified documents on the Parrish's home PC put an exclamation mark on that point."

"Notice the lack of Dayna's signature on the note. Davidson said it was a minimized Word document that the taskforce first spotted when they cracked Dayna's login."

"Although we now know the salacious details, this note is old news."

"In other words, Gallion's CIC hasn't given us much more to chew on than we already knew or assumed to be the case," Cady finished Preston's line of thought. "What's your take on Peter Gallion?"

"I wish we had some wiggle room, but at this point, I'm afraid we have no choice but to trust him."

CHAPTER FORTY-NINE

"The Wolf didn't show."

"What?"

Cady had been momentarily confused by the number displaying on his caller ID, but he recognized David Davidson's voice.

"We had our take-down team ready at JFK this morning, Agent Cady—for the Estonia flight—but Stepan Volkov was a no-show."

Damn, Cady thought. This was a setback. He'd hoped they'd be able to link Volkov to Assistant Director Litchy or squeeze some truth out of the Russian agent.

"Were you able to track Volkov through his Sanford Gilreath alias to a car rental or hotel room?"

"We tried, but it's standard operating procedure to swab out once you enter a hostile country for local travel, in case the natives crack your passport. For all we know, the Wolf is on his third ID by now. But," the CIA analyst continued, "Gallion believes that if Roland Jund is telling the truth, then it was the Wolf who paid Dayna Parrish a visit on the night of September 17 and jerry-rigged the evidence to point to Jund."

"And since Volkov didn't leave as expected?"

"One of two reasons, Agent Cady. Either he's on to us and he dumped the Gilreath persona, or he's tending to unfinished business."

"You're in my nightmares now, Cady," Lieutenant Deb Rohr told him upon answering her phone.

"Hello to you, too, Lieutenant."

"You're not the nightmare, though. I dream of recurring variations of that night at Quillings."

"Sorry to hear that."

"Don't be—they're kind of fun. When I realize I'm in a dream, I try to make it lucid and see if I can pop Evan when he's crouching behind the elevator frame—you know, before he starts cutting."

"How's that going?"

"Like trying to get a toy out of one of those claw machines," Rohr said. "You know, Cady, people are always asking about you."

"What do you tell them?"

"I say we're the trauma twins. You're blunt force and I'm sharp."

Cady hadn't known Deb Rohr long, but he missed her dark quips and quick insights. He imagined they were forever bonded after that night at Quilling manor, not unlike a couple of grunts in a foxhole who'd managed to survive.

"You know Evan cut me through to the bone in both places with that scalpel? Face and wrist?"

"Even in my condition that night, Deb, it looked bad."

"I'm glad I killed the fucker," Rohr said. "I've added it to the top of my résumé, above my name."

"Good to hear you won't be needing counseling."

"To be honest, I wish I could do it again. It happened so goddamned quickly, I wasn't able to appreciate it in the moment."

"Anything new on Sister Quilling?"

"Lucinda's not looking so youthful anymore. Detention brings out the gray roots. I'd say she's been doing some soul-searching, but that would require a soul. She keeps asking to speak with you, though."

"I don't do follow-ups," Cady said. "Tell her I'll see her in the tabloids."

"What do you think makes a pair of sickos like those two tick?"

"You know what the shrinks say?"

"What's that?"

"We're only as sick as our secrets."

"Well Jesus Christ, Cady—they had one hell of a secret."

"Can I ask you a favor, Deb?"

"Saving your ass wasn't good enough?"

"You know I can't walk down the hallway without some smartass making the sign of a crucifix, thanks to your quip about the garlic."

"The assholes here have given me enough stakes and mallets to host a croquet tournament," Rohr replied. "What do you need from me?"

"I'm wondering if you could check in on Terri at the resort?" Cady said. Cohasset was about a ninety-minute drive from Duluth. "Quietly look around, see if anything is out of the ordinary."

"What's going on?"

"It turns out I'm going to be in D.C. a while longer than expected. A few loose ends on a pain-in-the-ass investigation," Cady said. "And I hate leaving Terri alone this long."

"Does this have to do with your old boss being on a rampage?"

"Don't believe everything you read in the paper, Lieutenant."

"What should I be looking for?"

"It's a small town, so anything that seems out of place. Anyone hanging about who shouldn't be."

"What the fuck, Drew?" Rohr asked. "Are you in someone's crosshairs?"

"Shouldn't be," Cady said. "Quite frankly, I'm a bit jumpy after the past month. This is more for my peace of mind, Deb. To know Terri's safe and sound without getting her wound up."

"You talk to Chief Irwin about this?"

"I asked the chief if he could run a squad by every few hours if they're not busy. Keep a high profile on Terri's side of the lake. Unfortunately, Chief Irwin and Terri have some bad blood between them."

"What happened there?"

"It's a long story." Terri thought Grand Rapids Police Chief Leigh Irwin to be an incompetent who had bungled the investigation into the death of her former husband some years back. Turned out Mr. Ingram's death had not been an accident, as Chief Irwin had assumed, but had been the first volley in the Chessman killings that had led Agent Cady to Terri's door. "Needless to say he won't be dropping in for cookies."

"I have a consult with a plastic surgeon before lunch, but I can leave after that and poke about."

"Thanks, Deb. I'll let Terri know you're coming and she can rig up one of the cabins."

"Those made when Truman was president?"

Cady began the mental gymnastics.

"Just your pause tells me all I need to know. I never stay any place built pre–Jimmy Carter, just on principle. Plus, Terri won't get concerned if she thinks I'm just blowing through town and stopped by to say hi."

"You sure? You can stay in the main house. Terri would love the company."

"No, I'd only wind up stealing her from you," Rohr said. "And then you'd unfriend me on Facebook."

CHAPTER FIFTY

Assistant FBI Director Accused of Treason by Murder Victim
By E. Duranty Walters, The New York Times

In a startling turn of events in the investigation of the September 17th murder by hanging of Dayna Parrish, a source close to the investigation has shared a typewritten confession left for authorities by murder victim Dayna Parrish, which alleges that both she and her FBI agent husband Steve Parrish were spies for the Russian Federation. In what she refers to as her "last testament," Dayna Parrish states that the couple's handler was none other than Assistant Director Roland Jund of the FBI's Criminal Investigative Division.

As previously reported in the New York Times *on September 15, Assistant Director Jund claimed self-defense in the strangulation death of an at-the-time unidentified intruder, who Assistant Director Jund alleged had broken into his home in Leesburg, Virginia, in the early morning hours of September 14. In the days that followed, the intruder was identified as fellow FBI Agent Steve Parrish, who was none other than the husband of the late Dayna Parrish. Murder victim Dayna Parrish's "last testament" goes on to state that if she is "met with a suspicious or untimely demise"...*

"Christ, Liz. Do I want to read on?"

"It depends on what you had for breakfast," Agent Preston replied over the phone.

It was the first morning since he'd been in D.C. that Cady had allowed himself to sleep in, all the way to seven a.m.—one of the benefits of his limited partnership with Peter Gallion's Analysis Group. He had dive-bombed a shower and was out the door when Preston called to insist he pick up a copy of the *New York Times* on his way to his perch at the foreclosure in Belle Haven. He'd speed-dialed Preston as soon as he parked and began reading the above-the-fold article.

"Clearly this reporter has someone spoon-feeding him bits and pieces of the investigation damaging to Roland," Preston said.

"Clearly it's Mike Litchy."

"The article goes on to talk about the 'treasure trove' of classified data the investigators found on Parrish's home PC."

"You call Jund on this?"

"Right after I hung up on you. He's already talked to his attorneys, which is something, considering it's not quite eight. They want him to keep quiet, but he told them it's gotten too far out of control for that. They're going to release a brief statement to the effect of: Jund denies everything in the article, including the punctuation."

Through the trees Cady spotted a car winding down the street—a Jaguar XF. He simultaneously put his phone on speaker and brought the binoculars to his eyes.

"Litchy's heading in," Cady spoke aloud. "And the son of a bitch is smiling."

"He probably read the morning paper."

"No offense," Lieutenant Rohr said, "but I'm glad I stayed in town last night."

"Should I cancel your booking for next summer?" Cady was heading back to the Hoover Building after forty minutes of physical therapy and had called Rohr to check in on her trip to Cohasset.

"I'm a city gal, Cady. I don't do bears and raccoons."

"I've yet to see a bear, but I've heard tales," Cady replied. "What's the news, Lieutenant?"

"The news is no news. I showed up early afternoon yesterday and checked around. No one hanging about, no unknown cars parked where they shouldn't be, nothing bothering the neighbors down the lakefront. You only have three cabins rented—two today, since a

couple was going to leave this morning. One cabin has a group of
fishermen up from Iowa. These guys are all retired and look to be in
their upper hundreds. They're taking their limit and heading back
to Hawkeye via the casino at Mille Lacs, but, as one of the geezers
told me, don't tell their wives that. Your other cabin guy is waiting
to close on a townhouse in the Twin Cities."

"You meet him?"

"He was helping Terri haul a couple rocking chairs she picked up
at Goodwill when I got there. Seemed like a nice enough guy. Terri
served us lemonade and we shot the shit about Bob Dylan."

"Dylan, huh? Kinda retro, isn't he?"

"Oh, well, this guy, see—Jarvis is his name, I think—he says Bobby
D's the greatest poet since Shakespeare." Deb laughed. "I'm a Bono
fan myself."

"What's he look like?"

"He's a good enough looking guy, if you're into that. Medium
height, forty or so. A bit wiry."

"What about his face?"

"You coming out, Cady? 'Cause I can help you with that."

"We got a guy in the wind that's got shrapnel wounds to his face
or something."

"Jarvis had nothing like that going, although he had a pair of
wraparounds and a baseball cap on, you know, like every fisherman
ever." Rohr cleared her throat. "Look, Drew, Terri and I grabbed a
pizza in town last night and it's clear she's worried sick about you.
Said you can't let go of what happened in Duluth…of what happened
to Hannah Erickson."

This was the last thing Cady wanted to talk about. But Rohr had
been there—she of all people would understand. "I should have had
us there two hours earlier. Yeah, it bothers me. A lot."

"As far as I'm concerned, you did a phenomenal job in a phenomenal
timeframe."

"The bottom line is that I dotted every i and crossed every t for
hours after I *knew*."

"You were doing your job."

"I dotted i's and crossed t's while a young woman lay on a cold
table having her life pumped out of her."

"You've got to knock that shit off. Or tell it to a counselor," Rohr insisted. "What happened at Quillings' is not on you."

Cady chose not to continue the discussion. "Anything else for me?"

Several seconds passed, and Cady could tell that Rohr was weighing whether to push it or not. Thankfully, the lieutenant backed off.

"Let's see—this Jarvis guy was heading down to St. Paul after the lemonade to see if he can at least store his crap in the basement of his new townhome. I guess there's some bullshit with the closing date. And I talked to Chief Irwin," Rohr said. "You're right, he doesn't want to touch Terri with a ten-foot pole, but he told me his squad cars haven't seen anything outside of kids farting around and throwing rocks."

"Good to hear."

"Life in Mayberry continues."

"Look, Deb, I can't thank you enough for checking in on Terri."

"Don't give it a second thought—and hey, I see your old boss is a commie."

"Yup, a Marxist through and through."

"Someday, over a beer, I expect to hear the true story."

"I hope that's sooner than later, Lieutenant."

"I hate to make you jealous, but you better solve this case and hustle back to Terri. You've got that handsome thing working for you, but this Jarvis guy knows love songs and quotes poetry. I'm just sayin'."

"I didn't hear anything you said after the handsome part."

"Don't let it go to your head, Cady. Handsome in a bland, peanut-buttery sort of way," Rohr replied. "We'd have never dated."

CHAPTER FIFTY-ONE

"I came to say goodbye."

It was after midnight when Assistant Director Mike Litchy let the blond man into the basement of his colonial in Belle Haven.

"That seems a bit risky," Litchy said, glancing about the darkness of his backyard before shutting the door.

"Agent Cady kicks off at dusk. People are creatures of habit, and I think you've given him reason to believe that once you're in for the night, you're in for the night."

"You want a drink? Can I get you a Glenlivet or some brandy?"

"No thanks," the blond man responded. He could smell the whiskey on Litchy's breath from yards away. "I've got a little driving to do tonight—'miles to go before I sleep.'"

"Thank you, T.S. Eliot."

"Robert Frost."

"What?"

"The poet was Frost, not Eliot."

"Well pardon me all to hell," Litchy said. "How 'bout we cut the shit and you tell me why you're here."

The blond man had buzzed Litchy's iPhone and mumbled "wrong number" when the AD answered before clicking off. It was a code they'd established over the years for the handful of times a face-to-face was required.

"I've got some bad news to share, Michael," the blond man said. "A little bird told me that Special Agent Cady is now connected with Peter Gallion's group."

"Bullshit." This time Litchy's denial could pass a polygraph. "I spent yesterday morning on the taskforce sitting next to Gallion, and all we talked about was the hot water that Roland fucking Jund is in."

"The man's a spook with a Mensa-level IQ."

"I don't give a rat's ass about Mensa IQs. CIA's been pointing the finger at us since the Lynchpin taskforce was created. This thing with Jund plays to their convictions; it feeds their suspicions of how the FBI leaks like a sieve." Litchy paused to look the blond man in the eye. "We've been all over this. Hell, it was your idea to go this route. And I hate to remind you, but it was also your idea to use the Parrishes instead of doing the job yourself. Look what that got us…hah!… almost screwed, blued, and tattooed."

"Your disclosures to the press haven't helped."

"The *New York Times* was an act of genius," Litchy said. "You should be kissing my ass instead of kicking it, for Christ's sake. It's hurrying things along."

"It was a controlled burn that felt organic. We just had to be patient and let nature takes its course. But with the *inelegant* leaks to the *Times*, Gallion and company are going to give Cady's tale of assistant directors and cell phones more credence. The leaks to the *Times* will lead them to believe that a big fish still hides in the weeds, manipulating events. It won't be long before they come around to Cady's way of thinking, that Jund is not the Lynchpin."

"Jesus Christ. It was your idea to feed them a Lynchpin in order to protect the real McCoy." Litchy jammed a forefinger against his chest repeatedly. "And I warned you about Cady—how he needed to be taken care of—but you went with half measures in Duluth, and after that blunder you've opted to sit with both thumbs up your ass." Litchy frowned. "And now you come here to say goodbye and leave me to deal with your fuckups?"

"No." The blond man shook his head. Litchy was an unpleasant drunk, even more unpleasant than when sober, but the AD had been right about the threat posed by the investigator from the FBI. The agent had an uncanny ability to connect subtle dots. Leaving Cady alive would not be prudent—and that would be dealt with, just not in Washington, D.C.

"So Cady will be taken out of the equation?"

"I've got Agent Cady under control."

"So you've said before."

The blond man began looking about Litchy's lower-level man cave of comfy chairs and big-screen TVs. "Quick question, Michael. You wouldn't have anything *remiss* lying about your house, would you?"

"Of course not," the AD said, exhaling. "I'm not a fucking idiot. And no one's going to be kicking down my door. Ever."

It was easy to tell Litchy was lying. The blond man could make the assistant director talk. The blond man could make the assistant director scream. But with the CIA sitting on the front of the house, that might not be the most discreet avenue to pursue. It had taken Volkov nearly two hours to comb the woodlands behind the Litchy residence to verify no sentry had been posted there before he dared approach the back door. A quick glance at his watch told him he needed to move the evening along.

Volkov needed the AD to disappear—to vanish into thin air as if the man had never been born—with none of that pesky deoxyribonucleic acid smeared hither and yon to dispute the case. Litchy was lying, but it didn't matter. In an odd way, it would help the cause. Any eventual *findings* in the AD's residence would help supplement the small package Volkov planned to stash in Litchy's office. As for the threat posed by Special Agent Cady, Terri Ingram had cheerfully informed him earlier in the week that her "G-Man" had made plans to come home Friday...and Volkov would be there to greet him.

"Your cyber geeks convinced Shuffle's going to work?" Litchy asked, steering the conversation in a different direction.

Shuffle was a technologically sophisticated computer virus that had been custom made to attack the heart of the Haystack database and render the spycatcher DB of little or no value. By the time Shuffle's lines of computer code finished rearranging Haystack's data files, with the virus's malicious variations of *if this–do that* and *if that–do this* computations, the powers-that-be at both the FBI and CIA would be polygraphing the cleaning crew.

"It's a fait accompli." The blond man smiled. "Our programmers are brilliant. It'll take a half decade before they realize they can't trust the Lynchpin's search results."

"Brilliant, are they now?" Litchy said. "Bunch of goddamned whiz kids, right? Must be real fucking hard since they had the specs to the goddamned database handed to them."

"I cannot argue that." The blond man's smile broadened into a grin. "You need to lighten up, my friend."

"Lighten up? My ass has been out on a limb for you for years. And you stingy bastards refuse to open the purse strings wide enough to get a rubber nickel out."

"Michael." The blond man held his palms up, asking for peace.

"Don't Michael me. I'm bone tired and I have a big day tomorrow. But—hey—thanks for making my night. So kind of you to stop by and bid farewell as you leave me to mop up your clusterfuck. I wish you safe travels. Bon voyage." Litchy kissed his fingertips and threw them in the air. "Arrivederci. Fuck off."

"I was speaking metaphorically."

"What?"

"I was speaking metaphorically about coming here to say goodbye."

The two men stared at each other for the several seconds it took for the reality of the situation to dawn on the assistant director.

Litchy turned and bolted for the wrought-iron steps leading up to his main floor, but the blond man had the rope around the AD's neck before he'd reached the first step. Volkov yanked to tighten the noose, cutting off Litchy's oxygen. The AD fell backward, but the blond man stepped sideways and used the rope to swing Litchy onto the basement carpet with minimal impact. It was the first death in a long time that he felt good about. Assistant Director Mike Litchy had been superbly useful to the cause over the years, but he was nevertheless an exceptionally weak link whose shelf life had expired.

Volkov knelt down on Litchy's spine and leaned forward as the gurgling sounds began to wane.

"'The unexamined life is not worth living,'" he whispered into the choking man's ear. "That was Socrates."

CHAPTER FIFTY-TWO

The limited partnership with Peter Gallion's CIC Analysis Group was paying dividends, at least as far as Cady was concerned. No longer was he dragging himself back to his motel room by midnight every night for a four-hour nap before bouncing into a quick shower and shave, and then out to his rental car for a slow drive by of Litchy's domicile, and then digging in at the foreclosure and sipping lukewarm coffee from five thirty on. In fact, Cady had his nights free and clear since David Davidson had stated the obvious: "If Litchy spots you circling his orb, then we're all screwed. But if Litchy sees one of us in aisle five at the local hardware store, hell, we're just looking for duct tape."

Cady still kicked in for AD Litchy's morning commute. Always an early riser, Cady would grant an early reprieve to an always-appreciative Ross Bakken—the tower of muscle who had been driving Davidson in the Lincoln Town Car.

Cady now had time to throw himself into physical therapy—Evan Quilling had indeed caused him about a twenty percent loss of movement in his gimp hand. And Cady liked the therapist that he'd randomly selected based on the close proximity to the Hoover Building. He also now had time to work his way through the Mount Kilimanjaro of e-mails that had been stacking up in his absence. He had time to contact Special Agent-in-Charge Ron Bergmann of the Minneapolis field office to let him know he'd soon be ready to resume his role on the Medicare Fraud Strike Force, the plan being for Cady to return to his normal schedule by the first of November.

Unless something broke.

At this juncture, Cady wasn't sure what more he could do for his one-time boss. He had met with Jund earlier in the week, at the Starbucks off East Market Street that had become their usual rendezvous point, and, between sips of joe, the two had made small talk, which was an art form foreign to both FBI agents. Jund's gray stubble had developed into white whiskers, and the assistant director looked as though he'd put on the ten pounds Cady had lost. For a second, Cady thought of handing Jund the bag of junk food Preston had most recently given him, but decided against it.

Instead, Cady jotted a brief note on a Starbucks napkin, updating Jund on current events that he'd likely already heard from Agent Preston. Jund smiled and nodded, even gave Cady a weak thumbs up, but the AD wasn't himself. Cady dropped the napkin in the half cup remaining of his dark roast, swished it about, and then tossed it, cup and all, in the trash bin. Cady shook the assistant director's hand with his southpaw and left, wishing there were more he could do for the man.

Though days away, Friday could not come soon enough. Cady couldn't wait to jump on the plane back to Minnesota, back to Cohasset, back to Sundown Point Resort...back to Terri. He couldn't wait to hold her in his arms, smell her hair, fall into those blue eyes, and feel her breath in his mouth. No, Friday could not come soon enough.

But that morning, a few hours after he relieved Ross Bakken at the foreclosure in Belle Haven...something broke.

CHAPTER FIFTY-THREE

Where the hell was Mike Litchy?

Cady looked at his watch again and then checked the time on his smartphone. It was nine thirty a.m. and still no sign of the man. No Jaguar XF flying past the foreclosure. No smiling AD. Nothing. Cady called Liz Preston to check Litchy's online calendar for schedule hours.

"He should be attending a nine o'clock meeting," Preston informed Cady, "unless he's got that time blocked for work. Let me call you back."

Cady waited, eyes glued to the road, wondering if he'd have to use his empty coffee mug for something unintended if much more time went past. Five minutes later, Preston called back.

"Litchy's admin is trying to get hold of him. I told her I needed to set up a meeting regarding taking some time off, and she mentioned she'd not seen him yet and was rearranging his schedule for today. From what I could tell, it appears he blew off his nine o'clock."

Cady drove by Litchy's house slowly, staring at the front windows. The drapes were drawn. The house was still. He parked farther down the block, out of view of the colonial, and stared at the front yard for fifteen minutes.

After relieving himself into a mug he'd never use again, Cady called David Davidson.

At eleven o'clock Cady watched as a FedEx van turned into Litchy's driveway. He inched his rental car forward so he could watch the scene unfold from the periphery. Davidson himself stepped out of the van holding a small package and approached Litchy's front door. The parcel was filled with two of the latest Belle Haven phone books, and Davidson would pretend to require a signature.

Cady watched as Davidson rang the doorbell for several minutes, then began rapping on the front door with his knuckles, louder and louder still until Cady could hear the thumps from where he was parked. Davidson walked over to the window, saw his view was blocked, and began rapping on the windowpane. This went on for another eternity before Davidson surrendered and stood in the driveway, and then called what Cady assumed to be Litchy's home number. After another minute, Davidson walked around the side of the house and disappeared from view.

Eventually, Cady's phone rang.

"His Jag is still in the garage," Davidson said.

"The way you banged on his house, if Litchy were there, I guarantee he'd have come out and ripped you a new one."

"I did the same thing in back, but all the windows have shades and everything's locked down. We followed him home from that club of his after eleven last night; there's been no movement since and, like I said, his car's still here."

"I don't know about you," Cady said to the man from the CIA, "but I say we gotta get inside that house."

It was a black bag job in the midafternoon.

The four of them approached Litchy's colonial from the tree line in the back, where they couldn't be seen. The four included Cady, Davidson, Bakken, and a short gentleman with a shaved head for whom Davidson did not provide a formal introduction and from whom Cady did not request one. Shaved Head got through the two backdoor locks in about the same amount of time it would take Cady to tie a shoelace. Although Shaved Head held some kind of jamming device the size of a walkie-talkie, he still bolted up the steps to deal with Litchy's electronic security system. Shaved Head needn't have exerted himself—Litchy's alarm system had been turned off.

They had a surveillance car at the foreclosure home as well as one near where Cady had parked on the periphery of Litchy's property line. Both cars were in constant communication with Shaved Head, in case Alexandria PD showed up or, worse yet, Assistant Director Mike Litchy made an appearance after nearly a day of doing god-knew-what with god-knew-who. Ross Bakken took the garage, David Davidson the upstairs, and Cady the main floor office. In addition to monitoring surveillance, Shaved Head would drift the kitchen, dining, and living rooms—the areas not likely to bear fruit. The search of Litchy's colonial was timed for under half an hour, with the last five minutes allotted for all four men to search the lower level on their way out.

Cady, wearing a pair of examination gloves, nudged the mouse to Litchy's office computer with a forefinger. It was off. He began pulling open drawers, rifling through papers, taking only the time needed to ascertain the irrelevancy of the files before moving on. In ten minutes he was done with Litchy's desk—it did not appear Litchy did much work at home—and he moved on to the bookcase that lined one wall. Litchy had classics, reference books, and even a thirty-something-volume set of *Encyclopedia Britannica*. None of the books appeared to have seen much wear; Cady figured Litchy kept them for show.

Cady moved the leather couch at one end of the office out from the wall to see if anything was stuffed underneath, and then popped up the separate cushions. Nothing but an old cough drop. Cady put the sofa back exactly as he'd found it and then pulled Litchy's chair from around his desk and used it as a stepstool to see if anything lay on the top of the shelves. Again, nothing.

Cady checked his watch, then began pulling books off the shelves, glancing at the tops to see if any of the reference books or novels had something stuffed between the pages or if anything was hidden on the shelf behind. He made it to the eighteenth volume of the *Encyclopedia Britannica* before he saw the side of an envelope tucked in back behind the books. Cady pulled out the next five encyclopedia volumes, grabbed the seven-by-ten envelope, opened the clasp, and peeked inside.

Lightning in a bottle.

CHAPTER FIFTY-FOUR

"Early last week, Special Agent Drew Cady informed the CIC Analysis Group of having witnessed Assistant Director Mike Litchy deposit this prepaid cell phone into a trash bin at Oronoco Bay Park," Peter Gallion said, holding up the evidence bag containing Litchy's prepaid for the executives seated around the conference room table.

Cady sat motionless in a chair along the back wall of the mid-sized meeting room at the CIA's headquarters in Langley, Virginia. Sitting to his left was CIA Analyst David Davidson; to his right, Special Agent Elizabeth Preston. The trio remained silent, as this was their first time in attendance at a meeting of the Lynchpin taskforce.

Gallion had requested an emergency meeting of the taskforce members and invited the two FBI agents and his analyst to attend, but he had cautioned each against speaking unless directly addressed by him. Now Gallion presided over a meeting that included Director Connor Green and Assistant Director Paul Speedling on one side of the table and Gallion's three counterparts from the Central Intelligence Agency on the other. Gallion looked to Cady more like a tenured philosophy professor at Berkeley than the head of the Counterintelligence Center Analysis Group inside the Directorate of Intelligence for the CIA. The man's slim physique provided the optical illusion of more height than his five-ten frame would attest, and his graying hair looked a half-month shy of fitting into a ponytail.

"How exactly did Agent Cady stumble upon this *information*?" Director Green did not appear to be in the most charitable of spirits.

Gallion waved a hand. "Just as we suspected, Connor. Agents Cady and Preston are Roland Jund loyalists, a trait most administrators would find admirable in their subordinates, and they took it upon themselves to poke about the embers."

"What led these—and I'm going to label them *rogue agents* over loyalists—to surveil an assistant director of international operations at the Federal Bureau of Investigation?"

"It's my understanding that an assortment of items aimed the two in AD Litchy's direction. His erratic, passive-aggressive treatment of Agent Preston raised some red flags," Gallion said and smiled. "And— what did you call it, Liz?—his Benedict Arnold profile?"

Agent Preston nodded.

"Evidently, the two agents felt the profile matched Mike Litchy more than the rest of us on the taskforce."

"And how exactly did these rogue agents come by the names of those of us sitting on the Lynchpin taskforce?"

Nothing was said, but Cady noticed AD Speedling sink a little lower in his chair.

"I see," Connor Green said, breaking the silence. He gestured toward the agents in the back of the room with a nod of his head. "There will be two badges in my briefcase when I leave here today."

"I do wish you would withhold judgment, Connor, if only as a personal favor for me, until the end of the meeting."

"This may be par for the course in your world, Peter, but I consider it a betrayal in mine. If what Cady and Preston did was not technically illegal, it broke protocol, it broke the Bureau's code of conduct, it interfered in an ongoing investigation, it misused FBI resources—not to mention a half-dozen other firing offenses I can rattle off the top of my head." Green turned and stared at Preston. "I stood up for Agent Preston when Mike wanted her out because, until exactly five minutes ago, I held Agent Preston in the highest of regard. And as far as Agent Cady is concerned," Green said as he flung a hand in Cady's direction, "Jesus Christ—we've all heard things about him."

Cady crossed his arms and wondered what the hell they had all heard about him.

"Connor, please." AD Speedling spoke for the first time. "I'd like to hear why Peter summoned us here today before there's talk of taking badges."

"Sorry, Paul," Director Green said. "This meeting is over. We're in a room full of spooks that have been chomping at the bit to put Lynchpin on the Bureau. Evidently, Jund wasn't good enough for them, so they've scraped together a couple of backstabbers and, meanwhile, they don't even have the common decency to invite Mike Litchy here to defend himself." Green shook his head. "Fucking Stalin had more class."

"I wonder if you can shed some light on that," Gallion said.

Green glared at the leader of the CIC Analysis Group. "On what?"

"On the fact that Mike Litchy has not been seen in nearly two days."

"Bullshit." Green took out his cell phone and stabbed at something on his screen.

Within seconds a buzzing rang from one of the varied evidence bags sitting on the cherry wood in front of Peter Gallion.

"Perhaps you'll grant me a minute, Director, to explain how in addition to the prepaid purchased by Mike Litchy," Gallion said, holding the evidence bag he'd previously shown the attendees in one hand and the buzzing evidence bag in his other, "I've also come into possession of Mr. Litchy's personal iPhone."

CHAPTER FIFTY-FIVE

"Why didn't you tell us you were surveilling Litchy?" AD Speedling asked. "Why didn't you tell us you knew Stepan Volkov was in the country?"

"It was a matter of trust." Gallion let that linger in the air before continuing. "Remember the reason we set up the Lynchpin taskforce in the first place—to smoke out the identity of a high-ranking mole that we all knew existed. In a most surreal manner our prayers are answered when, out of the blue, Roland Jund strangles a fellow FBI agent who turns out to be the husband of the woman Jund spent a small portion of his summer romancing. Suddenly this woman hangs herself—no, scratch that—she has been hanged on a night when Assistant Director Jund has no alibi. We then take credible evidence and highly classified documents from the Parrish household that implicate not only Mr. and Mrs. Parrish, but also Roland Jund as their leader. Like I said, it's a surreal situation that has literally disentangled itself before our eyes. In addition, the entire mess is sloppy, which, frankly, gives it an added air of believability." Gallion stopped to take a sip from his bottle of Perrier. "There are, of course, loose ends. Roland Jund sticks by a story that strains plausibility in the face of the mounting evidence against him. However, no trace of physical evidence indicates that AD Jund ever set foot in the Parrishes' Kings Park household. And if Jund did in fact kill Dayna Parrish, why would he leave evidence of his duplicity on their computer for all the world to see?"

"I brought those same items up in every meeting," said Speedling.

Gallion nodded. "But you were his friend and confidant, so your objections were taken with a grain of salt. Stepan Volkov's entry into the country immediately prior to Dayna Parrish's death raised red flags that something was, in fact, for lack of a better phrase, out of whack. You see, the Wolf is a proficient sniper. We also know he is an expert with any type of handgun. However, a lesser-known skill set of Volkov's is his dexterity with a rope." Gallion glanced around the table. "The Wolf was known to personally hang political prisoners during his days of service for the Serbs in the Bosnian War."

"So Volkov is the Lynchpin's enforcer?" Green asked.

"Handler. Enforcer. Troubleshooter. What's in a name?" Gallion looked at the trio sitting in the back of the room, then at the two FBI agents. "When I talk about keeping you in the dark being a matter of trust, understand: I couldn't very well tip my cards and inform the real Lynchpin of my growing suspicion that he was still in play or that we were aware that his aide had recently entered the United States under a false identity."

"Yet you informed Agent Cady?" asked Green.

"That was a judgment call made when Agent Cady informed us what he had observed about Assistant Director Litchy."

It occurred to Cady as he listened to Peter Gallion's narrative of mostly-truths that none of Gallion's CIA colleagues had entered the fray. They sat quietly while Gallion spoke. Cady suspected Gallion had held an earlier meeting in which his counterparts had been brought fully up-to-date.

"When Agent Cady told you about Litchy dropping a phone, you took over surveillance?" Green asked.

Gallion nodded again. "And made a botchery of it, I'm afraid. We followed the assistant director home two nights ago. We had a man on the front of his house and we should have had one in the back, although if, as I suspect, Volkov came to whisk Litchy away, I'm afraid we'd have a dead or missing agent on our hands. Not to be overly melodramatic, but the Wolf would have been fed."

"So when Mike didn't show for work," Green said, "you tossed his house?"

"Please, Connor." Gallion allowed himself a small grin. "I know Hollywood paints us in one color, but we went through proper channels. Special Agent Elizabeth Preston, recently assigned to report directly to Assistant Director Litchy, was concerned for his well-being and, after checking the local hospitals, contacted the Alexandria Police Department, which covers Belle Haven. Agent Preston explained the situation to them and, as a result of Litchy's continued absenteeism, expressed her fear that he might be inside the house and in need of emergency aid."

"Liz's concern is very touching." Green again.

Gallion ignored him. "Agent Preston, Litchy's administrative assistant, and the Alexandria PD entered the assistant director's home at that point, but found no trace of him. However, they noted that his home alarm had been turned off, which raised additional concerns regarding foul play. At this point, Litchy's admin contacted Mike Litchy's only sibling, a sister in Baltimore, who had no knowledge of her brother's whereabouts. When informed by Agent Preston that her brother's Jaguar was still parked in his garage, Litchy's sister became apprehensive. Evidently, that Jag is Litchy's pride and joy and, according to his sister, he never leaves home without it. Additionally, the assistant director owns no other motor vehicles. Agent Preston— again, a concerned subordinate of the missing AD—asked his sister for permission to look about the AD's home for any clues as to her brother's whereabouts."

"Sounds like Liz was a busy girl," Green said.

Cady glanced over at Agent Preston, who appeared intent on examining the trim about the conference room's floor.

"We were all deeply concerned," Gallion replied. "Litchy's sister was exceptionally obliging, and exceptionally obliging on speakerphone right in front of Alexandria PD."

"That'll never hold in court," Green said.

"Who said anything about going to court?"

"When Mike appears, I imagine he will insist."

Gallion shrugged. "We were most fortunate to have on hand a couple of employees who have a certain level of aptitude in this area."

"I'll bet you did." Green looked across the table. "You spook bastards wanted to pin this on us since day one."

"Don't mince words, Director," Gallion said. "Tell us how you really feel."

"Fuck you." Green stood and began gathering his papers.

"Connor." An Asian gentleman on the CIA side of the table named Nguyen spoke for the first time. "You and I have worked together for many years. I consider you not so much a colleague as a friend. I have been to your house for occasions outside of work, and you to mine. I trust you and I believe the feeling is mutual. And I know the Steve Parrish matter is eating you alive."

"Jesus Christ, Lan," Green replied, looking at Nguyen. "I wouldn't know Steve Parrish if he up and puked on my shoes."

"I know that, but the thought of an agent like Parrish foraging about your division for national secrets is killing you, just as it would me. Then there's the Roland Jund issue to contend with, and now it's become the Mike Litchy situation. I know you're probably punch drunk at this point, Connor, but consider this: if Litchy is guilty," Nguyen said, "then Jund is not."

Green gave an almost imperceptible nod.

"If Litchy is guilty and Roland Jund was set up as the fall guy—"

"Then it's a push," Green completed Nguyen's thought.

"Then it's a push." Nguyen gestured at Green's chair with an open hand. "Please, Connor. This taskforce needs you, now more than ever."

Connor Green bit his lower lip and sat back down.

After a respectful moment or two, Gallion resumed the floor. "Everything we are about to show you stems from a thorough search of Assistant Director Mike Litchy's Belle Haven residence. David, if you would be so kind."

Davidson cleared his throat and stood. All eyes turned toward the CIA analyst and, for Cady, it was impossible to misinterpret the outright hostility in Connor Green's gaze.

"To cut to the chase, a ladder was found in the assistant director's walk-in closet connected to his master bedroom. It was a typical wood foldout, heavy, the kind normally stored in a garage as opposed to inside the living quarters. Besides being out of place, its bulk took up space that could be used for additional garments."

"A ladder in a closet. He's clearly KGB."

Davidson smiled at Director Green as though he were in on the heckling and continued. "We noticed a rectangular hatch for the ceiling attic."

"Hence the ladder."

"Hence the ladder." Davidson turned and began speaking directly to Connor Green. "A man of less girth than I climbed up into Litchy's attic, only it wasn't so much an attic as an insulated but unfinished space. A plank of plywood on top of the two-by-eight floor joists stretched diagonally from the hatch opening to one corner of the space. Our man up there began lifting insulation as he crawled along this oddly positioned plank. When he lifted up a bulging piece of insulation in the corner of the attic, he found a fireproof safe, compact and much like the kind used for handguns, fastened to the side of a two-by-eight."

"Litchy was being responsible with his firearms," Green said.

"That's what we were expecting, only the safe did not contain firearms," Davidson replied. "Hanging from a nail on a nearby ceiling rafter was the key to the safe."

"And I imagine Mike's sister was there every step of the way, nodding her avid approval."

"Again, Connor, what we found at the Litchy residence will never see the inside of a courtroom," Gallion interjected, then looked back to Davidson. "Tell them what was in the safe, David."

"We found two small brown envelopes and one large envelope. Let me preempt any questions and say that Assistant Director Mike Litchy's fingerprints were all over the safe, the key, all three envelopes, the contents inside of each envelope, as well as on the ladder used to access the attic."

"What was in the envelopes?" It was the first time Green had said something that lacked at least a hint of derision.

"The largest of the three envelopes contained eighty thousand dollars in hundred-dollar bills. One of the two smaller envelopes contained what a preliminary estimate values at nearly half a million dollars in round, brilliant-cut diamonds."

If a nurse were in the room, she'd have demanded to take Connor Green's temperature.

"What was in the third envelope?" Green asked.

"A Belgian passport for an individual whose name I fear I cannot pronounce correctly, but bearing an image of Mike Litchy with blond hair and a moustache."

The room sat in silence for several moments.

"Another envelope was found behind some reference books on a shelf in the assistant director's home office," Peter Gallion said, taking the floor back from Davidson. "This envelope contained nothing as sexy as diamonds or hundred-dollar bills or fake passports. This particular envelope contained numerous photographs. Pictures of Litchy and a *houseguest*. Now, for the purpose of this gathering, please understand that these are not the original images found in Litchy's home office, but copies of the found images."

Gallion pressed buttons on the console in front of him. A screen lowered next to where Cady sat with Preston and Davidson. Gallion stepped back and flicked off the lights. Four separate images of a younger Mike Litchy and a younger Dayna Parrish filled the screen. Four images of the naked duo engaged in four dissimilar sexual acts.

"The envelope found hidden behind the reference books in Litchy's office contained another twenty images," Gallion told the conference room, "but I suspect you get the gist of it."

If a nurse were in the room, she'd have demanded that Connor Green be rushed to the ER.

CHAPTER FIFTY-SIX

"Is Roland going to be all right?" Terri asked.

"There's a mountain of detail to sort through, but I think Jund will be back to driving his staff apeshit any day now."

Having landed at the Minneapolis St. Paul International Airport, Cady was taking the light rail downtown to pick up his Ford Escape, which he'd parked at the Minneapolis field office. Since this last stretch in Washington, D.C. had been pro bono, Cady didn't want to eat the costs of parking his SUV at the airport.

"What's your ETA, G-Man?"

Cady glanced at his watch. It was a quarter past seven and the sun had already set. "There shouldn't be much traffic. I'll be there by eleven."

"We'll celebrate."

"Yes, we will."

"That's a mighty big smile, Terri," Bob Jarvis said as he entered the resort's office, waving a fistful of twenty-dollar bills.

"My fiancé is heading home right as we speak."

"That's great news," Jarvis replied. "Wish I could meet him, but I got some good news myself."

"You finally get the okay to move in?"

"Yup. I'm heading out in a few minutes so I can get an early start in the morning." Jarvis started stacking crisp twenties into multiple hundred-dollar piles. "Thought I'd come settle up."

"In cash, no less."

"I sold off the rest of the meth I've been cooking back there." Jarvis gestured toward Terri's cabins and they both laughed. "Actually, the ex and I are divvying up accounts, so I'm using cash until my new checks arrive."

"Cash'll work." Terri wrote out a receipt. "Bob, you've been a gem. If you ever need to come *Walden* it again, please keep us in mind."

"Sure will. I'll even let my friends know."

"Word of mouth is always welcome."

"Sundown Point's been everything the doctor ordered." Jarvis pocketed the receipt and change and stood up. "I'm going to miss it here."

"Well, I wish you best of luck with your new life. I think things are going to work out for you."

Jarvis stood still for a few seconds. "Okay, Terri—I thought I could sneak out and not say a word, but you know those Northerns I hauled in?"

Terri nodded.

"I was frying them up and my arm hit the cord and, I don't know how it happened, but the pan and everything wound up on the floor."

"You didn't burn yourself?"

"I jumped fast and far," Jarvis said. "But I screwed up your carpet."

"Don't worry about it. I've got an industrial cleaner that takes out everything."

"I don't know…it looks like hell."

"I can do a patch. It's really no big deal. Cabin five's on the carpet replacement list anyway."

"Tell you what," Jarvis insisted. "Come take a peek at it, and if it's all good, I'll leave in peace, but I think I may owe you another hundred for the damage."

Terri held up both hands in surrender. "Let me grab the cleaner and I'll be there in five."

CHAPTER FIFTY-SEVEN

"Gallion and Director Green allowed me to tag along for their meeting with that numbskull reporter at the Gray Lady," said Davidson.

Cady was heading north on I-35, passing the Forest Lake exits, and David Davidson was on speakerphone, letting him know how the meeting at the *New York Times* had gone.

"That E. Walters reporter guy is sitting there, looking all pointy-headed and full of himself, but so is the publisher, about seven editors, and what must be their entire legal department. The newspaper folks are seated around the conference table and Gallion and Connor Green are shown to the head of the table in the, you know, turkey-carver seats. And I'm a fly on the wall in the corner of the room."

"You're a glutton for punishment."

"No, this was priceless," Davidson said. "The Gray Lady's lead attorney starts off doing this holier-than-thou Atticus Finch impersonation, you know, spouting the usual stuff about the First Amendment to the United States Constitution and freedom of the press and blah, blah, blah. Meanwhile, Gallion and Green are sitting there, hands folded, nodding at every rehearsed point the lawyer makes. After about ten minutes of the dance, the lawyer explains that this is why the paper will never reveal E. Walters' source, not even to the FBI or the CIA."

"Then what?"

"Gallion says, 'Okay.'"

"He just says okay?"

"Well, he also compliments the attorney on his presentation. A hush falls over the conference room, and finally the publisher asks

Peter if there's anything else they can help him with. Peter looks around the table for a second and asks if anyone has seen Assistant Director Mike Litchy."

"Gallion asks if *they* know where Litchy is?"

"Yes, it was great—and even though most everyone at the table knows exactly who Litchy is, they act all confused and ask Peter who he's referring to. And Peter says—no shit, Agent Cady—Peter says, 'Why, Mike Litchy is E. Walters' source, of course.'"

"And they deny it?"

"The lead attorney jumps back in, acting as though he'd been slapped in the face, and starts in on how they 'refuse to play a game of speculation' and 'will neither confirm nor deny' any names that are put forth. Peter nods again and looks at E. Walters, you know, Litchy's reporter *be-yotch*, and informs him Litchy intentionally misled him and that Litchy himself is currently under investigation."

"What did the reporter say?"

"Well, first off, Mr. E. Walters has no poker face to speak of. He's turning redder by the second and keeps sipping his glass of water. Walters finally mumbles something about how Peter should take it up with 'this Litchy fellow.' Peter then informs the room that Assistant Director Mike Litchy has not been seen in three days, that Litchy's not reported for work or returned messages, that he's missed numerous meetings, and that friends, colleagues, and family members have no idea where he is. Peter reminds Walters that he and Director Green represent the CIA and FBI, respectively, and that both organizations have had some experience locating missing people, but if Walters is still in touch with Litchy, it would behoove E. Walters—I love that word, behoove—to tell the missing agent to turn himself in immediately."

"So essentially Gallion was telling the Times folks that they'd been scammed."

"It gets better. The reporter guy asks Gallion about Roland Jund's role, about how culpable Jund is in all of this, and Peter tells him Roland Jund is in the process of being cleared, and that any information leaked to the media by Assistant Director Mike Litchy likely reflects Litchy's duplicity in the matter. Peter then looks at the lead attorney and lets slip that Jund's personal attorneys may be in touch."

"Jund has fantasies about suing the *New York Times*."

"I hear that's common," Davidson replied. "Finally, Walters asks if there's any hard evidence backing up this assertion of Litchy's guilt. Peter reminds Walters how he's written extensively about Dayna Parrish, about her and her husband's roles as Russian operatives. E. Walters nods his head, and then Peter informs the room that Mike Litchy himself had been in a long-term relationship with Mrs. Parrish. Walters asks if there's any proof that such a relationship existed. Peter nods and then takes his time fumbling open his briefcase—even mister doom and gloom Connor Green is stifling a smirk—and Peter finally pulls out an eight-by-ten picture, you know, one of *those* pictures, and informs the room that this photograph was one of several found in Litchy's residence and, though it appears to be a decade old, it should act as proof positive of their relationship."

"Sounds like Jund might be getting some better press in his immediate future."

"Ya think?"

After a second, Cady asked, "Litchy's dead, right?"

"There are two schools of thought. The first view is that he left the house feet first, carried out. Why else would he leave his treasure and his new identity? The competing view is that Litchy left of his own volition—on his own two feet—and that the fake passport was left to send us in the wrong direction."

"But the cash and the diamonds?"

"Considering what Litchy had been up to, that's chump change—walking-around money. And he'd have a pot of gold or two hidden elsewhere."

"What's your take?"

"I waver back and forth. Perhaps he knew the jig was up and slipped out the back to begin a new life," Davidson said, "or else the Wolf read him a line of verse."

"What do you mean, read him a line of verse?"

"Stepan Volkov fancies himself some kind of poet laureate, philosopher king. Our intel, mostly from Volkov's time in Bosnia, indicates that when the Wolf does an up-close-and-personal-hit, he likes to assign his victims a line of verse or a famous quote right before sending them off to the great beyond. Some shtick, right?"

"Charming."

But something scratched at the back of Cady's mind. Something Lieutenant Rohr had mentioned recently. Something about the divorced guy renting one of Terri's cabins, claiming Bob Dylan was the greatest poet since Shakespeare. Jarvis was his name. Something about Jarvis loving to quote poetry.

"Can you send that image of Volkov at JFK to my cell phone?" Cady asked.

"I can get you a JPEG," Davidson replied. "What's up?"

"Just want to satisfy an itch."

CHAPTER FIFTY-EIGHT

"I'm sending you an image."

"What?" Lieutenant Rohr asked. "We're sexting now?"

"I don't want to taint it by saying anything," Cady replied. "Just open it up and tell me what you see."

Cady hit Send with his thumb, his eyes darting back to the interstate. He'd flown past the Pine City exit, the speed of his Escape inching toward ninety miles an hour.

"Okay," Rohr said a moment later. "It's a picture of what's-his-name."

Cady's stomach dropped. "The cabin guy?"

"Yeah, divorced guy between homes. Why?"

For a couple of moments, no one spoke.

"Say something, Cady. You're scaring me."

"My God, Deb," Cady said, his voice breaking. "I just killed Terri."

Cady called Terri's cell phone, the same number she used for the resort so potential guests could reach her in real time. It kicked immediately over to voicemail. In the message he left, Cady stayed as upbeat as possible, said he was hungry, and told her to call him as soon as possible so they could plan to meet at the Sawmill Inn in Grand Rapids for a late dinner.

"Jesus Christ," Davidson said into the phone, stunned at the revelation that Stepan Volkov—a.k.a. the Wolf—was holed up at Sundown Point Resort. "You know what that means?"

"It means he's there for me." Cady sighed. "One fuckup and Terri pays with her life."

"Even if your callback on Litchy's throwaway phone gave you away, Volkov's not going to fly across the country to target you and your family. There's no point. They generally fold the tent and disappear into the night."

"I need you to contact Agent Preston, ASAP. If they're playing for keeps, Liz Preston is in danger. She had more to do with knocking Litchy off his perch than I did."

"I'm on it," Davidson replied. "But let me take this to Gallion. We can get a team there in under three hours."

"I'm a little more than an hour out," Cady said, now speeding west on US-2. "Terri'll be dead in two if I don't show up...if she's not already."

"I've got to take this to Gallion," Davidson insisted.

"Do what you've got to do."

Cady clicked off.

"Hey, Andrew—it's about time you called."

Cady's gut clenched. Not only had Terri used the wrong name for him, she'd also put the call on speaker, atypical of her.

"Didn't you get my message?" Cady strove to speak casually, naturally. "I'm almost at Grand Rapids. How's a late dinner at the Sawmill sound?"

A moment passed.

"I'm a mess," Terri replied. "Bob Jarvis checked out of cabin five today and he managed to dump a ton of grease all over the carpet, so I'm ripping it up."

"Did you charge him for it?" Cady shifted into what he hoped sounded like landlord mode.

"No."

"You need to do damage deposits, Terri."

"He 'fessed up, and five needed replacement anyway."

"No Sawmill, then?"

"Not tonight, Andrew. Just get your rump to cabin five so you can help me pull up all these staples."

"I'm starved," Cady said. "I'm going to hit the drive-thru at Taco Timmy's. You want anything?"

There was a long pause and Cady prayed she understood.

"Get me the combo that comes with the tamales."

"You got it, Ter."

"I love you, G-Man."

"I love you too, Ter."

"He's got her?"

Lieutenant Rohr had beat Cady to a bait shop halfway between Grand Rapids and Cohasset. The bait shop was closed, but Cady knew the owner. Rohr dumped her Mazda and jumped in Cady's Escape, barely shutting her door as Cady raced from the parking lot.

"Volkov didn't let her answer the phone until I was nearly here—to give me less time in case Terri screwed up the call, no doubt."

"She say anything?"

"A ton," Cady responded. "First, she wasn't her normal smartass self. And then she called me *Andrew*."

"She used your full first name?"

"My full first name is Drew. There's no *Andrew* anywhere. Never has been."

"Smart girl."

"Then she ordered a combo from Taco Timmy's."

"So?"

"The Health Department shut Timmy's down right after I moved here," Cady said. "Food poisoning."

"Where are we going now?"

"The other side of the lake."

CHAPTER FIFTY-NINE

"I'm the bait?"

Cady looked at Lieutenant Rohr. "Yes."

The two pulled into an empty cabin across the width of Bass Lake from Terri's resort. It was empty in the sense that the cabin owners, likely city dwellers, were not currently there and had, evidently, put off taking in their dock for the last possible weekend. Cady wasted no time stripping down to his boxers and popping the Glock 22 in a Ziploc bag. The rear cargo area of Cady's Ford Escape was continually awash in resort supplies, and chief amongst the clutter hidden in back were shopping bags stuffed full of the Ziplocs and wrap Terri required for the weekly fish fry she put on every Wednesday for her guests. A running joke between the two had been that if Walmart ever ran out of Saran Wrap, they could send their customers to Sundown Point.

It wasn't that funny of a joke, but it gave Cady the idea.

He stood by the dock, arms in the air like a suspect under arrest, as Rohr ran yards of Saran Wrap around his torso, securing the ziplocked Glock to his chest and keeping it waterproof.

"The lake road ends at Sundown Point, and a dirt road cuts another sixty yards through the resort, all the way to cabin five—that last cabin by the woods—where Volkov is waiting to kill me. Before the lake road ends, I need you hunkered down and steering from the passenger seat, just letting the engine drive. Jack the parking brake when you hit the playground, next to that miniature schoolhouse the kids play in."

"Swing set then schoolhouse, right?"

Cady nodded. "As far as you can to the right. Get edged up right against the playhouse. Then hit a couple friendly beeps of the horn, but don't go farther. You'll be about forty yards out and that'll confuse him. Do not raise your head above the dashboard, Deb. Not even for a second."

"And I roll out the side door and get behind the schoolhouse," Rohr said, "because I don't do fish in a barrel."

Cady nodded again. "By then I'll have killed him."

"What if he's not in the end cabin?" the lieutenant asked. "What if he's roaming?"

"Then it gets a hell of a lot harder. Volkov's the only remaining guest, so you're good as long as you don't shoot Terri or the wet guy in his underwear."

Rohr looked out at the lake in the October night. "That's a quarter mile away."

"Give me fifteen minutes, Deb. Twelve for the lake and a few more for twenty yards of brush to get to the cabin's back window."

"Can't we cut through the woods?"

"We'd need lights and he'd pick us off."

Rohr looked at the lake again. The day's high had been an invigorating forty-eight degrees and the sun had been down for hours. "You're going to freeze to death."

"I know."

"Let's find you a boat."

"He'd hear the motor or spot me in the moonlight," Cady said. "Plus, we don't have time to mess around."

"The shit you get me into."

"Deb, I don't know how to say this, but…"

"I know." Rohr nodded. "Let's just get this fucker done. Your plan's dumb enough to work."

Rohr ran to Cady's idling SUV. Cady stepped quietly to the end of the dock and, without hesitation, lowered himself into the ice-cold waters of Bass Lake.

CHAPTER SIXTY

The idea struck Lieutenant Rohr as she jumped behind the wheel of Cady's Escape. She poked at the FM settings until she found a classic rock station out of Grand Rapids. Rohr lowered all four of the Escape's windows, cranked the rock station to a level that portended hearing loss, and stepped on the gas.

Cady wasn't up on his Minnesota state history. He assumed the Land of Ten Thousand Lakes had been carved out by glaciers a million years or so ago—but after submerging himself into the frigid waters of Bass Lake, he wasn't so sure the glaciers had ever left. Cady kicked off hard from the dock post and glided underwater for as long as his lungs held out, and then cracked the surface and began swimming the crawl.

Cady heard blaring music, maybe a Rolling Stones song, that seemed to be coming from anywhere and everywhere. It had to be pissing off those trying to catch some shuteye in the homes around the lake. The lake dwellers would blame high school kids, and one or two of those awakened might even call the cops, but Cady knew it was the lieutenant ad-libbing, buying him cover as he swam the lake in order to come up on Volkov's flank.

On his tenth kick, Cady's underwear washed off. He felt the boxers begin to slide but made no effort to save them, as he'd then have to *Laurel and Hardy* the shorts for the rest of the trip. Besides, Cady thought, considering the temperature of the lake water, what they'd been covering up were now the size of raisins.

—

Rohr killed the radio when she hit US-2. She figured the Stones and the Who had gotten Cady through at least half of Bass Lake unnoticed. The agent was now on his own. Rohr turned west on US-2 and a minute later was in a blip on the map known as Cohasset. She pulled into a SuperAmerica gas station and poked around on the radio for the classical music station she'd bumped into when she'd come to check on Terri late last week. Rohr figured she'd keep that station at half level as she approached the resort. Not loud enough to piss off neighbors, but enough to help distract this Volkov motherfucker from anything going bump in the night.

Rohr had five minutes to make her agreed-upon entrance at Sundown Point Resort, even though she had doubts Cady could really swim the lake in that short timeframe. She felt for the FBI agent, recalling the strain in the agent's face and eyes, and knew that if anything happened to Terri, Cady would be a shattered man...and likely turn his Glock 22 on himself.

At the halfway point, Cady felt as though he'd been jabbed in the side with an ice pick. Repeatedly. He'd turned over to do the backstroke, but soon found it messed with his trajectory. He thought he was making great progress, only to flip back onto his stomach and find that he was aimed yards farther down the lakefront than where he needed to land. He did a stretch on his side until he heard the music disappear, and then he went breaststroke again.

He knew what it felt like to be caught inside an ice cube. He knew what the doomed souls on the *Titanic* felt like in their final moments. But he never stopped moving, as the realization slowly began to sink in that he might not make it across to the cabin to save Terri—and that drowning had suddenly become a possible outcome.

Rohr turned the Escape left onto Sundown Point Road, the path that traveled down Terri's side of Bass Lake. It was a dark gravel road, deserted at this time of night, which gave Rohr another idea. She flicked the SUV's headlights over to brights. There was no oncoming traffic for her to piss off, and if she was going to be a sitting duck.... why make it easy?

With a third of the lake left, Cady went underwater; whipping both legs and arms in a synchronized motion and gliding as far as he could before repeating the movement. Then he'd surface for a gulp or two of air before going back under. His heart beat so hard he thought it'd jackhammer through his ribcage.

During one stretch underwater, Cady flashed back to Quilling manor and their hidden basement room. Only it wasn't Hannah Erickson pale and motionless on the death table—it was Terri. The image made him snap his arms faster, his legs harder. He'd made a deadly mistake calling back the number on the prepaid cell, and it had brought the Wolf to Terri's door. If he'd gotten Terri killed, he'd find a way to take out Stepan Volkov if it was the last thing he ever did. Then he'd return to Bass Lake, swim out to the middle...and let go.

The last thirty yards, Cady dog paddled. And a piss-poor dog paddle it was. He was spent. His lungs were on fire as he glided toward the woods, until he was walking on his hands and knees through the wet muck of the weed bed, never stopping, pulling himself onto dry land by the branch of a dead tree. He feared his gasping for breath could be heard in Grand Rapids, but then he heard another sound off in the distance—a symphony, something classical, Mozart or someone else Terri might recognize.

Lieutenant Rohr had arrived.

Rohr threw the Escape into park on the final curve of Sundown Point Road, before it dead-ended at Terri's resort. She turned Beethoven down a notch and dialed Grand Rapids Police Chief Leigh Irwin's cell phone number, in her log from a call she'd made the previous week.

The chief answered groggily, as though he'd been asleep or on the verge of it. After forty seconds of Rohr speaking, Chief Irwin was wide awake. Words like *armed intruder* and *hostage* and *send ambulance* tended to have that effect on small-town chiefs of police.

Lieutenant Rohr turned Ludwig back up, slid across to the passenger seat, awkwardly got the Escape into drive, and headed into Sundown Point Resort.

Cady took a knee, groping the wet ground until he found what he needed: a jagged stick to slash at the Saran Wrap holding the Ziploc to his chest. He'd shaken uncontrollably for ten seconds before his mind commanded his body to stop. He wrenched and tore at the wrapping with the broken branch, gouging at his chest until he got a grip and was able to rip apart the layers of wrap, freeing the baggie containing his Glock. He zipped the bag open and pulled out his pistol.

Cady grimaced. Now came the hard part.

CHAPTER SIXTY-ONE

Cabin five was shrouded in darkness.

Terri stood atop one of the mismatched dining chairs, the noose around her neck snaking through a pulley that the man who called himself Bob Jarvis had attached to the wood ceiling. Her hands were loosely tied in front of her, the rope below her chin held slack.

"I'm not a barbarian," Jarvis had informed her. He hadn't even tightened Terri's bonds after she flung the water bottle he'd given her in his face.

The point of utmost discomfort came when Drew called. Jarvis had told her what was expected, but when the cell phone buzzed, Jarvis gave a quick tug to the line above her head to draw the noose taut, to focus Terri's mind on her own mortality. Jarvis placed the bottom of his boot against the lip of her chair—the implication clear—and then pressed speaker and held the phone in her direction.

After the call, the man she knew as Bob Jarvis had loosened her bonds.

Stepan Volkov had taken the screen off of the cabin's side window that faced the dirt road, and it was from here that he planned to shoot Cady in the head once the FBI agent parked on the grass and stepped from his car. He had a K100 Whisper with suppressor, and it would be impossible to miss from this distance. He would then bring Terri outside and use the K100 on her as well. He didn't have the heart to kick the chair out from under such a lovely soul, to leave Terri gasping and choking, clawing at her throat, her eyes bulging in a slow and cruel demise.

Plan B—and there was always a Plan B—lay across a dresser that Volkov had dragged from one of the cabin's two bedrooms and set in front of the side window. Plan B was a SIG SG 550 assault rifle… just in case he needed to take Sundown Point apart piece by piece in pursuit of Special Agent Cady. The SG 550 could be set for one round per trigger pull, bursts of three, or full auto, which Volkov would only use as a last resort. If Plan B came into play, he would have to disappear via the boat he'd rented from Terri. It was a rowboat with a nine-horsepower boat motor clamped on the back, more than enough to spirit him and his duffel bag away to the Pincherry Grove Resort on the farthest end of Bass Lake. Volkov had another car tucked away at Pincherry as part of Plan B.

Plan A, though, was the most desirable option, as Agent Cady and Terri Ingram would—like Assistant Director Mike Litchy—simply cease to exist. No bodies would ever be found, and even when friends and family eventually came looking, all they'd find would be Sundown Point Resort, apparently locked down in winter mode and—thanks to Volkov—several Las Vegas and Carnival Cruise brochures, which he'd already placed on top of Terri's desk. The lovebirds must have eloped to Vegas and then on to a cruise, all would think, and the trail would grow cold and colder yet, even after law enforcement got involved.

The sixties rock had faded and disappeared. Volkov had looked across the lake, thinking it a nice night for a bonfire, but couldn't spot any light or tell where the music was coming from. Maybe some teen hot-assing it in Daddy's car with his wingmen. It worked much the same in Russia—youngsters, lakes, liquor, cars, and fire. Strangely, though, the nights at Sundown Point Resort had been unusually peaceful, both quiet and serene.

"You know Drew's going to kill you." Terri spoke for the first time since the brief conversation with her fiancé.

Volkov checked his watch. He stood again on the neighboring chair and peeled off a strip of duct tape. He placed the tape gently across Terri's lips and stepped down in front of the resort owner.

He hated this part. Hers would not be a good death, not like Litchy or Dayna Parrish. He'd actually grown attached to Terri over the past two weeks and, in a different life, Volkov imagined she might be what he was looking for.

When Terri had come to cabin five with the cleaner—as well as a glass of homemade lemonade—it had pained him to sneak up from behind and slip the noose about her throat. Volkov had actually felt pleased when Terri managed to tag him in the ribs with an elbow before he'd gotten her under control. He hoped it would bruise.

A woman like Terri should leave a mark.

"If it comes to it, please don't struggle," Volkov said and gestured as though grasping at a rope about his neck. "Just let it happen, Terri, so it'll be quicker."

Terri blinked back tears from the corners of her eyes. She clearly didn't want to let him see her cry.

Volkov was famished. He had been pleased to hear Special Agent Cady was unknowingly preparing to cater his own funeral. The Mexican food would hit the spot, as Volkov had a long night of clean-up ahead of him.

He turned again to the resort owner. "Situations like these tend to take on a life of their own. Later—I may not have the appropriate amount of time." Volkov cleared his throat. "You're a beautiful spirit, Terri. I wanted to go with, 'Death lies on her, like an untimely frost,' from *Romeo and Juliet*, but you mentioned studying Thoreau at university, and perhaps one of Henry David's might be more apropos." Volkov turned his attention to the side window as he intoned, "'Truth and roses have thorns about them...'"

CHAPTER SIXTY-TWO

Lieutenant Rohr passed Terri's lake house at the entrance of Sundown Point Resort, and a second later beeped "Shave and a Haircut" on the horn as she passed the equipment barn. She was getting ahead of herself, and would save the "two bits" for when she pulled up against the schoolhouse, but she wanted all eyes on her for this portion of the performance. Cady had the herculean task—to cross the lake and slay the beast—whereas hers was more a form of art.

Lieutenant Rohr's task was misdirection.

Cady slogged through the undergrowth, making his way through yards of brush on the woodland side of cabin five. Every few steps he paused to shudder, to let his body shake out a spasm of shivers. He might not have hypothermia yet—what with traipsing about naked in forty-something degrees after swimming a quarter of a mile in forty-something degrees—but he was certain he'd caught its kissing cousin. At one point something dark moved across of his left foot. Cady jumped back and almost swore. He thanked god for Rohr's ingenuity, as the strains of classical music helped cover his footfalls. He prayed the Wolf's attention was focused solely on the Ford Escape.

Even before Cady hit the tree line, the headlights from the approaching SUV danced around the edges of cabin five, casting a chiaroscuro of light and shadow. He looked down and noticed that most of his lower body was blackened with mud from the lake weeds and the dirt of the brush. If Volkov covered his bases by peeking out the kitchen window, the window facing the forest, Cady would be fully exposed in the five steps required to make it to the side of the cabin. Point blank. Cady heard Rohr's friendly beeps of the horn and cursed silently.

He was running late.

Volkov pulled the curtain on the side window open a quarter inch and watched the oncoming SUV. He squinted against the bright headlights, wondering if that was how the townies drove at night on this stretch of lake road, constantly on the lookout for deer or coyotes or crossing turtles.

Volkov held the silenced K100 in his right hand, his shooting hand, and listened to what he pegged as Beethoven's Fifth. He heard Cady honk out a silly tune and watched as the Ford Escape passed the barn, the agent heading slowly toward his fate. Suddenly the Escape twitched to a halt. Mildly annoyed, Volkov waited for Cady to get out of the driver's seat and hike the remaining distance to cabin five, but instead he received two more beeps of the SUV's horn and then nothing.

This smelled wrong. First, why would Cady park the Escape way back by the playground, and second, why was the agent not exiting his vehicle? Volkov set the K100 down on the dresser and reached for the SG 550.

Looked like it would be Plan B after all.

Terri lifted her bound hands up to her throat and slipped the tips of her fingers over the noose. This son of a bitch was about to murder the man Terri loved, and she wasn't going to let that happen…not if she could help it.

Hidden in the tree line, Cady gave a two-second scan of the immediate area—lake, dock, cabin, trees, grass, dirt—in case he could spot a roving Volkov. He then ran the five paces to the side window and came face to face with his mistake. Terri's cabins all sat on concrete blocks, which made the windows a bitch for Peeping Toms, and it was all Cady could do to get an eyeball in the lower corner of the windowpane.

His heart caught in his throat.

All the windows in Terri's cabins swung in sideways, with hinges on one edge and a latch on the other. The kitchen window was latched shut, but enough light seeped in from the Escape's headlights for Cady to make out shapes and, through the ill-fitting Goodwill drapes, Terri standing on a chair, a rope around her neck somehow attached to the ceiling. Her hands appeared bound, yet she was struggling with the noose around her throat. A dark figure stood beside the window, facing the dirt road. Volkov, his back to Cady, peeked out an edge of the window frame, a pistol with an extension in his right hand and pointed at the ceiling.

Cady heard two final beeps from the SUV and watched as Volkov set down his handgun and picked up an assault rifle.

Volkov flipped open the window and leveled his SG 550 when Terri made her swing.

The thought had occurred to her when Bob Jarvis, or whoever the bastard really was, suggested she not struggle when the time came. What her would-be killer failed to realize was that *not struggling* was a concept foreign to Terri Ingram. And though her hands were bound, she worked eight fingers down into the slack between the noose and her throat and brought her thumbs up from underneath. She gripped the rope like a trapeze artist clutching the horizontal bar and kicked off from her chair.

Terri hit the man's shoulder as hard as she could with the heels of both feet, hoping to knock him off-kilter, to buy Drew a second or two to duck down, but the man was a rock. He quickly realigned himself and began to fire.

And Terri Ingram began to choke.

CHAPTER SIXTY-THREE

Rohr punched two finals honks on the Escape's horn and then threw herself backward and down into the passenger-side footwell. The doors were locked, but the windows were open and strains of Beethoven continued to fill the air. The lieutenant's main fear was that this Wolf motherfucker might not be holed up in cabin five, but, instead, roving the campground. He'd see an empty vehicle and would have to step up to the driver's or passenger's side window in order to spot her. But that was a two-way street, and Rohr had her Beretta 92 at the ready, aimed at the driver's side window while her head swiveled back and forth between both side windows.

The serenity of Bass Lake was shattered a half instant later as repeated bursts of 5.6 millimeter rounds cut a line across the dashboard of the Ford Escape, chest level, spraying the safety glass of the windshield and shredding the driver and passenger seats, as well as the seats in back. Anyone sitting up would have been cut in half.

Jesus Christ! It was all Rohr could do to contain herself, to keep from jumping out of the SUV and bolting for the barn. Cady was right—Volkov was in cabin five, but the prick had brought a goddamned howitzer to a gunfight. In the hush that followed, Rohr realized Volkov's first victim had been Beethoven.

She couldn't stay in the footwell. If Volkov's cannon could take out the radio, another spurt might puncture the dashboard and footwell. *Probably cut right through to where I'm hidden. Fucker thinks I'm done, but he'll be out to check in another second or two... and where the hell is that goddamned Cady?*

Rohr put two fingers on the door latch. *Fuck it*, she thought as she shoved open the passenger door and dived behind the schoolhouse. Another spurt of bullets turned the car door to Swiss cheese; more rounds ripped apart the cheap plywood of the playhouse. Rohr rolled sideways as though she were on fire until she came up even with the kids' slide, now blocked—thank God—from cabin five by the corner of cabin one. The schoolhouse was a pile of toothpicks.

Although it seemed an eternity, Rohr figured maybe ten seconds had passed since that first burst of gunfire. That's when she heard the individual gunshots.

Special Agent Cady had arrived.

Metal lawn chairs.

Terri had several of those relics peppered about the resort; the weather couldn't hurt them, and they allowed guests to sit and gawk at the lake. If Cady could stand on one, Volkov would become the fish in the barrel. He spotted one of the chairs at the front of the cabin across the dirt path, but that was a world too far.

A burst of gunfire cracked his thought process down to one word: *Rohr*.

Cady backed up several steps and then literally ran up the side of cabin five. He slammed a left forearm down on the one-inch ledge outside the window, both his feet planted against the siding. Volkov was huddled in front of the window, blowing the shit out of Cady's Escape, and...*my god*...Cady saw Terri swinging from the ceiling rope, hands clutching at her neck, legs kicking at Volkov.

Cady shot through the window, nailing Volkov between the shoulder blades.

He smashed his right forearm against the window frame as hard as he could, bursting the screen, popping the side latch and screws out of the woodwork, the window bouncing sideways on its hinges against the wall. Then Cady was slipping through the opening, a peculiar birth, gun in front of him, his second shot striking Volkov in the left shoulder, spinning the Russian about and causing him to lose control of his rifle. Volkov now faced Cady, his mouth open in confusion.

Cady squeezed twice more, center mass, driving Volkov against the wall. Then he wrenched himself the rest of the way through the window, sliding hard off the sink top and tumbling to the floor. He looked up in time to see that Volkov was somehow back in play, snatching the pistol off the dresser top with his right hand and swinging it back toward Cady. *He's got Kevlar* rang in Cady's mind as he raised his Glock 22, but he could tell he wouldn't make it in time.

The lieutenant peeked around the road side of cabin one. She spotted an arm and shoulder in the window from where she'd been taking fire. Rohr knew she couldn't hit him at this range with her handgun and feared her bullets would end up hitting Cady or Terri, so she began unloading her Beretta along the roofline near the bedroom. Let the fucker know he had it on two fronts.

More misdirection.

Volkov was shocked that Cady had survived to roll out of the passenger door. The SUV's headlamps made it impossible to distinguish a figure behind the wheel, but he didn't think Terri's kicking had bought the agent enough time to dodge the repeated bursts of three from the SG 550. His next—

Something struck his spine and then shoulder with the force of a baseball bat.

Volkov spun, dropping the rifle and spotting a naked Agent Cady, dripping with mud like something from a monster movie, squeezing through the opposite window. More of Cady's bullets knocked Volkov back against the wall, but Volkov's vest seemed to hold, and he went for the K100 as Cady nose-dived to the floor. Shots from whoever survived the Ford Escape batted against the cabin and Volkov jerked away from the open window. He had the K100 in his hand as Cady looked up.

He had the agent beat.

Terri did her best to hold the pull-up, like a kid in gym class. Her fingers were crushed into her throat when she left the chair, making it all but impossible to breathe. For a second she caught the chair with a tiptoe, swayed for several seconds, but lost it and began to swing. She saw Drew come in and fall to the floor, saw Jarvis smash against the wall but reach for his handgun. Saw him dodge toward her when someone outside began returning fire. Saw Jarvis getting the drop on Drew.

As she swung toward Jarvis, Terri aimed a desperate kick at his forearm.

Terri's foot caught Volkov's right hand, and the bullet meant for Cady's chest went into the ceiling.

Then Cady shot out the Wolf's eye—the one below his scarred eyebrow. Cady's next round missed, but his third passed through the base of Volkov's throat. There was no need for a fourth bullet. No Kevlar vest would bring the Wolf back this time.

Cady yanked out the silverware drawer, its contents raining to the floor. He grabbed the fillet knife and was on the kitchen chair in seconds, his good arm around Terri, supporting her, as he carved desperately at the rope above her head. A second later, they fell backward onto the floor. Cady rolled Terri onto her back, jerked her fingers from beneath the rope to help her breathe, arched her neck, and opened her mouth to make sure her airway wasn't blocked. Then he carefully worked the tight rope loose.

Terri took a huge gulp of air and began coughing uncontrollably.

"I knew you'd figure it out and come for me," Terri said when the coughing ceased, raspy voiced and choking on her words. "I knew you'd come." She took a real look at Cady for the first time, wondering if she'd sunk into shock. "Where are your clothes?"

A throat got cleared and Cady and Terri looked up.

Lieutenant Rohr stood outside the window Volkov had been firing through. She took in the scene for a beat or two as sirens blared in the background.

"You fucking Feebs ever make a normal arrest?" Rohr asked. "Nice ass, by the way."

CHAPTER SIXTY-FOUR

Cady, Terri, and Rohr walked to the entrance of Sundown Point Resort to greet Grand Rapids Police Chief Leigh Irwin and his brigade of squad cars and paramedics. As guns were drawn, the lieutenant held her badge in the air for all to see. Next to her came Cady, wrapped in a quilt pilfered from the bed in cabin five. Terri stood at his side, one hand on Cady's back, the other gently touching her throat.

After a five-minute pow-wow with Chief Irwin, two squad cars were sent back to town and Terri was sent to see the paramedics. The lieutenant walked the chief and two of his detectives back to cabin five, where they began to process the crime scene. Rohr played dumb, coughing up only the basics: *I got a distress call from Special Agent Cady and came to help. The dead guy with the elephant gun tried to kill me and Terri, but Cady popped a cap in his ass. End of story.*

Cady, on the other hand, took the world's longest shower. He let the hot water wash over him, pound away at his shoulder blades, and bring him back to the land of the living. He didn't plan on ever exiting the shower stall, but that decision was made for him as the water eventually turned lukewarm and then cold. Cady tossed on a pair of jeans and a sweatshirt, dry-swallowed four aspirin, and then went to hunt down Terri.

One of the paramedics informed him that Terri appeared okay, but they wanted to bring her to the hospital for X-rays. Cady walked his fiancée to the ambulance, told her how much he loved her, how sorry he was to have brought this to her door, and how he'd come to Grand Itasca hospital as soon as Chief Irwin was done with him. He started to say other things but Terri leaned in and kissed him on the lips.

"You saved me, G-Man."

"I put you in danger," Cady said. "You should slap me."

Terri squeezed his hand.

He squeezed back.

Peter Gallion's team of four no-nonsense-looking men, all dressed in black fatigues, arrived in a dark van a little more than an hour later. Gallion's operatives appeared genuinely disappointed that their services would not be required in those early morning hours, and, after a quick recon of Sundown Point Resort, went down to one of the docks to smoke cigarettes. Analyst Davidson and Peter Gallion himself arrived behind these men in a second car.

After surveying the crime scene—formerly known as cabin five—Gallion took control of the situation and gathered the two Grand Rapids PD detectives, Cady, and Lieutenant Rohr into the lake house's living room. The four sat quietly and avoided eye contact for five minutes before Gallion, Davidson, and Chief Irwin entered the room. Without so much as an introduction, Gallion informed them that tonight's incident was part of an ongoing federal investigation, and that the deceased gunman in cabin five was part of a gun-running cartel. Gallion's people had been investigating him as part of an interdiction operation targeting cross-border smuggling to and from Canada. It was imperative that those in attendance keep this information to themselves; leaks to the media would not be tolerated, as there were several undercover agents in play and reckless leaks would place their lives in jeopardy…and so forth and so on.

In other words, Peter Gallion lied through his teeth.

"I trust that, in a situation as crucial as this, we will have your complete cooperation," Gallion said. "Personally, I cannot thank you enough for your actions tonight in circumstances that, quite frankly, could have turned out very differently."

Cady didn't bother to ask Gallion exactly what identification he'd flashed at Chief Irwin, but the head of Grand Rapids PD seemed relieved to collect his detectives, head back to the city, and attempt to salvage what little might be left of a night's sleep. On their way out the door, the older of the two police investigators paused long enough to smirk at Cady and shake his head. Cady patted the detective on the shoulder.

Nice to know someone's BS detector was firing on all four cylinders.

"Deb," Cady said as he dropped Lieutenant Rohr off by her Mazda at the soon-to-be-open bait shop, "I owe you big time."

"Yes, you do." Then she said, "You know that rope he had around Terri's throat?"

"Yes."

"Kal Hoyer continues to plead innocent—keeps swearing he didn't strangle his *soul mate*."

Cady nodded. The lieutenant was a full step ahead of him, and he recalled how quickly he'd left D.C. on first hearing of Taylor Ganser's demise. He thought about Dayna Parrish's mock suicide, hanging by a rope from the garage rafters, as well as the rope that Stepan Volkov had tied around Terri's neck. And for the first time he began to believe that the pierced-faced boy with the lightning-bolt eyebrows was innocent.

"Is this thing over?" Rohr asked.

"Not yet."

"Be careful, then. I've grown kind of attached to you—you're like the pain-in-the-ass brother I never had."

Cady drove the resort's beater pickup through town on his way to Grand Itasca hospital. Gallion told him it'd take his crew an hour to scrub cabin five and then they'd vamoose. Gallion hoped Terri's X-rays checked out okay, and told Cady to call him and let him know—there were other issues, he added, that the two of them needed to discuss.

Cady felt as though he could sleep for a month, only he knew that wouldn't be happening because he'd been honest with Lieutenant Rohr. It wasn't over yet. There was one more thing he had to take care of.

The Lynchpin.

CHAPTER SIXTY-FIVE

"Either Litchy is dead," Cady explained the CIA's conundrum, "or the treasure and the fake passport were left behind as a ploy to make us believe he's dead."

"I think he's dead." Jund was ensconced behind his desk in his recently reopened office. "The Litchy I knew wouldn't have left the dirty pictures."

Cady shrugged at the AD's response. "Feet first or walking upright, without a body it's open for debate."

Terri was stuffed in the Sofitel near Dupont Circle—under a false name and on the Bureau's dime—with orders to text Cady at the top of every hour. Tomorrow he'd move her to the Avenue Suites Georgetown.

"The man brought pettiness to a new low," said Agent Preston. "He wasn't happy at being exposed for what he was, and he sent Volkov to kill Drew."

"But that's not how this works," Jund replied, "and Volkov was too valuable an asset to waste on small-minded vengeance."

"We're talking about a guy that had an innocent girl killed just to draw me out of D.C."

"I never thought the man had an IQ above freezing." Jund shook his head. "Clearly, I underestimated the son of a bitch. Jesus, we're linking that passport of his to all sorts of shiny things. It's a pretty big 401k to burn, unless Litchy's gone doornail or it's one of many identities he had access to."

Cady looked at Jund. "You mind if I wade through some of that information?"

—

Cady rubbed at his eyes as though that would help discredit the notion that had occurred to him as he reviewed the trove of financial treasures traced back from Litchy's alias. It was four o'clock in the afternoon. Terri had just texted to let him know that another hour had passed and all was well. He was working out of Preston's office, sitting on a folding chair in front of a folding table. Liz was busy tapping away at her keyboard.

The assistant director's falsified passport was in the identity of a Belgian citizen and international businessman who went by the name of Jens De Smet and, on paper, hailed from the seaport city of Antwerp. Amid De Smet's laundry list of nest eggs and other investments was an offshore shell company by the name of Starr Percussions, a corporation that the Bureau's forensic accountants had sunk their teeth into with gusto.

Starr Percussions, based in Costa Rica, made serious *dinero* supplying orchestra equipment from the four families of strings, woodwinds, brass and, of course, percussion—a full-service supplier of violins, cellos, and harps, oboes, flutes and clarinets, trombones and tubas, cymbals and snare drums—to vendors, which then turned around and distributed the instruments to schools, universities, and orchestra halls in Europe and South America. Starr Percussions professed to have warehouses in cities like Buenos Aires and Sao Paulo; however, Starr Percussions and all of its vendors and suppliers, as well as all addresses and locations of their operations, existed solely on paper.

With the Jens De Smet identity in hand, the forensic accountants were able to walk back the cat and fill in any missing pieces of the financial puzzle. Profits from Starr Percussions worked a byzantine path into a variety of De Smet's Swiss bank accounts, however briefly, then pinged their way into bank accounts in nations with notoriously laidback banking laws, such as—in Litchy-slash-De Smet's case—Panama and the Bahamas. At this point—and the accountants were currently digging deeper yet—De Smet's capital went on to entrepreneur endeavors of a more legitimate nature.

"You know the drill, Drew," Agent Preston said as they pored through the information linked to Mike Litchy's alter ego. "An elaborate front company used to make bad money good and return it to the bad guy."

Cady tapped at his smartphone absentmindedly. He had first dismissed the notion as lunacy. It couldn't be true. But the more he fixated on it, the more sense it made until…until it made perfect sense. Once convinced, he went over it again—and then again—trying to knock it down from each and every angle, trying to devil's-advocate the notion away.

Counterarguments were to no avail.

Cady was now certain that Assistant Director Mike Litchy had left his house feet first. In fact, Litchy was likely interred in a slab of cement at the bottom of the Atlantic Ocean or buried in a shallow bed of lime. Litchy hadn't sent Stepan Volkov to kill him. Not at all. In fact, Volkov held no deep allegiance to Assistant Director Litchy. And Litchy certainly was not the Lynchpin, but rather another spoke in the wheel of the intelligence network that the real Lynchpin had established. As for the Lynchpin himself, he was hiding right here in the stack of information Cady had assembled, and that explained why the Wolf had been sent in his direction.

How did Cady know this?

Because he now knew the Lynchpin's real name. And he now knew why Volkov had been sent to kill him.

Cady stared at Agent Preston, working diligently on the computer in front of her. After a moment, Preston sensed his gaze and looked up. Their eyes locked.

"What?" she asked.

"We've got to see Jund."

CHAPTER SIXTY-SIX

Cady handed in his resignation. Effective immediately. He was going to throw himself wholeheartedly into remodeling Sundown Point Resort, as well as price-to-sell his two-bedroom in Canton, Ohio, which had been sitting vacant for much of the past year.

It was all Roland Jund and Liz Preston could do to rent an event room at the Madison for a Thursday night shindig. Jund even presented Cady with a nice watch—not a gold one, but a high-end waterproof Timex. Liz found a bakery that baked a giant carrot cake—Cady's favorite—with a fishing pole in orange frosting on top. He got a card from Ron Bergmann and the Minneapolis bunch saying they had dibs on taking Cady and Terri out to The Melting Pot, a fondue joint, the next time the couple was in the Twin Cities.

Agents that Cady had not seen in years attended. Even Director Connor Green popped in with Paul Speedling for a minute to pat Cady on the shoulder and wish him well. Some of Cady's newfound CIA acquaintances stopped by. Peter Gallion offered him a job, to which Cady replied with a smile as he walked the head of the CIC Analysis Group over to the serving table and said, "Have another piece of cake, Peter."

Eggs Nolte, looking jubilant as ever, arrived with his chauffeur. Inquisitive as always, Eggs began peppering Cady with questions on what it took to run a resort in Minnesota. Cady, a novice in resort management, did his best to answer the old man's queries, but when Eggs started in on how big the walleyes got in Bass Lake, Cady pawned him off on Terri, who was only too eager to fill the ex-agent in.

Cady grabbed David Davidson and pulled him aside before Terri could meet him and begged the CIA analyst to visit Sundown Point in his Humdinger's persona. Davidson hemmed and hawed, expressed concern about getting punched by Cady's better half, and finally relented, telling Cady he'd only do it for an hour or until he felt Terri was about to explode, whichever came first.

After his longtime peers managed to squeeze a few drinks into him, Cady stood up and gave the world's shortest speech to a room full of friends and colleagues. Cady thanked one and all for coming and then informed the crowd that if any of them managed to get lost and found themselves in northern Minnesota, he had a twenty-five percent discount for any agents from the Federal Bureau of Investigation, as well as ten percent off for those from Langley.

All in all, it was a great going-away party...especially for someone who had no intention of going away.

CHAPTER SIXTY-SEVEN

The Lynchpin sat at the park bench and worked the crossword puzzle. He sucked the salt out of a shell before splitting it open with his teeth to get at the peanut beneath, then spit the sodden husk into an empty cup. He didn't need that level of sodium chloride intake in his diet, but it had been a habit since his childhood and, surprisingly, considering his *unique* line of business, he had never been at risk for high blood pressure.

The Lynchpin popped another peanut shell in his mouth.

Had he his druthers, he'd have gone dark for six months, but these were turbulent times—with Volkov's death and the debacle at Bass Lake—and, as a direct result, there remained infrastructure concerns and logistics to address, in addition to one hell of an outstanding issue. In other words, the show must go on. And the Lynchpin would be damned if he'd use a computer or phone line. Often, the old ways worked best.

Although his ledger had been filling with debits of late, there were two recent credits for him to reflect upon. Although the best-laid plans for Roland Jund had gone further than awry—they'd crashed and burned flamboyantly—the recent discoveries of just how far Assistant Director Mike Litchy had been burning candles on both ends were working their magic, encompassing all that the Roland Jund narrative lacked: the ring of truth.

Michael Litchy had betrayed his country, and had been doing so for many years. And though Litchy had been of tremendous value, the man was a first-class boor; he behaved erratically and had the impulse control of a toddler. None would shed tears over the

AD's disappearance. In fact, his departure worked to the Lynchpin's advantage in that many of Litchy's hunters still considered the AD to be in play, holding him responsible for Bass Lake; there were even signs they suspected Litchy of being the Lynchpin himself. The Lynchpin would play to the searchers' suspicions—movements in cyberspace attributed to Litchy, a sighting of the treasonous AD in Zurich perhaps, nebulous substance to keep the searchers forever on the prowl.

Litchy had sometimes even fancied himself the Lynchpin, as, among a variety of other tasks, he'd worked the Parrish cell and had the Wolf purportedly at his beck and call. But in the end, Litchy had been exactly like so many who came before him: a disposable instrument to be used only until it had served its purpose.

The second credit in the ledger was Special Agent Drew Cady's announcement of his immediate retirement. Evidently, what had occurred at the resort in Minnesota had rattled Cady to the core, given him pause to stop and smell the roses. The Lynchpin sincerely liked Cady and had already spotted the agent one life by giving Volkov the nod to lure Cady out of the nation's capital by creating mischief in Duluth. But Volkov's interference had only delayed matters, and now Cady knew something he didn't know he knew...yet...and it had to remain that way. The Lynchpin cursed himself for having a bit of fun when it came to setting up Mike Litchy's post-FBI nest egg. Cady might spot his lapse in judgment and, if Cady lived up to expectations, he'd deliberate upon the matter until the tumblers clicked into place. It was why Volkov had been dispatched to the resort on Bass Lake in the first place, when the decision to eliminate AD Litchy from the census had been made.

So, alas, Drew Cady remained a loose end, even in retirement. It was high time for Cady to be deactivated, permanently. The only question was: how?

The FBI agent, though youngish, had been in and out of hospitals for several years due to an assortment of operations on his wounded hand, as well as treatment for other injuries, including the ones suffered recently in a certain mansion on Lake Superior.

Perhaps a blood clot or stroke? A brain aneurysm, maybe, or a heart attack? Or perhaps the thin ice on that lake behind his resort?

—

The satellite views of the Lynchpin's house were worthless, Cady decided, since they weren't planning an all-out assault. Intercepting his mail had been a similar waste of time. The ten teams of two drivers made sure the Lynchpin never saw the same car twice in his rear or sideview mirrors. Director Connor Green made the decision not to go after the Lynchpin's landline, and no Internet provider was associated with his home address.

On the other hand, the unmanned aerial systems—surveillance drones—on loan from Homeland Security kicked ass. The two drones in use, which could operate undetected in both rural and urban settings, were able to track individual pedestrians and vehicles at altitudes of twenty-thousand-plus feet.

On the first of the Lynchpin's *chaperoned* outings, there were U-turns, bouts of speeding, sudden curb stops, and laps through strip-mall parking lots until Green had the coverage teams pull their cars back and left the chaperoning to the UASs in the air. When it became apparent that their target was on Nebraska Avenue heading toward Battery Kemble Park, Green ordered his team of undercovers to converge into Battery Kemble from the Chain Bridge Road and MacArthur Boulevard entrances. Young lovers holding hands, a dreadlocked man acting reckless on a skateboard, and even a woman walking a terrier were among the many surveillance experts to report back that the target had taken a brisk stroll along the walking trail and then returned to his car.

Yesterday, realizing that the Lynchpin was working his way toward Fort Dupont Park, Green ordered the surveillance experts to "kick it in the ass" to be on the scene ahead of the target. The two frat boys with the Frisbee, the middle-aged guy in the cheap suit camped on a bench with the want ads, the young woman pushing a stroller, the homeless man talking to himself—all undercover FBI agents.

"You've got enough characters for a Broadway musical," Jund said to Green. "I keep waiting for the Fiddler on the Roof to show up."

"He'll be next to the Indian chief from the Village People."

While the two Bureau executives chuckled, Cady and Preston

sat on a fold-down bench alongside the brown UPS delivery van/ command center and did their best to stay out of the way.

The Lynchpin meandered through Fort Dupont for nearly a half hour. At one point he bought a soft drink from a park vendor and then walked no more than twenty feet before depositing the unsipped cup into a trash bin and headed to a bench in the shade, where he worked his puzzle book in between glances toward the bin. After nearly an hour of this, the Lynchpin stood and headed quickly toward his car.

"He's testing the waters," Green said, but instructed the homeless man to stay on the trash bin and the fake cop to monitor the vendor. Hours later, as the bin was emptied by Park Services and an industrial garbage bag brought back to the main pavilion, the homeless man had a spiritually fulfilling time sorting through authentic trash and nothing else. The kid working the refreshment kiosk turned out to be a nineteen-year-old college dropout, making pocket change while trying to figure out what was next in his life's journey.

And this day, when it became clear that the target was advancing on Creek Hill Park, Green had a different cast of characters on scene with minutes to spare.

Yes, the drones kicked ass.

Cady and Preston had immediately brought Cady's hypothesis regarding Mike Litchy's offshore shell company to Roland Jund's attention. Jund, looking as though his kidneys had been polished against a cheese grater, led his two agents into the reception room of Director Connor Green's eleventh-story corner office. Jund barged past Green's administrative secretary and begged the director to exit a web conference and grant him fifteen minutes.

His meeting granted, Jund led his two agents into Green's inner sanctum and the four had a heart-to-heart. Green started out hostile toward Cady as the special agent began weaving his tapestry regarding Litchy's shell company, but the director of the Bureau's Counterintelligence Division became tightlipped toward the end of the explanation. Once Cady concluded, Green held up a palm, signaling those seated about his study to remain silent. The director stared at the back of his hand for several moments before saying four words.

"There are no coincidences."

With that, an ad hoc subcommittee of the Lynchpin taskforce was formed and Connor Green's opinion toward Agent Cady softened dramatically. It was in Green's inner office that Cady's immediate resignation was devised, the safe house for Cady and Terri reserved, and a surveillance strategy hatched against a most formidable adversary. Were Cady a cynic, he might have hazarded a guess that Connor Green's change in attitude toward him had more to do with being on the giving end in a turf war, at long last, than with Cady's charm and rapier-like wit.

Either way, it had all led them to where they stood now, in the back of a UPS van on the east side of Creek Hill Park, staring into a bank of monitors containing images of the Lynchpin as he sat on a park bench, working a puzzle book and munching on peanuts.

CHAPTER SIXTY-EIGHT

"He's under the bridge," the female of the necking duo on the picnic blanket alerted the command truck. "He just went under the bridge."

"You got a visual?" Connor Green asked.

"Can't see what he's doing," the necking woman replied. "Jim's adjusting the basket."

The necking couple was a hundred yards out. As she spoke, monitor seven tilted toward a walkway that arched over a thin stream of water and zoomed in on the wooden overpass. It was hard for Cady to decipher much of anything at this angle and distance. For once the drones were worthless.

"Team seven?"

"He's alone down there," a hoop shooter from the basketball court responded. "You want us to take him?"

"Sir," Cady cut in. "Couldn't he still be testing the waters?"

"We caught Robert Hanssen under a footbridge at Foxstone Park."

"That's why it seems so obvious—to draw us out."

"Negative, team seven," Green spoke into his mic and then turned to Cady. "Drawing us out or not, Drew, we'll have to take him at the exit."

"But what if that's a ruse?" Agent Preston asked. "What if he's got nothing on him?"

"Then we go with what we've got. Suspicious behavior and one hell of a coincidence."

"I'm afraid that won't be enough," Preston persisted.

"Then I'll have to bang on tables at Langley."

—

The Lynchpin came up the bank on the other side of the walkway, then took the footbridge halfway over the small river, leaned against the rail, and popped another peanut into his mouth. He scanned Creek Hill Park—a beautiful day for late October—and then spit the peanut shell into the water below him. After another minute of looking around, he sauntered back to the park bench he'd recently vacated, took the puzzle book from his jacket pocket, and resumed work on the crossword.

"I wonder if there's something in that book he hauls around," Jund said. "Codes or something. Or maybe that's what they swap."

Connor Green shrugged. "Could be."

"He's on the move again," said Cady.

The Lynchpin reholstered his puzzle book and walked onto the sand of the playground. He settled in on a swing for a few seconds, and then shoved off with his feet and began to swing back and forth.

"Fall back, team one," Green spoke into the mic. Monitor seven, transmitted from the necking couple's picnic basket a football field away, zoomed in on the park's playground.

The FBI agents in the back of the UPS van watched as a mother lifted her child off the little kids' slide, wiped his nose, and attempted to fit the now-screaming tot back into the stroller. It turned into a battle royale as the three-year-old's legs stiffened like planks and he fought mightily against vacating the play area.

"Is that her real child?" Preston asked.

"Yes."

"The joys of motherhood."

The Lynchpin walked over to an old-fashioned merry-go-round, a circle of heavy metal that could seat six kids between the rails with room for several more in the center. The Lynchpin placed a hand on one of the outer handles and swept it sideways. He repeated the process until the merry-go-round began to spin on its own head of steam. Then the Lynchpin stepped back and watched as it continued rotating of its own accord, gradually slowing until it came to a stop.

The Lynchpin walked halfway around the merry-go-round and sat down between two handrails. His back was now to the necking couple, but the images transmitted from the hoop shooter's gym bag caught him dead center on monitor three. He scratched at something on one of the rails with a fingernail.

"What's he pulling off?" Cady asked.

Connor Green had his eyes nearly flush with the monitor. "I think that's a piece of tape." Green looked from Jund to Cady to Preston. "Some kind of a drop signal."

The Lynchpin rolled the small piece of white tape into a tiny ball and flipped it off his thumbnail toward the grass. He leaned forward, reaching toward his feet as though stretching, and then both hands disappeared beneath the merry-go-round. A second later, he sat up and palmed something the size of a deck of cards into his coat pocket.

"We got him!" Director Green shouted as though welcoming in a new year. "We got him!"

The Lynchpin popped another peanut into his mouth as he followed the trail leading back to the park's entrance and the parking lot where his car waited. He sucked the salt from the shell, split it open with his tongue, and spit the empty husk onto the grass beside the walkway, and then looked up.

The Lynchpin swallowed the peanut in surprise.

—

Cady, Preston, Jund, and Green moved rapidly to meet the man they'd had under round-the-clock surveillance for the past several days. The Lynchpin spotted them heading his way; his head froze for an instant before glancing over his shoulder, noting the crowd of Green's park extras hustling his direction. He turned back toward the agents jogging his way, an amused smile on his lips at the folly of flight. As the group approached, the Lynchpin's eyes settled on Cady.

"That had to be the world's shortest retirement, Agent Cady."

Cady nodded but remained silent as the four agents stood in front of the master manipulator. The hoop shooter from the basketball court patted the man down from behind and removed both the puzzle book and a small envelope from the Lynchpin's jacket pocket.

"It was my 1858 Starr Percussion Army Revolver, wasn't it?" the Lynchpin asked, still staring at Cady.

Starr Percussions was the shell company set up by the Lynchpin for Assistant Director Mike Litchy's post-Bureau life of luxury. It was also similar in name to a certain six-shot, double-action percussion revolver that Cady had admired in a glass trophy cabinet of antique weaponry at a farm in Fauquier County.

"You never should have shown us your antebellum room."

"I'm getting senile," Eggs Nolte said. "Five years ago you'd never have set foot inside, but I wished to show off my collection of coins to a kindred spirit."

There would be a million questions to ask and then a million more when Connor Green brought Peter Gallion and the CIA into the mix. But Cady's part was done. He turned to leave.

"Agent Cady," Nolte called out.

Cady turned back. It was likely a trick of the sun, but Cady swore the old spymaster's trademark grin broadened, lighting up a wrinkled face.

"I warned you that the penetration was insidious."

"Yes, you did," Cady said, and turned and left the park.

CHAPTER SIXTY-NINE

"JoAnne is coming home tomorrow."

Roland Jund greeted them at the front door. He'd invited Cady, Terri, and Liz Preston over for a steak dinner on Cady and Terri's last night in D.C. before their return flight to Minnesota in the morning.

"That's wonderful news, Roland," Terri said, giving the assistant director a hug.

Jund led the trio into the living room, which seemed more a shrine to crushed beer cans and half-eaten pizza slices, and picked up a box of Hefty garbage bags.

"I let the cleaning lady go during my, um, sabbatical." Jund began divvying out individual garbage bags to his confused guests. "Unfortunately, I was never able to keep it as spotless as anticipated."

"We save you from being hanged for treason," Cady said, "and now we get to clean your house?"

The AD shook his head. "They never really hang anyone anymore." Jund handed Cady a bag. "And it's not really cleaning so much as getting rid of the clutter, you know, for JoAnne's arrival."

"I'm more than happy to help," Terri said, giving Cady a playful, chiding look. "Where do you want me to start?"

"I knew you'd be a sport. If I could have you take the lower level, and, Liz?"

"Reporting for duty, *sir*."

"If you could take the kitchen, that would be greatly appreciated."

Terri headed for the basement staircase. Liz rolled her eyes as she passed Cady and headed for Jund's kitchen.

"Now, Drew," Jund instructed, "the main floor needs just a tad bit of touch-up."

"What area of the house will you be taking?"

"Why, I'm tossing the shrimp and steak on the barbie." Jund marched off as though deeply offended by Cady's insinuation.

It was all Cady could do to keep from lifting the beer cans from the bottom and letting the backwash drain over the carpet and furniture, but he kept telling himself he was doing this for Jund's wife. The office was a muddle of Styrofoam cups and fast-food wrappers. One abandoned cup on a bookshelf was half full of old coffee with green fuzz growing around the rim. Other cups smelled of whiskey, and one next to Jund's PC still contained a splash of what Cady pegged as peppermint schnapps. Microwave containers of chili and stew lined the wastebasket. Cady was in the process of tying off his trash bag when the assistant director returned, a barbecue fork in one hand and a Dos Equis in the other.

"Drew," Jund said. "I didn't want to mention this in front of the others. In fact, it's kind of a difficult topic for me to bring up in the first place."

Cady looked at his ex-boss. My god, he thought. The man's about to *thank* me.

"Here's the deal." Jund put his beer down on the desktop. "Remember that phony retirement party we had for you, you know, to make Nolte think you were leaving the Bureau?"

Cady nodded, now uncertain where this conversation was heading.

"Well, because it wasn't a *real* retirement party, that watch I gave you came out of my own pocket." Jund stared at Cady's left wrist. "I've been dropping hints like mad, but you haven't picked up on any of them."

Cady stared back at Jund. Unbelievable. If Terri, Agent Preston, and himself had not all come in one car, he would have walked out the front door and left. Instead, he took the Timex from his wrist and handed it over to Jund.

"Would you happen to have the box it came in, with the instructions?" Jund asked as he slipped the watch onto his wrist.

Cady stared at the assistant director and said nothing.

"What say we not worry about that," Jund said and picked up his Dos Equis. "When you finish up here, toss the bag in the garage and come join us on the deck." Cady leaned back against the desk until the assistant director was out of view.

Jund had mentioned earlier that a detained Nolte alternated between playing games and remaining silent, but the packet of information the old man had palmed at the dead drop had led to the roundup of two separate cells of illegals with reach inside the State Department.

Only one thing about the Lynchpin case was still puzzling Cady. He walked to the front of Jund's desk and sat down. He pressed the enter key a few times to wake Jund's computer, but saw it was password protected. He looked at the center drawer for several seconds before pulling it open. A wooden lip along the front acted as a container for pens that Jund had likely filched from the office, a box of staples, a bamboo letter opener, and a small mountain of paperclips. In the center of the drawer sat two folders. The folder on top contained mortgage documentation, and Cady got the feeling Jund would have put the place on the market had he and JoAnne not been in the process of reconciling. The second folder contained current household invoices—that is, Jund's monthly bills.

None of this interested Cady.

He tried the upper right-hand drawer. Locked. He thought for a second, then reopened the center drawer and ran his hand along the back for a key. No luck. He pushed aside the mound of paperclips. Sure enough, in the bottom of the concave sat a small key, which he used to open the right-side drawer.

It was a typhoon of stationery, cards, letters, and thank-you notes in no particular order. One of Jund's Styrofoam whiskey cups, fortunately empty, had even worked its way into the desk drawer. He raked a hand through the avalanche of papers until he got to the bottom of the pile. Buried at the base, he found what he was looking for. Although there were several of the identical envelopes sitting at the bottom of Jund's desk drawer, Cady slipped out only one to examine.

It was empty, of course, as it had yet to be mailed, and perhaps now never would be. The return address in the upper left was exactly like the two he had seen recently—the District of Columbia's Department of Motor Vehicles.

Cady set the single DMV envelope on top of Jund's keyboard, locked the desk drawer, and returned the key. Then he took his bag of trash out to the garage and went to join the barbecue.

EPILOGUE

"I don't want to tear it down," Terri insisted. "I laugh uncontrollably every time I walk by cabin five and picture you slipping through that window in your birthday suit—looking like the Swamp Thing—and giving Volkov a thorn instead of a rose. It does my heart good."

Terri had come to refer to that evening as *the night my G-Man skinny-dipped Bass Lake and saved my life*. Cady, on the other hand, was embarrassed by the image that the rescue brought to mind.

"That's a national security secret, Terri. If you so much as breathe a word of it to anyone, I'll have you in Guantanamo so fast it'll make your head spin."

"Do it soon; winter's on the way," Terri replied. "They got conjugal visits down there?"

"If not, it's a deal-breaker." Cady looked at Terri. "What do you want to do with Gallion's money?"

Cady figured Peter Gallion's offer of employment at the CIA had expired after the recent Eggs Nolte shockwave, but the head of the Counterintelligence Center Analysis Group had made good on his promise to reimburse Cady for his shot-up SUV—Davidson had made arrangements to have the Bonnie-and-Clyde-looking Ford Escape towed away to parts unknown—and funds to replace the infamous cabin five, as well as purchase some new playground equipment.

"Did you drop those cruise brochures on my desk?"

"No."

"Oh, hmm," Terri said. "Well, they have some great deals this time of year."

—

They got home from Washington, D.C., on Halloween evening and, to Cady's surprise, Terri slipped into the Catwoman costume that he had ordered months back off the Internet. Cady had been physically exhausted, ready to drop, but looking at Terri, he felt a second wind and crossed the living room to…but the doorbell rang. Some friends from town had brought their children by, and Terri slipped back into the bedroom to change into something more kid-friendly and less revealing.

Two weeks later, while sitting at the Minneapolis St. Paul Airport awaiting their flight to Tampa for a spontaneous Caribbean cruise, Cady read Eggs Nolte's obituary in the *New York Times*. The Gray Lady gave the old spymaster quite the write-up—a hero's sendoff— praising the patriot's never-failing service to the country he so deeply loved. Evidently, per the article, the Cold Warrior had died of heart failure—not surprising, considering Nolte's advanced age. The article went on to state that Nolte's death symbolized the end of an era.

Let's hope, Cady thought as he tossed the newspaper on a chair for other travelers to enjoy.

Let's hope.

ACKNOWLEDGMENTS

I would like to thank Ed Stackler, editor extraordinaire, for burning off the lame parts; Michelle Dotter, for finding all the bits and pieces my eyes were too glazed over to notice; Alison Crellin, for the great cover art and a dozen other tasks; and, of course, my father, Bruce W. Burton, for his several reviews and warped sense of humor.

Any mistakes in the novel are mine.